bear bottom

Also by Stuart Gibbs

The FunJungle series

Belly Up
Poached
Big Game
Panda-monium
Lion Down
Tyrannosaurus Wrecks
Bear Bottom

The Spy School series

Spy School
Spy Camp
Evil Spy School
Spy Ski School
Spy School Secret Service
Spy School Goes South
Spy School British Invasion
Spy School Revolution
Spy School at Sea

The Moon Base Alpha series

Space Case
Spaced Out
Waste of Space

The Charlie Thorne series

Charlie Thorne and the Last Equation
Charlie Thorne and the Lost City
Charlie Thorne and the Curse of Cleopatra

The Once Upon a Tim series

Once Upon a Tim

The Last Musketeer

STUART GIBBS

bear bottom

A *funjungle* NOVEL

Simon & Schuster Books for Young Readers

New York London Toronto Sydney New Delhi

SIMON & SCHUSTER BOOKS FOR YOUNG READERS
An imprint of Simon & Schuster Children's Publishing Division
1230 Avenue of the Americas, New York, New York 10020
This book is a work of fiction. Any references to historical events, real people, or real places are used fictitiously. Other names, characters, places, and events are products of the author's imagination, and any resemblance to actual events or places or persons, living or dead, is entirely coincidental.
Text © 2021 by Stuart Gibbs
Cover design and principal illustration by Lucy Ruth Cummins © 2021 by Simon & Schuster, Inc.
Jacket background imagery by iStock
Interior map art by Lucy Ruth Cummins © 2021 by Simon & Schuster, Inc.
All rights reserved, including the right of reproduction in whole or in part in any form.
SIMON & SCHUSTER BOOKS FOR YOUNG READERS and related marks are trademarks of Simon & Schuster, Inc.
For information about special discounts for bulk purchases, please contact Simon & Schuster Special Sales at 1-866-506-1949 or business@simonandschuster.com.
The Simon & Schuster Speakers Bureau can bring authors to your live event. For more information or to book an event, contact the Simon & Schuster Speakers Bureau at 1-866-248-3049 or visit our website at www.simonspeakers.com.
Book design by Lucy Ruth Cummins
The text for this book was set in Adobe Garamond Pro.
Manufactured in the United States of America
0322 OFF
First Simon & Schuster Books for Young Readers paperback edition May 2022
2 4 6 8 10 9 7 5 3 1
The Library of Congress has cataloged the hardcover edition as follows:
Names: Gibbs, Stuart, 1969– author.
Title: Bear bottom : a Funjungle novel / Stu Gibbs.
Description: First edition. | New York : Simon & Schuster Books for Young Readers, [2021] | Audience: Ages 8–12. | Audience: Grades 4–6. |
Summary: While visiting a ranch near Yellowstone National Park with his parents, Summer, and her parents, Teddy Fitzroy investigates the disappearances of bison and an irreplaceable necklace.
Identifiers: LCCN 2020050896 |
ISBN 9781534479463 (hardcover) | ISBN 9781534479470 (pbk)
ISBN 9781534479487 (ebook)
Subjects: CYAC: Mystery and detective stories. | Stealing—Fiction. | Ranch life—Fiction.
Classification: LCC PZ7.G339236 Bc 2021 | DDC [Fic]—dc23
LC record available at https://lccn.loc.gov/2020050896

For Andrea Lee Gomez,
who was there for my family
when we needed her the most

RODEO
GROUNDS

Spooner
Ranch

OY VEY CORRAL

GRASSLAND

RANCH HOUSE

KRAUTHEIMER CREEK

BUNK-
HOUSE

FOREST

SPOONER
HOME

TO
BACKCOUNTRY
ACCESS

OLD
ABANDONED
MINE

SCALE
ONE
INCH
=
ONE
MILE

West
Yellowstone

MADISON RIVER

TO OLD FAITHFUL

YELLOWSTONE
NATIONAL PARK

Contents

THE SELFIE OF DOOM

My family was delayed on our return to the ranch because we were trying to prevent a tourist from getting mauled by an elk.

We were leaving Yellowstone National Park, having spent the day exploring, on our first vacation in two years. My parents had been working overtime at FunJungle Adventure Park, the world-famous theme park/zoo, since before it had even opened. Mom was the head primatologist and Dad was the official photographer, and their jobs kept them extremely busy.

I had always thought that FunJungle attracted an unusual number of dumb tourists. But at Yellowstone, I discovered that there were dumb tourists *everywhere*.

It was the week after the Fourth of July, and thus the

height of tourist season; Yellowstone was flooded with visitors from all over the planet. That day we had witnessed dozens of people doing incredibly boneheaded things, often directly in front of signs warning them not to do them: attempting to pet wild animals, climbing over the safety railings at scenic viewpoints, swimming in rivers with life-threatening rapids—and positioning their young children dangerously close to bison for photographs. Two rangers had to arrest a college student who was about to use Monarch Geyser as a hot tub; apparently, he hadn't realized that the 204-degree water would have boiled him alive.

I had also overheard tourists ask the park rangers startlingly uninformed questions, such as: "What time do you turn off the Old Faithful Geyser every night?" "Why do we have to stay on the hiking paths when the deer don't?" And "Where can we see the presidents carved into the mountain?" (The answers were: "It's a geological feature, not a fountain"; "The deer are wild animals"; and "You're thinking of Mount Rushmore, which is five hundred miles away in South Dakota.") I also heard one person angrily claim that a raccoon had stolen his bag of Cheetos and demand that the park service refund his money. Tourists did things like this so often that the park rangers had a name for them: tourons.

Despite all of that, it had been a good day. Yellowstone featured some of the most beautiful scenery I had ever encountered, and we had also been lucky enough to spot three bald eagles, a moose, and a pair of wolves. Plus, my girlfriend, Summer, was with us. Summer was fourteen, a little bit less than a year older than me. She was smart and fun and liked seeing wildlife and hiking as much as I did. Her father, J.J. McCracken, was the owner of FunJungle, and he had invited us to join him—along with a few other FunJungle employees—at his friend's ranch in West Yellowstone for a week. While my parents were big fans of Summer and her mother, Kandace, they were a bit wary of J.J., whose actions often concealed ulterior motives. However, the offer had been too good to pass up: a free place to stay, a flight on J.J.'s private jet, *and* a visit to one of Dad's favorite places on Earth. (Mom and I had never been to Yellowstone, and Dad had always wanted to take us there.) We had eagerly accepted the offer.

Our group had arrived the evening before, too late to visit Yellowstone, so my parents and I had been raring to go that morning. J.J. had some business to deal with, while Kandace hadn't arrived yet; she was flying in from a fashion shoot in New York City that afternoon. So Summer came with my family to see the park. Sidney Krautheimer, the owner of the ranch, happily lent us a car.

We were leaving the park in the late afternoon, on the road to West Yellowstone, when we saw the biggest touron of the day.

The road was a picturesque, winding route along the bank of the Madison River. It was relatively free of traffic, which was unusual in Yellowstone, as the roads in the park were prone to traffic jams. Usually, these were due to wildlife sightings; a bear, a moose, or even a common white-tailed deer could cause backups several miles long. But there were also plenty of car wrecks, often caused by tourons who had rented massive recreational vehicles that they couldn't control. So a wide-open road through the gorgeous landscape was a pleasant surprise.

The first thing that tipped us off that we were dealing with an unusually dumb tourist—even by Yellowstone standards—was the fact that he had abandoned his car in the middle of the road. Rather than taking a few seconds to pull over onto the shoulder, he had simply stopped, put on his hazard lights, and leaped out. He hadn't even bothered to shut his door. We nearly plowed right into the car as we came around a bend.

For a moment, we feared we had stumbled upon an emergency situation, but then we saw what had caused the man to abandon his car in such a hurry: a small herd of elk, grazing by the river. The touron was trying to get a photograph of them.

I understood why he wanted the photo; it was a spectacular scene. There were five females, four fawns, and a large bull watching over them. The fawns were adorable, certainly only a few weeks old, while the bull had an impressive ten-point rack of antlers. And amazingly, there were no other tourists around. Still, the man was making a very big mistake—in addition to having left his car in the road.

Instead of keeping a respectful distance, he was trying to get as close as possible to the elk, tramping directly across the meadow toward them. This had put all the elk on the alert. The bull looked particularly agitated, but I knew that a mother elk who felt her young were threatened could be very dangerous as well.

Dad parked our car on the shoulder. "I'm gonna see if I can talk some sense into this guy before he gets himself killed," he said, and hopped out.

Mom climbed out too, so Summer and I did the same. After all, it was a beautiful spot and there was no point in sitting in the car.

It was only then that we discovered the man's family was still in his car. His wife was in the passenger seat, while his two teenage children sat in the back. All three were making it obvious that they were irritated with the father. None seemed remotely aware that their car was a serious driving hazard.

"Dad!" the daughter yelled out the window. "We've seen, like, ten million elk already today and you've taken pictures of every one of them! We don't need any more!"

"These are *better* elk!" the father yelled back. "This photo's gonna be amazing!"

"Yeah right," the son said sarcastically. He wasn't even looking at the scenery; instead he was riveted to his phone. "It's just a stupid deer."

"Morton!" the wife called. "Enough is enough! I'm hungry!"

"I'm sorry to bother you," Mom said as pleasantly as possible, "but do you think that maybe you could move your car? It's blocking the road."

The woman sighed with annoyance, as though my mother had asked her to do something unreasonable. "I can't move it. That darn fool took the keys." She pointed toward her husband.

Her daughter noticed Summer and gaped with astonishment.

Summer was famous—although she didn't want to be. Since her father was a famous businessman and her mother was a fashion model, she'd never had any choice in the matter. She usually did her best to keep a low profile; today she was wearing sunglasses and had her blond hair tucked up under a baseball cap. We had made it through the entire day without anyone recognizing her—until now.

So Summer resorted to her usual trick in such circumstances: She pretended to be someone else.

"You're Summer McCracken, aren't you?" the girl asked. She was staring at Summer in the same way that a bird watcher would have regarded a bald eagle.

"Sorry, no," Summer said, speaking with a fake western twang. "I get that all the time, though."

The daughter narrowed her eyes suspiciously. "Are you *sure* you're not her?"

"Oh, I'm positive," Summer said.

The daughter started to press the issue, but her brother cut her off. "It's obviously not her. Do you really think Summer McCracken would be driving around Yellowstone in that car?" He pointed toward our run-down loaner. "Summer wouldn't come here. She goes places like Paris. Or Dubai."

The daughter looked from Summer to our car and back to Summer again. "I guess you're right," she said.

Meanwhile, their father, Morton, was now attempting to sneak up on the family of elk, even though they were all staring directly at him. He had uprooted a small shrub from the ground—killing it in the process—and was holding it front of him while he waddled across the meadow in a low crouch, apparently hoping that the elk would think we was just a walking bush.

The elk did not appear to be fooled by this at all. Instead, they were growing increasingly upset as Morton approached. Due to the bend in the river, they had water on three sides of them, and Morton was coming from the only land direction; they were boxed in.

"Hey!" Dad shouted at Morton. "You're getting much too close to those elk! You need to come back to the road!"

"Shhhh!" Morton hissed. "You're going to scare them away! I'm trying to sneak up on them!"

"Well, you're not doing a very good job of it!" Summer shouted. "They're looking right at you! And if you get much closer, they're going to attack!"

"I saw people getting way closer than this to plenty of animals today!" Morton told her.

"That doesn't mean it's right!" I yelled.

Morton ignored us and continued toward the elk, which were visibly nervous now. The fawns edged closer to their mothers, while the bull moved forward and gave an angry snort.

That was certainly meant as a warning to get Morton to back off, although Morton completely failed to comprehend this. Instead, he doubled down on his idiocy. Rather than retreating to his car, he turned his back on the herd of elk— and tried to take a selfie.

"Of course," Dad said, exasperated.

As a professional wildlife photographer, Dad was extremely annoyed by the proliferation of phone cameras. He had spent his entire life trying to take photos in ways that impacted his subjects as little as possible, like using telephoto lenses, which allowed him to work from so far away that the animals rarely even knew he was there. But even the best camera phones only worked from relatively close by, which often compelled inexperienced amateur photographers like Morton to get much too close to the animals.

However, it was the ability to take selfies that had caused the most problems. Since a selfie required photographers to turn their back on their subject, it led to even more disruptive—and often hazardous—behavior. At FunJungle, there was at least one incident each day of a tourist tumbling backward into an exhibit while attempting to take a selfie. In the national parks, there was even more potential for disaster; a ranger had told me that selfie takers at Yellowstone were regularly falling off scenic viewpoints, riverbanks, canyon edges, and cliffs. Or, like Morton, they were getting dangerously close to wild animals and then not paying attention to them.

Mom, Summer, and I all started shouting at once, trying to get Morton to listen to reason—or scare the elk off. I figured we had a much better chance of scaring the elk. Even Morton's family now grew concerned. They started shouting at him too. They even got out of the car to do it.

Morton ignored us all. Even worse, he ignored the bull elk behind him, which was growing more and more perturbed.

Since elk look somewhat similar to deer, many people don't realize exactly how powerful and threatening they can be. A bull elk can grow to over eight feet long and weigh 750 pounds, which is far bigger than a black bear. With their sharp hooves and multipronged antlers, they can fend off full-grown mountain lions—or do serious damage to dumb tourists.

The bull behind Morton was a large specimen. It now pawed the ground and lowered its head, pointing its rack of antlers toward Morton's backside.

"Morton, you idiot!" his wife screamed at the top of her lungs. "Look behind you!"

"Why?" Morton asked. "Is there something better to get a photo of?" He finally turned around—just in time to see the bull charge him.

Morton yelped in fear and fled across the meadow as fast as he could—which wasn't very fast at all. He had the build of a man who hadn't done much exercise in the past decade, and the bull quickly closed in on him.

I almost felt bad for the guy—until, in the midst of his flight, he actually tried to take a selfie. While he should have been completely focused on his own well-being, he stiff-armed the phone in front of him and clicked away.

Meanwhile, his own children were also recording the event. Both had their phones trained on the chase and were laughing as they watched their father run for his life, as though the entire event were taking place on TV.

There was nothing my parents, Summer, or I could do to help Morton. He was too far away from us.

While Morton focused on his selfies rather than fleeing, the bull elk lowered its head—and rammed its antlers into Morton's ample bottom. Then, with a heave of its powerful neck, it scooped him up and flung him aside. Morton tumbled across the meadow while his phone sailed through the air and plunked into a beaver pond.

I was worried that the bull might now trample Morton, but thankfully it stopped, gave one last snort, and then trotted back to join its herd.

"Morton!" his wife shrieked. She ran across the meadow toward her husband. My parents, Summer, and I joined her, although Morton's children remained on the shoulder of the road, trying to upload their videos to YouTube.

Morton was howling, which made me fear he was badly hurt, but as we got closer, it became clear what was really upsetting him. "My phone!" he wailed. "That stupid deer made me lose my phone!"

I kept a wary eye on the bull as we approached. "Do you think he might attack again?" I asked my parents.

"No," Dad replied confidently. "I think he knows he got his point across. Literally." He pointed to the bull, which still had a shred of Morton's boxer shorts impaled on the tip of its antler.

Tires screeched on the road behind us, followed by a loud crash. We turned around to see that a large recreational vehicle had plowed into the rear of Morton's car. (As we would learn later, the driver had been so focused on watching the elk gore Morton, she had taken her eyes off the road until it was too late.) The car slid off the side of the road and smashed into a tree, while the front end of the RV crumpled. A geyser of steam erupted from its radiator, like a miniature Old Faithful.

"My car!" Morton wailed. "And my phone!" He rolled over and shook his fist at the bull elk. "You stupid deer! I'm gonna sue this park for everything they've got!"

The bull ignored him and resumed grazing by the river.

We finally arrived at Morton's side. Given what I'd seen the elk do to him, the injury wasn't nearly as bad as I'd expected. Morton had a small gouge in the right cheek of his rear end but was otherwise all right. Physically, at least. Mentally, he was enraged over the loss of his car and his phone.

"You saw what that crazy deer did to me, right?" he asked us. "It just attacked me out of nowhere!"

"No, you provoked it," Mom told him, without an ounce

of sympathy. "After we repeatedly warned you not to."

"How was I supposed to know it was dangerous?" Morton demanded. "There's no warning signs!"

He was completely wrong. There had been plenty of signs throughout Yellowstone warning visitors that the wildlife was dangerous.

By the roadside, the driver of the RV was now arguing with Morton's children, most likely about who was at fault in the accident. Just as Morton's daughter leaned in to let the driver have it, the family car burst into flames.

Morton screamed again. So did his wife. She seemed to forget that her husband was wounded and raced toward the flaming car. "Our clothes!" she shouted to her children. "Get our clothes!"

Mom sighed heavily. "I think we're going to have to take this guy to the hospital."

I wasn't happy about that. And I could see that Dad and Summer were disappointed too. But we couldn't leave Morton wounded in the middle of the wilderness.

"Darn right I need to go to the hospital," Morton said. "Lousy, no-good deer! This is the last time I ever go on vacation in a national park!"

"I'm sure the park service will be happy to hear that," Summer informed him.

Morton ignored her and kept on ranting. "We should have gone on a cruise. They don't have any homicidal deer on cruise ships."

Dad looked to me and rolled his eyes. "Welcome to Yellowstone," he said.

I laughed, figuring this was the strangest thing that would happen to me that day.

It wasn't even close.

THE RANCH

We only had room for one extra person in our car, so we took Morton to the hospital in West Yellowstone while his family waited for a tow truck. Morton continued to rage the whole way, mostly about how he was going to sue the park service for allowing an elk to maul him. He didn't even thank us for getting him to a doctor.

Afterward, the drive to the ranch where we were staying seemed blessedly quiet. West Yellowstone was a small town that mostly catered to tourists, with plenty of souvenir shops, motels, and family-owned restaurants. The ranch was located a few miles south of it, situated along a narrow dirt road.

I had never seen any place like it. For the first ten years of my life, I had lived in a tent camp in the Congo while

Mom researched gorillas. Now my family lived in the Texas Hill Country, at the FunJungle employee housing complex. (It was called Lakeside Estates, but it was really only a trailer park.) Since moving to Texas, I had spent plenty of time on ranches; several of my friends from school lived on them, including Summer—although raising cattle was only a hobby for the McCrackens, rather than their main source of income. However, the landscape of the West Yellowstone ranch was vastly different from Texas, with great, wide fields of grass, forests of evergreens and aspens, and snowcapped mountains looming in the distance.

Plus, instead of cattle, this ranch raised bison.

American bison—or buffalo, as most people call them—are the largest land animals in North America. Some big males can weigh well over a ton. In part, this is due to their enormous humps. Many mammals, like camels, have humps that are composed of fat, but bison's humps are solid muscle, situated directly over their shoulders. The muscle is necessary to support the bison's giant heads, giving the animals the bulked-up appearance of people who have spent way too much time at the gym. This effect is enhanced by the bison's shaggy brown coats, which are so thick that, during the winters, snow can accumulate on bison's backs without melting.

Since my family and I had arrived at the ranch at dusk the night before and left early in the morning to visit Yellowstone, we didn't really get a good look at the herd until we returned. The ranch's owners, Sidney and Heidi Krautheimer, were happy to take us out to see the bison, along with J.J. and Summer. We didn't have to go very far; a few hundred of their bison were grazing in a wide meadow right by their ranch house. They were visible from the house itself, but the Krautheimers took us out on foot to get a closer look.

Even though it was close to dinnertime, the sun was a long way from setting. Yellowstone is located quite far north in the United States, and it was only two weeks past the summer solstice, the longest day of the year. It was hot out in the fields. The buffalo were shedding their thick winter coats, which were sloughing off them in sheets.

"Originally, my family raised cattle out here," Sidney explained. "We started the shift to bison around twenty years ago. Now we don't have any cattle at all. But we have nearly eight hundred bison, of which about a fifth were born last spring."

There were plenty of young calves about. They didn't have their humps yet and their coats were reddish-orange, so they looked like an entirely different species from the adults. Due to their coloring, the Krautheimers called them "red dogs." They were energetic and rambunctious, frolicking in the fields, while the adults were far more serene; most of them were calmly grazing, although we spotted a few rolling around in the dirt. It was amusing to see such a big animal waggling its legs in the air.

"That's called wallowing," Heidi said. "They're scratching themselves. Plus, a nice layer of dirt helps repel insects."

Sidney waved a hand toward the entire herd. "Not that long ago, a sight like this would have been incredibly common. In the late 1800s, there were sixty to eighty million bison in North America, ranging from Alaska all the way to Pennsylvania. The herds were so big they could take days to pass. And then, in the space of only a few decades, European settlers nearly wiped them out. Tourists shot at them from passing trains, like they were targets at a shooting gallery. Hunters amassed piles of their skulls that were several stories high."

"Why would they do that?" Summer asked, looking horrified.

"Some of the hunting was for sport," Heidi answered. "And some was done to clear land for ranching. But most of the slaughter was due to the government's campaign against the Native Americans. For the Shoshone, the Crow, the Blackfoot, and many other Plains tribes, bison were the main source of food, and their hides were used for clothing and shelter. Those tribes' ways of life couldn't exist without the bison, so the thinking went that if the bison were gone—then the tribes would be too."

"That's awful," Summer said, and I echoed her in agreement. The idea that one group of humans had been willing to drive an entire species of animal to extinction in order to harm another group of humans was disturbing on multiple levels.

Sidney said, "Thankfully, attitudes have changed where our culture and the environment are concerned. In fact, bison were really the beginning of the wildlife conservation movement in America. Until the early 1900s, no one had ever considered trying to bring an animal back from the brink of extinction. But lots of people were horrified by the thought that such an amazing animal could be gone forever due to shortsighted human behavior. Teddy, I understand you're named for one of those men."

"I am," I agreed. My full name is Theodore Roosevelt Fitzroy. My parents had always admired Teddy Roosevelt's commitment to nature and the environment (although some of his other ideas, while common to his time, would be frowned on today).

"Yellowstone might not even exist if it wasn't for Roosevelt," Heidi added. "He started the park service. He also sent federal troops out to protect the remaining bison while a few were rounded up and brought east to be bred in captivity—at the Bronx Zoo, of all places."

"In New York?" I asked, surprised.

"That's right," Sidney agreed. "A good portion of my

herd—and most of the bison in this entire country—are descended from those New Yorkers."

We came to a small rise from which we had a great view of the herd, spread out across the grassland below us. There were so many brown, shaggy animals clustered together that it looked sort of like the land had been covered with shag carpeting.

We had walked only a few hundred yards from the ranch house, which was a sprawling two-story building made of local timber and surrounded by wraparound porches. The bunkhouse, where the ranch hands stayed, was just ahead of us. The ranch had been in the Krautheimer family for over a hundred years, although both buildings had been remodeled and modernized recently.

Upon immigrating to the United States from Germany, the Krautheimer family had somehow made their way to West Yellowstone and staked a claim to a great swath of land. The family was Jewish, although they had worked hard to assimilate when they arrived. However, in recent years, Sidney had been far more open about his religion. He wore a yarmulke instead of a cowboy hat, dropped the occasional Yiddish word into his speech, and had even changed the name of his ranch. It had originally been called the Bar Lazy Seven; now it was the Oy Vey Corral.

"I used to be a New Yorker myself," Heidi told us.

"Park Slope in Brooklyn. Sidney and I met on a teen tour in Israel. When he told me he'd grown up on a ranch in Montana, I thought he was joking. So he challenged me to come see it for myself. The moment I got here, I decided I didn't want to go home. It was the most beautiful place I'd ever seen."

The Krautheimers were dressed in standard ranching gear: blue jeans, denim shirts, and cowboy boots. They were the same age as my parents, and they had two children. Their sixteen-year-old daughter, Melissa, was practicing her horseback riding, as it was rodeo season; we could see her astride her horse, Sassafras, in the distance, galloping around the fields. The Krautheimers' son, Evan, who was thirteen like me, had passed on our tour in favor of playing video games. "I've seen this ranch plenty," he'd explained.

J.J. McCracken and the Krautheimers were old friends; they had met through ranching circles twenty years earlier. J.J. had brought his family to visit many times over the years— although they hadn't been since FunJungle had opened, as running the park had eaten up much of J.J.'s time.

Beyond the fields and the bison herd, a small tributary of the Madison River snaked across the ranch. Trees grew thick upon the banks, and the forest continued on the far side, stretching toward the western boundary of Yellowstone, which was also the boundary of the ranch. A few pronghorn antelope, the fastest land animals in North America, were grazing along with the herd, looking delicate and spindly compared to the bulky, muscular bison.

It was a spectacular view, although I couldn't help but feel a little bit sad. In a sense, the scene I was observing was somewhat fake. This wasn't a natural, free-range herd of bison; those didn't really exist in America anymore. Instead, this was a captive herd, ranched for their meat and their hides. It was like I was in a zoo where the animals would eventually be eaten.

I asked, "Is it any harder to raise bison than cattle?"

"Not really," Sidney replied. "In some ways, it's much easier. After all, bison evolved here. Cattle didn't. So they're built for this landscape."

"More or less," Heidi put in. "Oddly, a lot of people think of bison as being from mountainous areas, because they're used to seeing them in places like Yellowstone, but in truth, they're much more suited to the Great Plains. It's just that the ones on the plains were all wiped out, and the only bison left were the ones living in the parks."

"That's true," Sidney agreed. "But still, the bison are really at home here. They eat what grows naturally in this area, and they're built to survive the long winters. They thrive here."

"Then why would anyone have cattle here at all?" Summer asked.

"A lot of it's tradition." Heidi plucked a wildflower and tucked it into her hair. "And lifestyle. People have been raising cattle here for generations, not bison."

"Plus, it's not so simple to switch from one to the other," Sidney said. "Any time you make a big shift like that, it costs money. And ranching operates on a thin margin." He turned to J.J. "Which is why you're all here right now."

My parents, Summer, and I looked to Sidney, wondering what he was talking about.

Sidney noticed our reactions and then grew slightly embarrassed. "You didn't tell them?" he asked J.J.

"I thought I'd keep it a surprise," J.J. said. "Though now's as good a time as any to spill the beans. I'm thinking about buying the Oy Vey Corral."

Summer immediately grew worried. "Why? Do you want to move here?"

"No, no," J.J. said quickly. "I have no intentions of leaving Texas, especially while you're in school there. I'm thinking of this place as more of a new tourism concept."

Now my mother looked concerned. "You're not thinking of building another FunJungle here, are you? Because a tourist attraction like that so close to Yellowstone would be a disaster. . . ."

"Whoa." J.J. held his hands out, palms up, signaling Mom to calm down. "I'm no fool, Charlene. What I'm thinking of is something much more appropriate to this area. I want to build a small safari lodge, just like the sort they have in Africa . . . but in a place where folks can experience the best of American wildlife." He waved a hand toward the herd of bison.

"It *does* feel kind of like the Serengeti," I observed.

Since I had grown up in Africa, one of the things that had always surprised me about America was how little wildlife there was. If you went on a hike, even in a national park, you'd be lucky to see so much as a white-tailed deer, whereas the parks in Africa were rife with animals. In the Serengeti, at the right time of the year, you could see thousands of zebras, wildebeests, and antelopes at once. And there were plenty of other places on the continent where great herds could be observed. That wasn't to say that Africa didn't have problems with poaching and animal management, but overall, the wildlife was in better shape there than in America.

Dad asked J.J., "So that's why you invited us up here? To get our approval for this idea?"

"I'm not looking for your approval," J.J. said. "I'm looking for your *input*. If I do this, I want to do it right."

"Oh," Summer said. "*That's* why Pete's here."

Pete Thwacker, the head of FunJungle's public relations department, had also come to the Oy Vey Corral with us, along with his husband, Ray. Pete was very good at his job—

although, ironically, for someone who worked at the world's most famous zoo, he didn't care much for animals. Or nature in general. Since arriving at the ranch, he had barely stepped foot outside; instead, he had spent most of the day reading. Pete didn't really even seem to know how to dress for the outdoors; he had mostly brought custom-made suits to wear. (At FunJungle, he was the only person who dressed like this—besides the lawyers; even J.J. was partial to jeans and denim shirts.) Meanwhile, Ray was much more of an outdoorsman; he was having a great time and had spent the entire day fly-fishing in the ranch's river.

"Exactly," J.J. said. "Pete knows the marketing angles. While the Fitzroys know all about the environment and such. And I know a good investment when I see—"

"Sasquatch!" Heidi exclaimed, so suddenly it made everyone jump. She pointed toward the trees down by the riverbank. "He's here!"

For a moment, I thought she was playing a trick on us, claiming that there was a bigfoot on the property, but then I saw what she was talking about.

There was a grizzly bear down by the trees. And he was enormous.

This, I figured, was Sasquatch.

We were quite far away, but I could tell that he was much larger than the grizzlies on display at FunJungle. With his thick, shaggy brown coat, he looked to be almost the size of a bison. He was shambling along the edge of the forest at a leisurely pace, pausing every few feet to uproot something and consume it.

I knew that I didn't really have anything to worry about. Grizzlies rarely attack humans unless they're provoked. In fact, they don't even hunt other mammals that often. As omnivores, they are far more likely to eat plants or insects. In fact, in some places, grizzlies survive almost exclusively on insect larvae, which have a much higher fat content than most other animals.

The reason grizzlies aren't particularly aggressive is that they have to conserve as much energy as they can. Their year is essentially split into two parts: hibernation—and preparing for hibernation. During the active months, they consume as much food as possible, while trying to expend a minimum amount of energy. Chasing down prey often isn't worth the work; attacking a human makes even less sense. Statistically, the bison were a far bigger threat to us than the grizzly. (And technically, the animal that had been by far the most dangerous to humans in Yellowstone was the horse.) It almost seemed as though the bison were aware of this; they didn't appear concerned by Sasquatch's presence at all and continued grazing calmly.

And yet, I was still unnerved by the sight of the grizzly. It was much bigger than a lion or a tiger and several times the size of a black bear or a wolf. Its presence triggered something primal within me.

Summer must have been feeling the same way, because she asked, "Should we get inside?"

"No," Sidney said reassuringly. "Sasquatch is nothing to worry about. He comes around most nights and we've never had an issue with him."

"We have to be much more worried about our garbage," Heidi said. "If we don't lock it up tight, Sasquatch will devour it."

"Plus, we'll lure every other bear for a hundred miles," Sidney added. "Folks around here take a lot of precautions to make sure the local bears don't get used to handouts. We want to keep them like that." He pointed to Sasquatch again, just as the bear lumbered into the shade of the trees and disappeared from sight.

"Wow," J.J. said. "That was incredible. I don't remember seeing any bears like that here before."

"We've been having more grizzly sightings in recent years," Sidney reported. "Seems the population is rebounding. In fact, we're seeing more of all the local wildlife. But Sasquatch is special. I get *farklempt* whenever I see him."

"Farklempt?" Summer repeated.

"It's Yiddish," Heidi explained. "It means 'choked up.' You see an animal like Sasquatch, and you have an emotional response."

"You sure do." J.J. had a dreamy look on his face. I had spent enough time with him to recognize it. He was imagining a successful business, probably envisioning excited safari guests oohing and aahing over a Sasquatch sighting.

"Why would you ever want to sell this place?" Summer asked the Krautheimers.

"If it were up to me, we wouldn't," Sidney replied. "But we can't maintain it forever—and our kids have made it very clear that they don't want to be ranchers."

"We're working out a deal," J.J. said. "I wouldn't really be buying the ranch so much as becoming a partner in it. The Krautheimers will stay to manage certain parts of the operation, and they can phase out whenever they want."

The Krautheimers nodded in agreement, although both of them looked a little sad about it.

Summer said, "Well, Dad, if you want my opinion, I think this would be a fantastic location for a safari lodge! How about you, Teddy?"

"I think it's a great idea," I agreed. "This is a really amazing place."

"I'm glad you think so," Sidney said. "Obviously, we feel that way too. Although, to be honest, Teddy, there's another reason we invited you here besides the lodge."

"Oh?" I asked.

I noticed both my parents tense slightly, as though they suspected what was coming next.

"J.J. told us you're quite the amateur detective," Heidi said to me. "You've solved quite a few cases down at Fun-Jungle. . . ."

"And you have one?" I guessed.

"Sadly, yes," Heidi said. "Our bison have been disappearing. We were hoping you could figure out what's going on."

THE DISAPPEARING BISON

"Two bison from our herd have vanished over the past month," Jasmine Creek told me over dinner. "I assume they were stolen, but I can't guarantee it."

Jasmine was the foreperson for the Oy Vey Corral's bison operations. She was in her thirties and was still dressed for work, in dusty blue jeans, boots, and a well-worn cowboy hat.

The Krautheimers had arranged for a welcome barbecue for their guests, and they had invited their ranch hands as well; in addition to Jasmine, there were three men named Gavin, Arin, and Zach. We were all eating on the porch of the ranch house, which afforded a great view of the bison herd.

The bison were also dining; as herbivores, they ate almost

constantly. There was an endless chorus of grunts and belches from them as they chewed.

Jasmine's mother, Daisy, ran the Krautheimer household—and cooked as well. She was overseeing a large grill loaded with ribs, steaks, and sausages, all of which she had carved from one of the ranch's bison.

It always struck me as odd to eat meat on the very ranch that it had come from, but for the McCrackens and the Krautheimers, who had grown up doing it, it was a natural part of life. (Summer had once told me that, if anything, more people ought to see where their meat came from, so they would have a better understanding of what it took to put food on their tables.) So I had piled my plate high with ribs and steak, along with corn on the cob and heaping scoops of Daisy's homemade coleslaw and potato salad.

The Krautheimers had asked Jasmine to sit with Summer and me at the kids' end of the table to explain what was happening with their bison. Evan and Melissa Krautheimer were also with us, while all our parents dined with Pete and Ray and the other ranch hands.

Pete seemed to be uncomfortable with eating an animal that had been grazing nearby a day before, and had opted only for the vegetarian side dishes. In addition, his allergies had flared up and his nose was so raw from blowing it that he looked like a proboscis monkey. And if that wasn't bad enough, every mosquito in Montana appeared to have targeted him. I hadn't suffered a single bite, but his face was a minefield of little welts.

"Why do you think the bison were stolen?" I asked Jasmine.

"Because I can't find them anywhere," Jasmine replied. "And I've looked."

"Everywhere?" Melissa asked doubtfully, gnawing on a rib. "We have over six thousand acres here."

"I'm well aware of that," Jasmine said, looking slightly offended. "In fact, I'm pretty sure I know this land better than anyone in your family."

"The bison couldn't just be in some distant part of the property?" I asked. "Seeing as this ranch is so big . . ."

"Bison are communal animals." Jasmine took a sip of her beer. "They tend to stay with their herds. But even so, the hands and I have swept the ranch as well as we could. We didn't find any stragglers—and the fence is intact all the way around. All twenty miles of it."

"Maybe Sasquatch killed them," Summer suggested. "Or another grizzly did."

Jasmine shook her head. "I doubt a grizzly would go after a bison in the first place. Even the red dogs are too much effort for them, especially when there's so much other food around. But even if a bear *did* make a kill, there'd be evidence. A carcass would lure vultures. Like that." She pointed off in the distance with her fork.

Sure enough, to the north, several dozen vultures wheeled lazily in the sky. "That's because a deer got hit by an RV on the northern boundary road," Jasmine explained. "I know because I checked it out. If we had a dead bison, there'd be a cloud of vultures like that over the ranch. Plus, a bear doesn't eat the whole bison. Something would be left: skin, hooves, maybe some of the bones. I haven't seen any signs of a kill anywhere. Instead, these bison just vanished."

"Maybe space aliens took them," Evan said. "Like, for some sort of intergalactic zoo."

Summer and I looked to Evan warily. We hadn't spent enough time with him to know if he was being serious or not.

"They could get a lot of wildlife right here," Evan went on. "It's like one-stop shopping. They could pick up some bison, some cougars, some bobcats, some grizzlies—and whatever Melissa is." He burst into laughter.

His sister didn't think it was so funny. "You can be such a horse's patoot sometimes," she said, and bounced a dinner roll off his head.

Evan loaded a spoon full of potato salad and was preparing to fire it at her, catapult style, when his father snapped, "Kids! That's no way to behave in front of company!"

"I'm not doing anything!" Evan declared with fake

innocence, then shoved the spoonful of potato salad into his mouth, as though he had been intending to eat it all along.

Evan appeared to be in the middle of a growth spurt; the arms of his shirt and the legs of his jeans were an inch shorter than they should have been. He was nice enough, although he seemed more interested in playing video games than getting to know me. That made a certain amount of sense, though; I probably wouldn't have been thrilled to have a random kid suddenly staying at my house either.

Melissa was three years older than me and two years older than Summer. I had caught the end of her horseback riding practice right before dinner. Her specialty was barrel racing, where she galloped her horse at top speed through a looping path around three barrels. When I had first come to Texas, I had thought there wasn't much to riding a horse, seeing as the horse appeared to be doing all the work. But after riding a few times with Summer, I had learned that a good rider needed to be an excellent athlete, and that was certainly the case with Melissa. She was very talented and seemed to be in sync with her horse.

I said, "You guys must feel really lucky, getting to live here."

Evan laughed, then paused. "Oh wait," he said. "Were you being serious?"

"Of course," I said. "This ranch is awesome."

"Want to trade places?" Evan asked. "I live miles away from all my friends, the cell reception stinks, and you can't walk five feet without stepping in buffalo poop."

"I live in a mobile home next to the employee parking lot for a theme park," I said.

"Really?" Evan asked. "Forget trading places. Your home might actually be crummier than mine."

Melissa gave a dramatic sigh. "You have no idea how lucky you are, Evan. Can you imagine what life was like for our great-great-grandparents out here? Your friends are, like, five minutes away. It took our ancestors *hours* to get to town. And they lived in a log cabin without heat. Or air-conditioning. Or electricity. Or plumbing. Or anything, really."

"So when was this place built?" Summer asked, waving toward the ranch house.

"In the 1920s," Melissa replied. "The original log cabin is still on the property. Right over there." She pointed across the field.

Sure enough, there was a log cabin nestled in the trees down by the river. It looked straight out of a picture book about Abraham Lincoln's childhood.

Summer wasn't looking at the log cabin, though. She was scrutinizing the large ranch house carefully. "It's an awfully big jump from a log cabin to a place like this," she observed. "I guess your family did really well with ranching."

"Not exactly," Melissa said. "Our great-grandparents had a side business that covered the bills. They were bootleggers during Prohibition."

"Really?" I asked. "All the way out here?"

"This was a way station," Melissa explained. "The alcohol came down from Canada and then passed through here on its way to bigger cities. Although I hear the folks on the frontier drank plenty. Our great-grandparents didn't really run the operation. They just provided a place to hide everything. Some people say that Al Capone himself helped pay for this house. There's a secret storage area for booze under the kitchen. I can show it to you after dinner if you want."

"Sure!" Summer agreed. "That'd be awesome."

"It's not that big a deal," Evan said dismissively. "It's just a basement."

"A secret basement that Al Capone used to store illegal alcohol in," Summer corrected him. "My house doesn't have anything like that."

"My house barely even has a kitchen," I said.

"Hey, kids!" Daisy Creek was suddenly at our side, bearing a platter heaped with more meat. "Anyone want seconds?"

I had barely made a dent in the enormous first serving that she had given me. "I'm all right, thanks. But this is delicious."

"You should thank Jasmine. She's the one who raises all

this meat." Daisy beamed brightly at her daughter. To my eyes, Daisy didn't look old enough to have a daughter Jasmine's age. She was youthful and petite—although, despite her small size, she was tough as nails. Earlier in the day, I'd seen her haul a thirty-pound bundle of wood for the grill up to the porch as easily as most people would have hoisted a sack of cotton balls.

No one else at our end of the table needed any more food, although Gavin and Zach had already polished off their plates, so Daisy headed that way to give them seconds.

I returned my attention to Jasmine. "How long has your mother been working here?"

"Since she was a little girl. *Her* parents worked for the Krautheimers too. And my family has been in this area since long before any ranchers were here."

"Jasmine's Tukudika," Melissa explained.

I looked at her blankly, and so did Summer.

"It's a branch of the Shoshone tribe," Jasmine explained. "My people have lived in the Yellowstone area for as long as anyone knows. Sometimes, folks refer to us as the Sheep Eaters."

"Oh," Summer said. "That I've heard of. There was a Sheep Eater War in the 1800s. Although it really wasn't a war. It was the US government coming up with an excuse to kill Native Americans."

"That's right." Jasmine seemed impressed that Summer

knew about this. "The tribe was almost wiped out. We never even got our own reservation; our land was stolen to create Yellowstone. Instead, we got shipped off to other reservations in the area. Although, at least we got to stay somewhat close to where we were from. Plenty of eastern US tribes didn't even get to do that. They got booted off their land and sent to places like Oklahoma that they didn't have any connection to at all."

Melissa said, "Basically, the Native Americans got treated like garbage."

Her saying this seemed a bit ironic to me, given that she was certainly living on land that had once been inhabited by Native Americans. But then it occurred to me that I lived on land that had once been inhabited by Native Americans, as did everyone else in the Americas.

"We were called Sheep Eaters because we specialized in catching the wild sheep that live in this area," Jasmine explained. "Although, of course, bison were important to us too—as they were with so many tribes throughout the West. I come from a long line of bison managers—although the way I do it is a lot different from how my ancestors did."

"Mr. Krautheimer said there's almost eight hundred bison on this ranch," I said.

"Seven hundred and eighty-six," Jasmine reported. "At last count."

I asked, "With that many animals, how did you even realize that two were missing? I mean, they all pretty much look the same."

I didn't mean this only in reference to bison. Since my mother was a field biologist, I knew that it could be hard to tell animals apart even in populations that were heavily researched. Mom told me it had taken her nearly a year to learn each of her gorillas by sight in the wild, and there were only a few dozen of them.

"It took us a while to confirm they were gone," Jasmine admitted. "Which, I suppose, is what whoever stole them was counting on. I have ear tags on all of them, with a different number for each animal, but it's still a chore to keep track. We have to do a census every few days."

"You mean, you just count them?" I asked.

"Yes." Jasmine finished stripping a rib clean and dropped it onto her plate. "And if we come up with the wrong number, then we do it again the next day. And the next. Which was how we realized we were two short."

"Couldn't you just put microchips in them?" Summer asked. "That's what we do at our ranch."

"I suspect you might have more money for your operation than we do," Jasmine replied. "If we had the chips, then I could *prove* the bison had been stolen. But for now, well . . . all I can say is that there's two we can't find. I don't even know which two bison are missing. I don't know their ages. Or their genders. I can't even say when they were taken. Only that it's been a month since we noticed they were gone."

I chewed on a piece of steak thoughtfully. "So . . . you don't have any proof that they were actually stolen. And if they were, you don't know when it happened."

"Right."

"That's not going to be easy to solve," I said. Although, I could already feel myself growing intrigued by the challenge.

I had solved quite a few mysteries over the last year, most of which had been connected to the animals at FunJungle. For the last few cases, I had balked at the idea of getting involved, as crime solving was often dangerous, but now, to my surprise, I simply felt excited. I didn't know if this was because I had become more confident in myself—or if it was because I figured I couldn't possibly end up in *more* trouble than I had in the past. But something had changed in me.

"Do you have any clues at all?" Summer asked Jasmine. Summer had helped me solve almost every one of my cases and had a very deductive mind as well.

"No," Jasmine admitted. "Although, I have some ideas about how it might have happened."

"Like what?" I asked.

"It'd be easier to show you." Jasmine looked toward the

setting sun, judging how much light was left in the day. "Why don't we do it tomorrow morning?"

"All right," I agreed.

"Great!" Jasmine said. "Can you ride a horse?"

"Of course," Summer said.

I didn't answer quite so enthusiastically, as my horseback riding skills weren't very good. I was about to ask if there was another way to get around the ranch, but before I could, a pickup truck came down the long driveway toward the house. Since the drive was unpaved, a plume of dust rose in the truck's wake. The truck looked as though it might have a few hundred thousand miles on it; it was coated with dirt and dings.

"That's my father," Jasmine observed, then looked to Summer. "He must have your mom."

Summer sprang to her feet excitedly. She hadn't seen her mother in nearly two weeks, as Kandace had been in New York City to appear at some fashion shoots and charity events.

J.J. McCracken got up as well, just as eager to see Kandace.

The truck parked beside the house. Jasmine's father got out first. Arturo Creek showed his age a little more than Daisy did—he had gray hair and was slightly stooped—but he exhibited the same youthful energy as his wife. He was also quite a gentleman, as evidenced by the fact that he came around to the passenger side to open the door for Kandace.

I noticed there was a third person in the truck, in the back seat of the extended cab. I couldn't quite make out who it was, but figured it had to be Karina Soontornvat, the McCrackens' pilot. She had flown the jet to New York to pick up Kandace and needed a place to spend the night. Lots of employers might have put their pilot up in a cheap motel, but J.J. considered Karina a friend and had invited her to join us.

The truck was jacked up on large tires, so there was a good-size drop from the cab to the ground. Kandace took Arturo's hand to steady herself as she got out.

Kandace made no secret of the fact that she preferred the city to the country, and she often passed on trips like this, but Summer had told me that Kandace enjoyed the Oy Vey Corral. However, at the moment, she was dressed even less appropriately for her surroundings than Pete Thwacker was. She must have gone directly to the airport from a fancy event, because she was wearing a couture dress and lots of jewelry. Somewhere en route, she had swapped her dress shoes for sneakers that she could get dirty, which was a shrewd move. When she alit on the ground from the truck, tiny clouds of dust rose around her feet.

"Mom!" Summer exclaimed, and ran out to meet her.

J.J. started toward her as well, but then stopped suddenly, right beside me, as though something had upset him. "Dang it," he muttered under his breath. "Why's she wearing *that*?"

At first, I assumed he meant the dress, but then Kandace turned to face Summer and her necklace caught the sunlight.

It was a big necklace, in what I would later learn is known as the princess style, probably because princesses tend to have lots of money. Rather than being a single strand of silver or gold, it was encrusted with jewels for its entire length, all the way around Kandace's neck. Most of the jewels were small diamonds, which sparkled like a river in the sunshine, but at the very front was an enormous sapphire. The stone was the size of an egg and an iridescent dark blue that appeared to glow from within.

I didn't know much about jewelry, but I knew the necklace had to be expensive.

J.J. was obviously upset that Kandace had brought it to the ranch, although I thought he was overreacting.

But it turned out, J.J. was right to be concerned.

THE SECRET ROOM

Even though J.J. was upset, he didn't want to make
a scene in front of everyone. He kept his annoyance to himself until later that night, when he and Kandace were in the
privacy of their room, and he thought no one could hear
them.

But Summer, Melissa, and I *did* hear, because we were in
the hidden liquor room under the house.

As eager as Summer and I were to see the secret room,
we had waited until after dinner to explore it, mostly
because Daisy Creek had baked what was possibly the most
delicious-looking berry crumble I had ever seen. And it had
tasted even better than it looked, as it was stuffed with local
strawberries, blackberries, and huckleberries, then topped
with homemade whipped cream.

After that, we had watched the sun set, which was beautiful. Since we were relatively far north and it was the heart of summer, it was ten p.m. by the time the stars came out.

All the adults adjourned to the living room for after-dinner drinks, except for J.J. and Kandace, who went to their guest room, and Arturo and Daisy, who had gone home to their apartment in West Yellowstone after serving dessert. ("Once you get to be our age, you realize there's nothing better than turning in early," Arturo had explained.)

Jasmine and the ranch hands weren't concerned about having a drink before heading home, because the bunkhouse was only a short walk away. Each of them had an individual apartment, which the Krautheimers had refurbished a few years before. According to Jasmine, the rooms were small but still much better than the lodgings most ranches had. The Krautheimers had even offered her parents lodging there, but Jasmine said they preferred their independence and had opted for their own place.

After Daisy and Arturo had set off for town in the pickup, Melissa announced it was time to check out the hidden room under the house. Evan passed. "I've been down in that creepy place more than enough," he said, and went to his room to play video games.

The access to the hidden room was in the kitchen, which made sense, as the kitchen had its own entrance. This would have made it easy to move contraband in and out of the house. Like the rest of the ranch house, the kitchen had been modernized recently, although the Krautheimers had tried to maintain the original western style. That meant brand-new appliances, but everything else still looked quite rustic. Copper pots and pans hung from racks on the walls, the cabinets were fronted with etched glass, and the floor was the original wood.

The kitchen was a wide, open space with a large table in the center where the food prep was done. We had to slide the table aside to access the trapdoor to the liquor room, which was so cleverly constructed that it was hard to see, even when I was staring directly at it. The edges of the door matched up perfectly with the slats of wood in the floor, and the latch was concealed in a knothole.

The door was also much larger than I expected: four feet square and several inches thick. Once we moved the table, it took all three of us to lift the door, which we propped open against the kitchen counter.

It revealed a great dark space beneath the house, with an old wooden staircase descending into it. Melissa handed us each a flashlight and led the way. The stairs creaked ominously as we came down them, and the temperature dropped ten degrees. The air was dank and musty.

I had expected to find a room the size of the kitchen, but

it was far bigger, extending under much of the house, indicating that great amounts of illegal liquor must have been stored down there. Our flashlight beams didn't even reach the other side. It was a simple, large space dug into the earth. The height varied because the floor wasn't even. The ground beneath our feet was dirt, although the walls had been shored up with wooden slats, and every few feet there was a thick post to support the house above us. Some of the posts still had century-old oil lamps hanging from the hooks on them.

"That's how they used to light this room," Melissa explained. "They didn't get electricity out here until the early 1960s."

"This is so big," Summer said, playing her flashlight around the cavernous space. "How much liquor were they storing down here?"

"Plenty," Melissa replied. "This route supplied everywhere from Salt Lake City to Los Angeles. They were bringing it in by the truckload."

"Did they ever get caught?" I asked.

"No," Melissa said. "My folks say the government didn't really care to enforce the laws out here, but I'm betting that my ancestors bribed the Feds. I mean, if no one cared about the laws, then why bother going through all this trouble to hide the stuff?" She led the way deeper into the gloom.

As we passed beneath the living room, we could hear the

conversations of the adults above us. One of the ranch hands was telling everyone else about what to do if you ran into a grizzly bear.

I hadn't been able to spend much time with the three ranch hands yet, but Melissa had told me about them at dinner.

Gavin was the oldest by far. He was in his sixties, but he had been working ranches in the area ever since he was a teenager and was regarded as one of the best cowboys in the region. Melissa claimed that Gavin had never ranged more than a hundred miles from where he lived, although I didn't quite believe that. He didn't speak much; I hadn't heard him say a single word so far.

The other two hands were much younger. In fact, Zach had only graduated high school that May. He was a local kid, big and muscular after years of playing football. Even if Melissa hadn't told me about his serious crush on Jasmine, I would have known because he almost never took his eyes off her.

Arin was a bit older, a college graduate from Montana State University, which was ninety miles north in Bozeman. He was from Bangalore, India, and had come to MSU to study mathematical engineering, but he had fallen in love with the ranching business and wanted to learn how it worked.

Given the slight accent, I could tell Arin was the one

who was talking. "You don't want to catch a bear by surprise in the woods," he said. "So most local hikers tie little bells to their clothes to make noise. And you also want to be prepared to fend the bear off, so you should carry pepper spray."

"Or you could just avoid the woods completely and stay inside," Pete suggested.

"True," Arin admitted. "But if you go out, it also helps to know what kind of bears are in the area, which you do by looking at their scat. . . ."

"Scat?" Pete echoed, confused.

"That's their poop," Mom said. "When we track animals in the wild, that's how we refer to it."

"Exactly," Arin said. "Each species of animal leaves a different type of scat. Even different species of bears. Black bears aren't nearly as dangerous as grizzlies. Their scat generally has lots of grass and berry seeds in it."

"And what does grizzly scat look like?" Pete asked.

"It has little bells in it and smells like pepper," Arin replied.

Everyone in the room burst into laughter, although Pete's sounded very nervous.

Just then, I heard the sound of something scuttling in the basement behind me. I swung my flashlight that way, but whatever had made the noise was too far away or moving too fast for me to see it. "Do you have rats down here?" I asked.

"No," Melissa said dismissively. "That was probably a gopher. Or maybe a weasel hunting for gophers. Or a black-footed ferret. Or possibly a badger."

"And I thought Teddy lived in a zoo," Summer said.

It was spooky under the house and I was feeling as though I had seen enough, but both of the girls were pressing on. I got the sense that Melissa was testing us, seeing if we had the guts to stay down there with her. There really wasn't any other reason to keep going; there was nothing else to see. But I didn't want to seem like a wuss, so I stayed with them.

The house was designed so that the guest rooms were on the first floor, just beyond the living room, while the Krautheimers' rooms were upstairs. Thus, as we moved beyond the living room and passed under the guest bedrooms, we heard other voices. Heated ones. J.J. and Kandace McCracken.

"Why would you wear that necklace?" J.J. demanded.

"Because that's the whole point of jewelry!" Kandace replied sharply. "Why would you buy me something that you didn't want me to wear?"

I sensed Summer tensing beside me in the darkness, as though she was upset to hear her parents arguing.

"There are times when it makes sense to wear it," J.J. told Kandace. "Times when it can be protected. And this is not one of them."

"Relax," Kandace said. "Nothing's gonna happen to it

way out here in the boonies. It's probably safer here than it was in New York."

"Which is another problem! I can't believe you took it to New York without telling me!"

"Oh? What else do I need to ask your permission for? What shoes I can bring? What dresses I can wear? When I can go to the bathroom? I'm an adult, J.J. I'm allowed to make my own decisions."

"Well, maybe that shouldn't be the case," J.J. replied gruffly.

There was a pause, and when Kandace spoke again, her voice was cold; she was obviously bristling at the way J.J. was treating her. "What is that supposed to mean?"

"It means you showed terrible judgment here. So yes, I think we do need to discuss what you do before you do it."

"So you want to treat me like a child?"

"If you're going to act like one . . ."

"Well, here's another decision of mine that you probably won't like: You can sleep on the couch tonight."

Kandace was right. J.J. didn't like that at all, and things escalated quickly, with both the McCrackens talking heatedly at once. I glanced toward Summer, figuring she must be embarrassed that we were all hearing this, but she was turned away from me and I couldn't catch her eye.

I was about to suggest that we go back upstairs when someone suddenly grabbed Summer from behind.

A hand reached out of the shadows and seized her shoulder.

It happened so quickly, it scared me to death. I screamed in fright, so loud that the McCrackens heard it through the floor and were startled into pausing their argument.

Meanwhile, Summer handled things much differently, even though she was the one who'd been grabbed. Her parents had always been concerned for her safety, fearing that she was a target for kidnapping. When I had first met her, she'd had bodyguards with her at all times, but she had never liked this, as it made it hard for her to have a normal life. So she had asked her parents if she could lose the guards and take self-defense courses instead. She went twice a week and had improved quickly. Now she knew exactly what to do. The moment the hand touched her, Summer spun around and punched her attacker in the nose.

Her attacker gave a yelp of pain and collapsed on the ground.

"Evan?" Melissa asked, recognizing the voice. She aimed her flashlight toward the floor.

Sure enough, Evan Krautheimer was lying there, cradling his now-bloodied nose in his hands.

"Are you okay?" Melissa asked.

"No," Evan muttered. "She hit me!"

"Serves you right," Melissa said. "What were you thinking, sneaking up on Summer like that? She's our guest!"

"I thought she was *you*," Evan said bitterly. "You both look the same from behind in the dark." He got back to his feet. Summer had done quite a job on him. Blood was dripping from between his cupped fingers.

"I think we should put some ice on that," I said. "Does it hurt?"

"Of course it hurts," Evan replied sourly.

"Sorry," Summer said.

"Don't be," Melissa told her.

It was easy to find our way back to the exit, as the light from the kitchen was spilling down through the open trapdoor. Evan hurried in that direction and the rest of us followed. When we emerged back into the kitchen, I was able to get a better look at Evan. His nose was already swollen and black-and-blue, as if someone had swapped it out for a ripe plum—although it seemed to be his pride that was *really* hurting. He was certainly embarrassed by having his prank backfire. And that grew worse when his parents entered the kitchen. They had obviously heard his cry of pain.

"What happened?" Heidi asked, worried.

"I fell," Evan lied, grabbing an ice pack from the freezer.

"He did not," Melissa reported. "He tried to sneak up on Summer down in the liquor room and she popped him in the nose in self-defense."

"Evan!" Sidney exclaimed.

"I wasn't trying to scare Summer. I was trying to scare *Melissa*." Evan wrapped the ice pack in a hand towel and pressed it to his nose.

"That's not a great defense," Heidi informed him. "Do you need a doctor?"

"I'm fine. I just need to lie down." Evan quickly left the kitchen. The rest of us followed him into the living room.

This room was the focal point of the house, a large, open two-story space with exposed wooden beams and an enormous stone fireplace. It was decorated in a popular local style that Summer had called "aggressive frontiersman." All the furnishings were made from animals—or at least, parts of animals: The walls were adorned with the taxidermied heads of deer and antelope that generations of Krautheimers had killed, bison-skin rugs lay on the floors, and the chandeliers and light fixtures were made from elk antlers. (Elk shed their antlers every fall, leaving thousands strewn around the landscape, which makes them a very cheap building material.) The overall effect was somewhat creepy.

All the other adults had paused their conversation and were looking toward the kitchen, wondering what the commotion was about. Even J.J. McCracken was there, hovering in the doorway between the living room and the hall to the guest bedrooms, although Kandace was not, indicating that J.J. had in fact been booted out of their room.

"Is everything all right?" Mom asked.

"Fine, fine," Sidney answered. "A prank just got a little out of hand."

"Evan tried to scare Summer and she punched him," Melissa said in a cheerful voice that indicated she would be happy to tell people this over and over again.

The ranch hands all stifled their laughter, while J.J. McCracken beamed proudly at the way his daughter had handled herself.

Evan grew even more embarrassed. "It was an accident," he muttered, then hurried up the stairs to his bedroom.

Heidi followed him to make sure he was all right.

An awkward silence settled over the room. No one seemed quite sure what to say.

In addition to the ranch hands and Pete, my parents were also hanging out with Karina, the McCrackens' pilot, and Ray, Pete's husband.

Karina had been a test pilot in the air force but had served her twenty years and earned her pension, so now she had found work that was much safer, less demanding, and better paying. She still had a very military demeanor, right down to her crew cut. I had met her a few times but never really spent any time with her.

I didn't know Ray that well either, although we had

played cards on the flight to West Yellowstone. A carpenter at FunJungle, he was a lot different from Pete. He enjoyed being outdoors, he liked animals, and he was dressed in comfortable, well-worn clothes that probably cost less than what one of Pete's silk ties did. Unlike a lot of adults, he seemed to really enjoy being with kids and had happily talked to Summer and me about all sorts of things.

There was a loud bang from the kitchen, so sudden that it made everyone jump. This was followed by the sound of something large scraping over the floor.

Everyone turned that way, looking unsettled, wondering what was going on.

Jasmine entered from the kitchen, holding her phone to her ear with one hand and holding a set of keys in the other. "I've got your keys," she was saying into the phone. "They were in the kitchen." She noticed everyone was looking her way, then realized she needed to explain things.

"The kids left the trapdoor to the liquor room open," she said. "I closed it before anyone fell through. It was heavier than I expected."

That explained the bang. And the scraping must have been her shoving the table back into place over it.

Jasmine was about to return to her phone call but then grew worried. She looked back to the kitchen. "No one's still down there, are they?"

"No," Melissa said. "Everyone's out."

Jasmine sighed with relief, then got back on the phone. "I'll hold on to Mom's keys for her. . . . Okay. Love you too." She hung up, then held up the keys and explained. "Mom forgot these. And she wants everyone to know breakfast will be ready at seven a.m. tomorrow. If you want to eat, don't be late."

All the adults immediately checked their watches to see what time it was.

"Well," Dad said, "we have a big day tomorrow. I think maybe we ought to turn in."

Everyone else chimed in in agreement—although Zach waited to see what Jasmine would say before echoing her.

It took a few more minutes for everyone to leave, because adults never can say good night or good-bye quickly. Then the ranch hands all sauntered out and headed back to the bunkhouse. My parents, Karina, Pete, and Ray all headed down the hall to the guest rooms.

There were four rooms, although they all varied in size. The McCrackens and my family had the bigger ones because Summer and I each had to sleep on sofa beds in those rooms. Karina's room was on the same side of the hall as the McCrackens', while Pete and Ray's was next to ours.

J.J. didn't return to his room, although he obviously didn't want everyone to know he'd been kicked out. "I think

I might stay up for a while longer," he said as an excuse. "Maybe watch the stars for a bit."

"Are you sure, Daddy?" Summer asked. I could tell she was hoping he might change his mind and try to make amends with her mother.

"I'm sure. You know how I love the stars." J.J. headed out onto the porch.

Even though it was a bit sad, I found the whole charade amusing. J.J. McCracken was one of the most powerful and respected businessmen on the planet, with a reputation for being a ruthless negotiator. And yet, here he was, afraid to ask his own wife if she'd let him back into their bedroom.

Plus, it seemed to me that Kandace had been right. Maybe it hadn't been shrewd to bring an expensive necklace on her trip, but J.J. *had* bought it for her—and he had been awfully condescending during their argument.

I figured that maybe J.J. was gathering his nerve to face Kandace again. But he never did. He ended up sleeping on the couch in the living room.

Which was why he wasn't in their bedroom when Sasquatch broke in.

SASQUATCH

I happened to be visiting the bathroom when the bear showed up.

It was four a.m. Only the McCrackens' room had its own bathroom; we had to share one with Karina, Pete, and Ray. The Krautheimers had provided bathrobes for all the guests, so I pulled one on over my pajamas and headed down the hall.

Like the rest of the house, the bathroom had a somewhat eerie dead-animal theme. The handles for the taps and the towel racks were made from pieces of antler, and there was even a deer head mounted over the toilet, to give guests the unsettling experience of having a dead animal stare at you while you peed.

I had just washed my hands when I heard a very odd noise. It sounded like someone strangling a duck.

I went to see what it was.

I walked into the living room, which was a hundred times creepier in the dark than it had been with the lights on. The various disembodied animal heads on the walls stared vacantly from the shadows, while a stuffed bear loomed ominously by the fireplace. It took me a few moments to pinpoint the source of the duck-strangling noise. It was J.J. McCracken, snoring on the couch.

He was swaddled in a buffalo-hide blanket, so that even his head was covered. In the dark, he looked like an enormous woolly caterpillar.

I was about to return to my room when I heard a different noise in the living room. A soft snuffling from near the fireplace.

I looked back across the room, toward the stuffed bear. It was only now that my sleepy brain realized something very important: The Krautheimers didn't own a stuffed bear.

Plus, this one was moving.

Up close, Sasquatch was staggeringly big. With his shaggy coat, he appeared to be the size of a hippopotamus. His head alone, framed by a mane of fur, was as wide and round as a manhole cover. I was so close that I could smell him; he had the musky, grassy odor of a freshly mowed lawn.

Behind him, the front door was wide open.

The snuffling noise I had heard was Sasquatch sniffing

the air. He shifted his head toward me—and then froze.

He had smelled me.

Bears don't have very good vision, but they possess what may be the best noses in the animal kingdom. Some scientists estimate that they can smell seven times better than a bloodhound—or around two thousand times better than a human. Even though bear brains are smaller than ours, the olfactory lobe is five times larger. If a human can detect a scent from five feet away, a bear can detect it from a mile.

I had been given plenty of advice about how to behave if I ran into a bear in the wild. But I wasn't sure how much of it applied to encountering a bear in the living room.

The main rule is that you shouldn't run, because that will provoke the bear's instinctual attack response. But in the woods, there are no bedrooms that you can lock yourself into. So it seemed that maybe running back to my room was a good plan.

Only I didn't want to abandon J.J.

And it seemed that I should alert everyone else to the bear's presence as well.

I screamed at the top of my lungs. "There's a bear in the house!"

J.J. snapped awake, completely disoriented and tangled up in his bison blanket. "What?" he cried. "Where?"

There were immediately many other noises in the house

as well: shouts of surprise—or annoyance at having been woken—as well as the thumping of feet on the floor and the creaks of doors being opened.

Everyone was doing exactly the opposite of what they should have been doing. They were all coming *toward* the bear. But as I would later learn, everyone was thinking that there couldn't possibly be a bear in the house. Most of them assumed that I had run into a much smaller animal, like a raccoon or an opossum, and completely overreacted.

The only exception was Pete Thwacker, who simply didn't know how to behave around a bear. He appeared in the doorway to his room, wearing pajamas that looked like they had actually been ironed. My parents and Karina also came to the doors to their rooms. (The other downstairs guests hadn't awakened: Kandace had taken a sleeping pill, Summer was wearing earplugs because she had thought her father might return to the room and she knew how loud he snored, and it turned out Ray could sleep through anything.) Meanwhile, upstairs, the entire Krautheimer family gathered at the railing that looked down into the living room. Someone flipped the lights on, and everyone discovered that I hadn't been overreacting at all: There was really a bear in the house. And a massive one, at that.

Almost everyone screamed in shock, fear, or surprise. There was also a lot of shrieking, gasping, and gibbering.

Sasquatch, startled by the noise, the influx of people, and the sudden brightness, reared up on his hind legs and roared.

Outdoors, a grizzly roar is startlingly loud. Inside, it was as earsplitting as a bomb detonating. It made the walls tremble.

And if that wasn't scary enough, every one of Sasquatch's teeth was on display. His lips curled back, revealing fangs that were over three inches long, while long strands of drool dangled from his jowls.

On his hind legs, Sasquatch was over eight feet tall. His massive head clonked into the elk-horn chandelier, which swung away and then pendulumed back into his face, cracking him right in the nose. Sasquatch stumbled backward, pinwheeling his massive forelegs, and accidentally swatted the mounted head of a twelve-point buck with such force that it sailed across the room and embedded itself, antlers-first, in the far wall.

Then Sasquatch fell backward onto his bottom, landing on the coffee table so hard that he flattened it like a pile driver.

Now everyone raced back into their rooms. J.J. and I fled from the living room and down the hall. J.J. still had the bison blanket wrapped tightly around him, so he looked somewhat like a giant burrito. He tried to enter his room, but the door was locked from the inside, so he pounded on it desperately. "Kandace!" he yelled. "It's me!"

"J.J.?" Kandace asked groggily from inside. "It's the middle of the night!"

"Open the door!" J.J. yelled.

"Not until you apologize!" Kandace yelled back, apparently unaware there was a grizzly in the house.

In the living room, Sasquatch swatted a couch aside like it was made of tissue paper and started coming our way.

J.J. realized he didn't have time to explain what was going on to Kandace. He ducked across the hall into my room with my family and we slammed the door behind him.

The only lock on our door was a simple slide latch mounted to the frame. It was enough to stop a person from entering, but I doubted it could hold back a grizzly. We all grabbed whatever was close at hand to defend ourselves. Dad took an elk-horn lamp. I found a wooden duck decoy. Mom got two cans of aerosol hair spray. J.J. grabbed a shoe, although in his haste he dropped his blanket, revealing that he only slept in his boxer shorts.

Outside the door, we could now hear Sasquatch moving down the hallway. For a big animal, he was surprisingly quiet. There was no sound as his huge paws struck, save for the floor creaking beneath his massive weight, and his fur brushed lightly against the walls on both sides as he squeezed through the narrow passageway.

The grizzly stopped directly outside our door. We could

hear him snuffling again on the opposite side.

We all backed away from the door, holding our makeshift weapons at the ready. J.J. stumbled over the blanket that was bunched around his legs and toppled over onto his back.

Sasquatch made a huffing noise. The floor creaked again, like the bear had just shifted his weight. Then there was a thump from across the hall, followed by the sound of wood splintering. I heard a loud bang—and then screaming. It was Kandace and Summer.

"No!!!!" J.J. exclaimed, terrified for his family. He sprang back to his feet and, without even bothering to wrap himself up again, undid the latch and flung open the door to our room.

Across the hall, Sasquatch had knocked the McCrackens' bedroom door off its hinges, tearing it right out of the frame, and barged into the room.

J.J. raced over to protect his family, which was insanely stupid, given that he was almost naked and only armed with a shoe. But I couldn't really fault him for stupidity, because before I knew it, I was running across the hall to help protect Summer too.

My parents were right on my heels, although I'm not sure if they were trying to protect the McCrackens or me.

The McCrackens' room was significantly larger than ours, with a long table in the center, walls lined with bookshelves, and a separate nook for the king-size bed. Since there was more room, there was also more taxidermy. A small herd of sheep heads gazed blankly from the wall, while an entire mounted pronghorn stood by the bathroom door; Summer had hung her bath towel on its horns.

Kandace was sitting in her bed, screaming her head off, while Summer stood on her sofa bed, wrapped in a bathrobe. Their room had a vintage bow and arrow mounted on the wall as decoration. Summer tore it down and scrambled to load it.

Meanwhile, Sasquatch didn't seem to have any interest in the McCrackens at all. Instead, he was hungrily devouring the remains of Kandace's dessert, which had sat, forgotten, on the center table. The bear was licking the plate with great fervor, trying to hoover up every last molecule of crumble and whipped cream.

In his frenzy to protect his family, J.J. didn't quite comprehend this. Or maybe he figured the crumble was just an appetizer before Sasquatch ate his loved ones. So he raced in and flung Dad's shoe at the bear. "Get away from my family!" he yelled.

The shoe bounced harmlessly off of Sasquatch's head. The bear didn't even seem to notice.

Sasquatch was licking the dessert plate so feverishly that he was shoving it across the table with his tongue. He placed a great, meaty paw on the table to hold the plate still. One end of the table promptly collapsed, catapulting everything that had been stored on it—mostly Kandace's jewelry and makeup—across the room onto the bed. The plate slid to the floor and shattered.

Sasquatch realized there was no more dessert. He lifted his head back up and began sniffing the air again hungrily.

To Summer, it appeared that he was sniffing *her* hungrily. Summer loved animals, but not to the point where she was going to let herself get eaten by one. She pulled back the bowstring and fired the arrow.

Unfortunately, the bow was old and warped and Summer had only taken one archery class in her life. So even though Sasquatch was the size of a small car and Summer was firing from close range, she missed the bear completely—and hit her father instead.

The arrow struck J.J. right in his bare shoulder and he howled in pain.

Kandace screamed again. Summer gasped. "Sorry, Daddy!"

Through the wall, I could hear Pete Thwacker shouting in the next room. It sounded as though he had called 911. "There's a bear inside the house! Send the police, or the fire department, or the park service, or whoever you need to! No, I don't know what type of bear it is! It's not a panda or a koala! It's a brown one!"

From upstairs came the sounds of more footsteps. The Krautheimers were running about frantically. Then I heard them coming down the stairs.

Despite all the chaos around him, Sasquatch remained calm, continuing to sniff the air. It was strange, but I had the sense that the bear was being thoughtful about it, like there was a puzzle he was trying to solve. He slowly moved his head back and forth, his enormous nostrils flaring.

He was directly between Summer and the door, although Kandace could get to us.

"Summer," Dad said. "Don't make any sudden movements, but see if you can get out the window. Kandace, come to us. Slowly."

The McCrackens nodded agreement. Summer unlatched the window, while Kandace edged out of bed. J.J. plucked the arrow from his shoulder and waved for Kandace to join him.

"Where's the bear?" Sidney Krautheimer yelled from the living room.

"In our room!" J.J. yelled back.

"Well, get out of there!" Sidney exclaimed. "We're setting out some meat to lure Sasquatch back through the house—and we're armed to the teeth in case anything goes wrong."

"We're working on getting out!" J.J. replied. "It's not so easy!"

Summer propped the window open and quickly slipped outside into the night.

Kandace scurried from the bed to the doorway, but one of the sheets snagged around her ankle and she tumbled to the floor, letting out a cry of pain.

Sasquatch abruptly turned toward her. Even though he hadn't shown much interest in attacking any of us, he was highly attuned to the sound of a wounded animal.

Kandace screamed.

Sasquatch took a step toward her.

Mom quickly jumped into the bear's path, depressed the plunger on her aerosol hair spray, and stuck a lit match in front of it. The aerosol instantly ignited, creating a homemade flamethrower.

Sasquatch froze, warily eyeing the jet of fire.

"Nice going, Charlene!" J.J. crowed. "That's the idea!" Another can of hair spray lay on the floor, one of Kandace's that had been on the table. J.J. grabbed it, struck another match, and lit his own miniature flamethrower.

Sasquatch obviously didn't like the fire. He backed away.

"Ha!" J.J. cried. "Not so tough now, are you?" He took a step forward, trying to create more room for Kandace to get out the door.

Unfortunately, in his overzealousness, J.J. got too close to the stuffed pronghorn with his flamethrower. The bath towel that was hanging on its horns ignited, and suddenly, there was a fire blazing in the room.

"Uh-oh," J.J. said.

Sasquatch *really* didn't like this. And he didn't seem to like being boxed into the room, either. He shifted from side to side, huffing in distress.

"Everyone move!" Dad warned. "He's coming our way!"

We all raced out the door and across the hallway into our room—except for Kandace, who wasn't close enough. Instead, she leaped back into her bed and hid beneath the covers.

Sasquatch barreled out into the hallway, running from the fire. It was like a truck was moving through the house. The floor shook and the walls rattled as he thundered toward the living room.

A grizzly can run thirty-five miles an hour, which is startlingly fast for such a large animal. In his fear, Sasquatch appeared as if he might have been attempting to break that record. He tore through the house as fast as he could go, leaving destruction in his wake.

The Krautheimers had laid a trail of meat down the hall and toward the front door, but Sasquatch paid no attention to it as he fled. The Krautheimers themselves had gathered in the living room, and they were indeed armed. Each had a gun for self-defense, although all of them were still in their pajamas, making them look like the world's most casual commandos. Thankfully, they recognized that Sasquatch was running in fear, rather than attacking, so no one opened fire on him. Instead, they all scrambled out of the bear's way, clambering over the furniture. Sasquatch charged past them, knocking the armchairs and couches aside, sending them skidding across the floor like hockey pucks. He went right back out through the open front door and then kept on going.

I had followed him through the house. In theory, I should have been running away from a bear, rather than toward it, but Sasquatch seemed to have other things on his mind than me. By the time I reached the front door, he had already disappeared into the night.

Summer joined me at the door, having come along the outside of the house from where she had dropped out the window of her room.

"Are you okay?" I asked her.

"Yes. Freaked out, but okay." She slipped her hand into mine and held it tightly.

I turned back to the Krautheimers, who were surveying the wreckage of their living room furniture. It looked as though a steamroller had come through.

"Do you have a fire extinguisher?" I asked.

The same look crossed each of their faces at once, a fear

that somehow this evening was about to get even *worse*. Evan sprang into action. An extinguisher was mounted on the wall by the fireplace. He snapped it out of its bracket and asked, "Where's the fire?"

"The McCrackens' bedroom," I reported. "The pronghorn's on fire."

"The pronghorn?!" Heidi echoed. "How . . . ?"

"Long story," I said.

Evan was already racing down the hallway. We all followed him. We arrived in the McCrackens' room to find Mom, Dad, and J.J. fighting the fire, throwing wet towels over the blazing pronghorn. Evan dealt it the final blow, dousing the flames with the extinguisher—although in his haste, he also doused my parents, J.J., and much of the room with foam as well.

But the fire was out. The pronghorn was no longer burning. Instead, with its blackened face and coating of white foam, it now looked like a majestically posed sheep. The stench of its burned hair, combined with the musky smell of Sasquatch, was overwhelming.

The makeshift firefighting squad looked rather ridiculous as well. J.J. was still only in his boxer shorts, with a shallow wound in his shoulder where he'd been struck by the arrow. Evan wore pajamas decorated with beavers and had a rifle slung over his shoulder, and his nose was still swollen from Summer's punch. Both of them, and my parents, were dripping with foam.

Then Kandace started screaming again.

It startled everyone. In all the excitement, I had forgotten she was even in the room—and I think that my parents had too. She was still in the bed and had emerged from under her covers. My immediate thought, given the hysterical pitch of her shrieks, was that somehow Sasquatch had returned.

"What is it?" J.J. asked worriedly, sounding very much on edge himself. "What's wrong?"

"My necklace!" Kandace explained, pointing to the wreckage of the table in the center of the room. "It's gone!"

6

THE ASSIGNMENT

It took a while to confirm that the necklace was truly missing. My first assumption—and most everyone else's—was that it had simply been knocked aside during the chaos with Sasquatch. So we all set to work, cleaning up the McCrackens' room, while Kandace tried to recall the exact events of the night before.

She was a little hazy on the details, which made sense, as she had just been through a traumatic experience. To the best of her recollection, she had come directly to the room after dinner, bringing the plate of crumble and ice cream with her because she was in a hurry to get unpacked. (Kandace had arrived from New York with five large pieces of luggage, so unpacking was going to take a while.) She had still been wearing the sapphire necklace when she and J.J.

had their argument. After she had kicked him out of the room, she had gotten ready for bed, during which time she *thought* that she had taken off the necklace and placed it in her jewelry case, which was a large, sturdy box the size of a toaster oven. But Kandace wasn't completely sure of that. She admitted that she might have simply left the necklace on the table, intending to put it in the case but forgetting. She also wasn't sure whether she had locked the case or not. And, when pressed, she owned that she might not have placed the necklace on the table at all, although if she hadn't, then she didn't know *where* in the room she had put it.

In any event, as we cleaned the room, it became clear that the necklace was gone. Kandace's jewelry case had broken open, scattering earrings and smaller necklaces across the floor, but the expensive necklace in question wasn't among them. We also rooted through the wreckage of everything else that had been left on the table and scoured the rest of the room, thinking that perhaps the necklace had been catapulted into a distant nook or cranny when Sasquatch upended the table. We searched under the master bed and the sofa bed Summer had slept on, poked through the bookcases, and even checked the closet, just in case the necklace had skittered under the door. But we couldn't find it anywhere.

This left J.J. in an extremely foul mood. He was obviously still livid at Kandace for bringing the necklace to the ranch, although he was doing his best to not lash out at her, given that she was in a bad state, rattled by the experience with Sasquatch and feeling terrible about the loss of her jewels. On top of that, J.J. was embarrassed that everyone knew he'd been forced to sleep on the couch—and because we had all seen him in his underwear. Finally, he'd been shot with an arrow. The wound had turned out to be superficial and easily bandaged with gauze and surgical tape, but still, it looked like it hurt.

"That stupid freaking bear must have eaten our jewels!" J.J. fumed.

It was now just after five in the morning and the sky outside was beginning to show the faintest glow of light on the eastern horizon. We had finally finished cleaning the room, although the burned pronghorn still reeked and needed to be hauled to the trash. The Krautheimers had moved on to dealing with the wreckage of their living room, aided by Karina and Pete. (Ray had somehow managed to sleep through the entire ordeal and was still in bed.) So my family and the McCrackens were the only ones in their room.

"I don't think that's really likely," Mom said.

"Now you're a bear specialist?" J.J. asked testily. "In addition to gorillas?"

Mom gave him an icy stare to let him know she didn't appreciate his tone. "It doesn't take a specialist to know that bears don't normally eat jewelry."

"I'm not saying it came in here to eat the jewelry," J.J. argued. "I'm saying it came in here to eat the dessert Kandace left behind and gobbled down the necklace along with it."

"Dad," Summer said. "This wasn't a small necklace. How would a bear eat it by mistake?"

"Maybe Kandace got some whipped cream or pie on it," J.J. suggested. "The plate was right there next to the jewelry box. Or maybe the bear was so hungry, he decided to just eat everything in sight. You saw him. He was sucking up the contents of this table like an industrial vacuum cleaner. I know sharks eat weird stuff all the time. Well, maybe some bears do too."

My father said, "That's still a stretch."

"Well, what else could have happened?" J.J. demanded. "The necklace was locked in here with Summer and Kandace. Then the freaking bear got in. After that, the necklace was gone."

No one answered him right away, because none of us had another suggestion. Finally Mom said, "You're sure the room was locked?"

"I definitely locked the door before we went to bed," Kandace said. "I remember that for sure. I . . ." She glanced at J.J., embarrassed, then looked back to Mom. "I was angry at J.J. and wanted to make sure he stayed out on the couch."

"I remember her locking it," Summer added. "And the

windows were locked too. I had to undo mine to get out."

"That's right," I agreed, remembering it, then shifted my attention to the door of the room. It was no longer attached to its frame, as Sasquatch had knocked it clean off. We had propped it back against the wall. It had the same style of sliding latch that the door to our room had, and this was still screwed to the door. The latch had fitted into a metal sleeve on the doorjamb, but that piece was now missing. Instead, there were only four holes in the jamb where the screws that held the metal sleeve had torn free. I pointed them out to everyone. "That's definitely proof the door was locked. If it hadn't been, the sleeve for the latch would still be attached here."

Dad looked to Kandace and Summer. "Were both of you here in this room all night after you locked the door?"

Kandace asked sarcastically, "You mean, did we leave an extremely expensive piece of jewelry out in the open and then go take a walk in the middle of the night? No."

"I think he's just asking if maybe we ever went to get a drink of water or anything like that," Summer said diplomatically. "I was asleep in here the whole time until the bear showed up. Were you?"

"Yes," Kandace said. "You know me. Once I've taken my pill, I can sleep through anything."

"Except a grizzly bear coming into your room," I observed.

Dad leaned against the wall by the charred pronghorn,

trying to work things out. "So no one could get in until Sasquatch showed up—and then the necklace disappeared." He looked to Mom. "Maybe he *did* eat the necklace."

"That's what I've been saying!" J.J. declared, then thought to ask, "Either of you have any idea how long it takes something to go through a grizzly's digestive tract?"

"Er . . . no," Mom replied. "As you said, I don't study bears."

"I'd guess somewhere around eight to twelve hours," Dad suggested.

"Eight to twelve hours!" J.J. exclaimed. "We've got to track that dang bear down fast! Before he poops that necklace out in the woods somewhere. Then we'll never find it!" He stormed out of the room, calling for Sidney Krautheimer.

Kandace burst into tears. "J.J. was right. I should never have brought that necklace here!"

Summer put an arm around her mother to comfort her. "It's not your fault. No one could have imagined anything like this would happen. I mean, a grizzly breaking into our room in the middle of the night? That's crazy."

"It broke in because of me!" Kandace wailed. "I brought the dessert in here and then didn't take my dirty plate back to the kitchen! That's probably why the bear came in! That's why it ate my necklace! My beautiful necklace!" She put her head in her hands and cried.

I looked around the room, thinking. There was something about the dessert that bothered me, although I couldn't quite figure out what. All I could think was that Summer was right: It was odd that the bear had come into the house. On that night of all nights. I didn't know for sure, but I had to assume occurrences like this were extremely rare. Otherwise, the Krautheimers would have doors like the ones on bank vaults to keep the bears from getting in.

Which made me remember something important. "The front door was open," I said.

"What?" Summer asked. "When?"

"When Sasquatch first came into the house," I said, thinking back. "The front door was wide open behind him. He didn't knock it off the hinges like the door to this room. It was like someone had let him in."

"I can't imagine anyone would do that," Mom said. "Or *could* do that. How would you lure a bear into the house? And why?"

"To cover up the theft of a necklace," I suggested.

Everyone in the room looked at me with surprise.

"Teddy!" J.J. McCracken's voice rang out from somewhere else in the house. "I need to talk to you!"

I looked to my parents for an indication as to what I should do. They both nodded, so I left the room to go find J.J.

He was in the living room, by himself.

"Where are the Krautheimers?" I asked.

"Organizing a bear hunt," he replied. I must have made a face, because he quickly added, "They're not gonna kill Sasquatch. They're just gonna track him down. So we can keep an eye on him until he poops again. Sidney, Melissa, and Evan are upstairs, changing. Heidi went out to the bunkhouse to wake the ranch hands."

"And you want me to go with them?" I asked, wondering why he had called for me.

"Oh, gosh no," he said quickly, as if the idea of me going after a bear was ridiculous. "They're going on horseback. You'd fall off before you made it six feet."

"I'm not *that* bad," I told him.

"Point is, you have other talents that could be of use." J.J. glanced back toward the guest bedrooms, as if worried that we might be overheard, then took me by the arm and led me out the back door onto the porch, which was cold, as it was still fifteen minutes until sunrise. Even then, when we were far away from everyone else, he lowered his voice to a whisper. "Has anything struck you as odd about what happened tonight?"

"Yes—" I began, although before I could even explain what, J.J. interrupted.

"Me too!" he exclaimed. "Something here stinks like what bears do in the woods."

"So . . . you think that maybe Sasquatch didn't eat that necklace?"

"I don't know what to think. I mean, it certainly *seems* like Sasquatch ate it, but . . . I need to cover all my bases here. That necklace is worth a lot of money. *A lot.* Much more than my wife realizes."

"How much?"

J.J. hesitated, as though unsure whether or not to trust me, then gave in. "The fact is, I got a great deal on it when I first bought it for her. It was the deal of a lifetime. The value of that necklace—or really, the sapphire in the middle of it—has gone through the roof. Last time I had it appraised, which was over a year ago, it was worth eight-point-two million dollars."

I blinked at him in the dusky light, wondering if I had heard him properly. "Did you say eight-point-two *million?*"

"Yes. Which is why I wasn't pleased to see Kandace showing up here, wearing it like a piece of costume jewelry. And now exactly what I was worried about has happened. It's gone." J.J. focused his gaze on me. "And just in case that bear didn't take it—then I want you to find out who did."

"Me?" I asked. "Not the police?"

J.J. signaled me to lower my voice, then whispered, "You're smarter than any police detective I know, Theodore. And frankly, I doubt the police would even believe me if I told them the necklace had been stolen. But more importantly, there's another reason to not bring the police in. If I do that, the thief might realize I'm onto them."

"Oh," I said, understanding. "You want them to think you believe Sasquatch did it."

"Exactly! If someone really did steal that necklace, let's let them think they got away clean. Maybe they'll drop their guard. Some of these people know about your talent for solving crimes, but the others don't. Or maybe they think the stories are all overblown. You're only a kid, for Pete's sake. In the meantime, keep your eyes peeled and your ears tuned for anything suspicious. Can you do that for me?"

"I suppose." In truth, I was daunted by the case. I had no idea how someone could have stolen the necklace from inside a locked room, or how Sasquatch tied into it. But for the second time in a day, I was intrigued by the mystery and excited by the idea of solving it.

However, it seemed foolish to simply agree to something that would be time-consuming and potentially perilous, right in the midst of my first vacation in years. Especially when a billionaire was asking me to do it.

"This sounds pretty difficult," I said. "And I've ended up in a lot of danger when investigating cases before. . . ."

"I'll pay you," J.J. said quickly. "Seeing as you'd be working for me. Consider it a summer job."

"How much are you paying?" I asked. "If I recover the necklace for you, it seems that maybe I'd be entitled to one percent of its worth."

J.J. stared at me blankly for a moment—and then burst into laughter. "You're smart, all right, Theodore. I'm not gonna pony up that much, but . . . if you recover that necklace, I promise, I'll make it worth your while. Do we have a deal?"

"Can Summer help me? Like, as my assistant?"

J.J. considered this, then frowned. "To be honest, I'd prefer that even she didn't know you were investigating for me. She's a bright kid too, but I'm not sure that she could keep this a secret."

"I don't know if I can keep this from her. We're supposed to be on vacation together. Plus, I don't like lying to her."

"You won't have to lie if she doesn't ask what you're up to. Now, time's slipping away. What do you say? Will you take the case?"

I thought for a bit. The case was formidable, but I was excited by the challenge. There were plenty of things that bothered me about the events of the previous night, and I wanted to get to the bottom of it all. I wanted to find the necklace. And earning some money wouldn't be so bad either.

"Sure," I said. "I'm on the job."

THE DIRTY DISHES

When I came back into the house from the porch,
Sidney Krautheimer was downstairs, dressed to go hunt for
Sasquatch. He wore full camouflage gear and was holding a
double-barreled shotgun.

Worried, I said, "I thought you weren't going to kill Sasquatch."

"I'm not planning on it," Sidney replied. "Gavin and
Zach are bringing sedation rifles for us. We keep those over
by the barn because we generally use them for managing the
bison. But only a fool goes after a grizzly without heavy artil-
lery. Where bears are concerned, you need to be prepared for
things to go wrong." The shotgun had a strap attached to it,
which he used to sling it over his back.

I wasn't pleased that Sasquatch might end up getting

shot, but I understood Sidney's reasoning and didn't argue the point. After all, *he* was the one going after the bear. Not me.

The front door was wide open once again, although this time it was because the Krautheimers were in the process of heading out for the hunt. I noticed that Evan was crouched just off the front porch, shining a flashlight over the ground. Sidney headed out to join Evan, and I followed.

As we passed through the front door, I took a moment to inspect it. The door had a dead bolt lock, which needed a key to open from the outside but could be locked by hand from the inside. The doorjamb was completely intact, indicating that the dead bolt hadn't been engaged when the bear came in.

"Was this door locked last night?" I asked.

Sidney paused to think about that. "Honestly, I don't know. There's a good chance it wasn't. We don't usually lock it. That's one of the nice things about living out here. No crime."

Except for disappearing bison and stolen necklaces, I thought, although I didn't say it. My parents and I rarely locked our trailer, either, but the access to our trailer park was restricted because it was on FunJungle property—and we didn't have much worth stealing.

"Sasquatch came in this way last night," I said. "Or I

assume he did, because the door was wide open behind him. Can a bear open a door?"

Sidney thought about that for a moment. "I've never heard of it, but I wouldn't put it past them. Bears can be pretty darn smart when food is on the line. That's why we have to put three different latches on the shed for the garbage cans. If you only use one, they'll figure out how to open it. Even though your standard three-year-old human can't." He turned to Evan. "What've you got?"

"Not much," Evan replied. "It'd be a lot easier to read these in the sunlight."

"Read what?" I asked.

"Sasquatch's tracks," Evan replied.

The Krautheimers' house didn't have a lawn. There was only natural grassland around it, with a dirt path leading to the front door. In the beam of Evan's flashlight, I could see there were some scuffs in the dirt, although I couldn't make sense of them.

"Evan's one of the best trackers in the county," Sidney told me proudly. "He used to win all the competitions in it when he was younger."

"You're a tracker?" I asked Evan, surprised. "I thought you didn't like being outdoors."

"Just because you're good at something doesn't mean you have to like doing it," Evan said. He hadn't looked up once from the ground the whole time we'd been speaking. Now he pointed to the various marks in the dirt he'd been studying. "These are the tracks Sasquatch made when he came to the house. See? He's only using the pads of his paws. No claw marks. He was moving slowly then, taking his time. Looks like he pretty much followed the path to the front door."

"So he came from the road?" Sidney asked, sounding surprised.

"Or maybe the Spooner Ranch." Evan pointed toward the road, but it was far enough away that I could barely see it in the dim morning light. In the distance, well beyond the road, was a much brighter light, a lamp in the window of the home of their closest neighbor. It seemed to be at least a half mile away.

Sidney grunted at the mention of the Spooner Ranch. It was hard to get much meaning from a grunt, but it seemed negative to me.

Evan pointed to another set of bear tracks by his feet. "This is the trail Sasquatch left when he ran off. You can see how his claws were digging into the ground. He went around the house that way, past the kitchen." He pointed toward the opposite end of the house from the guest bedrooms.

I felt a wave of relief pass over me. If Sasquatch had gone the other direction, he would have run right into Summer, who had been heading toward the front door after having climbed out her bedroom window.

I heard voices in the direction Evan was pointing, coming our way. I couldn't quite make them out, as several people were talking at once, but they sounded breathless, like the people were walking quickly while they were talking. Mixed in with them, I also heard heavier footsteps and an occasional snort. Horses. And a bit of panting and whining. Dogs.

Several people emerged from the predawn gloom: Heidi Krautheimer was leading Jasmine and the three ranch hands back to the house. In her haste to go rouse them, Heidi had only pulled a heavy jacket and boots on over her pajamas, but the other four had been given time to dress. They were leading nine horses, each of which had already been saddled. Several of the saddles were fitted with slings to hold weapons. I noticed both sedation rifles and shotguns.

Zach had two midsize dogs with him. They were straining against their leashes, enthusiastically sniffing at the ground, eager to follow the scent.

"We're good to go," Zach reported.

"So am I!" Melissa bounded out the door, ready to ride, surprisingly chipper for someone up so early—not to mention someone whose house had been recently trashed by a grizzly bear. Like her father, she was dressed from head to toe in camouflage gear. She looked to her brother. "Ready?"

Evan made a face. "We might as well go back to sleep. We're never gonna find him."

"Not with an attitude like that, we won't," Sidney said. "We've got the dogs to find the scent. But we need you to follow the tracks. So stop kvetching and get your head in the game."

"I don't get why it's such a big deal," Evan groused.

Sidney pulled Evan aside and spoke to him in a low voice, although in his haste, he didn't seem to notice I was close enough to overhear. "J.J. McCracken is thinking about buying this ranch—and he's thinking about paying us very nicely for it. But now a grizzly bear has broken into his bedroom and eaten his wife's extremely expensive necklace. Do you honestly think, if we don't get that back, that J.J. will go through with this deal?"

Evan sighed heavily. "Fine. I'll do my best to find Sasquatch. But I can't promise anything."

"Your best is all I ask," Sidney said, then turned to his ranch hands. "Let's mount up."

Zach unclipped the dogs from their leashes. They bolted off into the darkness, howling with excitement.

Melissa, Gavin, Zach, Evan, and Sidney hopped onto their horses with the practiced ease of people who had done it thousands of times. Even though Gavin was older than my parents, and Zach was built like a brick wall, they still moved with effortless grace. The five of them set off around the house in the direction the dogs had gone.

Jasmine and Arin didn't go with them. They remained behind with the other four horses.

"Who are those horses for?" I asked.

"One of them's for *you*," Jasmine answered.

"Me?" I asked, surprised. "I can't go hunt for Sasquatch."

"We aren't going after the bear. We're going to figure out what happened to the bison, remember? Last night, I said we'd go first thing in the morning."

"It's not even six o'clock!" I exclaimed. "The sun isn't even up yet!"

"It will be soon," Jasmine said. "Best time of day to see the herd. Besides, you're already up. And I understand Summer is too. What were you thinking you were gonna do, go back to bed?" She said this in a tone that indicated only the lamest person on earth would do such a thing.

It occurred to me that I didn't really have a reason *not* to go with her. After all the events of the morning, I was wide awake, and since J.J. had told me to keep my investigation into who'd stolen the necklace a secret, I couldn't very well insist that I had to stay behind to do that. Plus, in a way, going along with Jasmine and Arin *was* investigating. I needed to question them. They hadn't been in the house when Sasquatch broke in, but they *had* been there earlier in the evening. I didn't know how they could have swiped the necklace, but I had to assume that anyone who had been around the night before was a potential suspect.

"Let me go get my clothes on," I said. I was still in my pajamas with the bathrobe over them.

"Make it snappy," Jasmine said. "And see if Summer wants to come."

I returned to the guest bedrooms. The door to the McCrackens' room wasn't shut, seeing as it had been taken off at the hinges. Summer was still in her pajamas, tending to her mother, who had lain back down in bed. Kandace had calmed down a lot since I had last seen her. In fact, she was asleep.

Summer put a finger to her lips, cautioning me not to speak. Then she came to the door and spoke in a whisper. "Mom was all worked up, so she took another pill to get some more sleep."

I explained that Jasmine had brought horses, ready for us to go investigate the missing bison.

Summer was as surprised as I had been that Jasmine wanted to go so early, but as usual, she was game for an adventure. She agreed to get dressed quickly.

I slipped into my room and informed my parents what I was going to do. In the past, they hadn't wanted me investigating mysteries, as that had often put me in danger, but they didn't seem too concerned about this one. Or maybe they were simply relieved that I was merely riding off to see some bison instead of joining the bear hunt.

"Have fun," Mom said.

"And try not to fall off the horse," Dad added.

"Why does everyone think I'm going to fall off the horse?" I griped. I got dressed as fast as I could, then headed back out again.

In the hallway, I ran into Summer, who was now dressed to ride.

"Can we swing by the kitchen?" she asked. "I want to get a quick bite. Just in case we're not back for breakfast."

That sounded like a good idea. To my surprise, despite the enormous amount of food I had consumed the night before, my stomach was grumbling. I figured that maybe the adrenaline rush of running into the bear had burned a lot of calories.

We popped into the kitchen and found a jar of home-made granola on the counter. Summer was grabbing baggies for us to put it in when my eyes fell upon the sink.

There was a pile of dirty dishes in it, the dessert plates from the night before. Heidi Krautheimer had told us all to stack them there, claiming Daisy Creek would clean them in the morning. Some of the guests had practically licked them clean, but most of the plates still had the remnants of crumble and whipped cream encrusted on them.

I suddenly realized what had been bothering me about Sasquatch's entry into the house the night before.

"What's wrong?" Summer asked.

"Hmm?" I pulled my attention away from the plates and shifted it to her. "Nothing."

"Don't lie to me, Teddy. I know the look that was just on your face. You know something's wrong. What is it?"

I decided there was no point in keeping what I had noticed to myself. "There's a dozen dirty plates in the sink."

"Right. Daisy went home while we were having dessert. So no one cleaned them."

"Everyone's been thinking that Sasquatch was lured to your room last night because your mother brought her dessert in there," I said. "But that was only one plate. There's much more dessert left in this sink. If that was all Sasquatch was interested in, it would have been a lot easier for the bear to come in here. This is much closer to the entrance, and he wouldn't have had to knock down a door to get to it. So why'd he go to your room?"

Summer gave me a look that said she was impressed by my realization. "I don't know. But I'm sure you'll figure it out."

I frowned, not so sure about that myself. I might have had success in the past deducing what humans had been thinking when they'd committed a crime. But I had no idea if I could figure out what a bear had been thinking.

"Hey," a voice said behind us.

We turned around to see Jasmine standing in the kitchen doorway, looking impatient. "We've got a mystery to solve," she said. "Let's ride."

THE FENCE

I did not fall off my horse while riding that morn-ing. Although I did come close a few times.

Summer had often told me that she loved horseback riding because she could free her mind while she was doing it. When riding, she could think about all sorts of things. I understood what she meant; I felt that way when hiking or riding my bicycle.

But when I was on a horse, all I could think about was trying to stay on the horse. That and how much my rear end was hurting.

Because of this, my plans to question Jasmine and Arin during our ride didn't work out so well. I had to wait until we got to our destination.

Luckily, that wasn't too far away. The ride was only about

fifteen minutes. The Krautheimers' house was located in the northwestern section of the ranch, so most of the property extended south and east. But we headed the opposite way, to the northwestern corner, which abutted the town of West Yellowstone.

Jasmine and Arin were riding their usual horses, Dyna-. mite and Bandit. Because Summer knew how to ride, she had been given a feisty young filly named Powder Keg. Meanwhile, I had been given the least spirited horse at the ranch, Molasses. He had been named that because he moved very slowly, which was just fine with me. While Summer spurred Powder Keg to run circles in the fields, I was happy to plod along at a leisurely pace on Molasses.

Despite my lack of skill on the horse, it was a beautiful ride. The sun had just come up and the fields were bathed in the first rays of light. Pronghorn and white-tailed deer grazed while jackrabbits bounded ahead of us. I even caught a glimpse of a long-tailed weasel darting through the grass.

Our route took us parallel to the dirt road that ran between the Oy Vey Corral and the Spooner Ranch. We were about halfway along when the Creeks' pickup came rumbling down the road, kicking up the usual plume of dust. Arturo was at the wheel, with Daisy in the passenger seat. They honked to get our attention, then pulled over and yelled out the window.

"What are you doing out so early?" Daisy called.

"The kids are helping me figure out what happened to the bison!" Jasmine called back. "What are *you* doing coming in so early?"

Arturo replied, "Heidi said Sasquatch got into the house! And now the whole place is a wreck."

Jasmine frowned, as though she was upset it hadn't occurred to her to call her parents. "Yes. But no one was hurt, thankfully."

Just then, the car we had borrowed to visit Yellowstone the day before came barreling down the road, heading toward town from the house. Whoever was at the wheel was a terrible driver. The car was veering back and forth wildly. It flew past the pickup without slowing down, cloaking it in a cloud of dust that made both the Creeks cough, then kept on going.

I caught a glimpse of Karina in the passenger seat, looking somewhat terrified, but couldn't make out who was driving.

"Who was that maniac?" Jasmine asked.

"I think it was my father," Summer said, looking embarrassed. "Sorry. He's the world's worst driver."

It occurred to me that, in all the time I had known the McCrackens, I had never seen J.J. behind the wheel of any vehicle. He always used a chauffeur. I had always assumed this was because having a chauffeur was a luxury, but now it occurred to me that maybe it was to keep J.J. from driving.

"They were sure in a hurry," I observed, then asked Summer, "Did he tell you he was going anywhere today?"

"No," Summer replied. "He said he had something to take care of, but I thought that meant he was staying around the house."

"We'd best be heading on," Arturo said. "Sounds like we have a lot of cleaning to do."

"Don't be late for breakfast!" Daisy warned. And then they continued on toward the house.

We resumed our ride, veering away from the dirt road until we came to the northern edge of the property. There, we found a great open field of grass, bounded by one of the main routes to Yellowstone. A few dozen of the Krautheimers' bison were grazing about fifty yards from the barbed-wire fence that marked the property line. We were much closer to them than we had been the previous night. I could see that each had a tag in its right ear with a number on it, as Jasmine had told us the night before. The tags were a variety of colors.

There was a good number of young calves in the herd, most of which had probably been born that spring, as well as quite a few midsize bison, the equivalent of teenagers. The young were far more active than the adults and seemed to be playing. The calves were cavorting about, while the teens were chasing one another and occasionally butting heads.

"This is why I like to come see them now," Jasmine said. "Once it gets hot out, all they want to do is graze and sleep."

Even though it was shortly after sunrise, there was a good amount of traffic on the road to Yellowstone, visitors getting an early start on the day. (We had done the same thing the day before, as Heidi had warned that on a busy summer morning, the traffic jams to get into the park could rival those in New York City at rush hour.) A steady line of cars and RVs was heading east, toward the park entrance, while only a single big old RV was heading out.

Several carloads of tourists had pulled over on the side of the road, eager to see the Krautheimers' bison. I had no idea if any of them realized it was a captive herd, but no matter what, the animals were impressive; it was possible these were the first bison many of the tourists had ever seen. Some tourists were staying in their cars, taking photos through the rolled-down windows, either in too big a hurry to get to Yellowstone to stop for long, or too lazy to get out of their vehicles. But a few had parked and come to the barbed-wire fence. Most were taking selfies with the bison in the background—even though the bison were so far away, they would probably only look like tiny brown dots in the photos. A few visitors were simply watching the herd with rapt expressions, awed by the magnificent beasts.

Jasmine stopped her horse at a spot along the fence where no tourists were gathered, then hopped to the ground.

The rest of us followed her lead and did the same. Arin and Summer got off their horses expertly. I did not. Instead, I got my foot stuck in the stirrup and fell on my butt in the grass.

This provoked some giggles from the tourists in the distance.

Jasmine said, "This is the only point on the whole property that comes close to a public road. If anyone was going to steal one of our bison, this is where it'd make the most sense to do it."

"A male bison can weigh over a ton," Arin added, by way of agreement. "And a female can weigh half that, so there's no easy way to move them unless you have a truck."

Jasmine left Dynamite behind and started to walk along the fence. She didn't even bother to tether the horse up, apparently confident that he wouldn't run off. Sure enough, Dynamite stayed exactly where she had left him and started grazing.

Most of the tourists now shifted their attention to Jasmine. "Look!" I heard one father exclaim to his children. "A real live cowgirl!"

I followed Jasmine, keeping an eye on the bison that were grazing nearby. Neither Jasmine nor Arin seemed concerned about them, but I figured I should stay on the alert while close to such large animals. Bison don't have the sharp teeth or claws of grizzlies, but they can still do a lot of damage with their horns and hooves. Plus, their great bulk alone is dangerous; animals that big can hurt you simply by bumping into you too hard.

I dropped in beside Arin and asked, as naturally as I could, "Did you guys see any sign of Sasquatch when you went back to the bunkhouse last night?"

"No," he replied. "And we didn't hear him either. We had no idea he was nearby until Heidi came and woke us."

"Have you ever seen him around at night?"

"Not directly, but we've seen evidence. Sasquatch leaves the biggest bear poops I've ever seen. They're the size of cantaloupes. And we've seen prints, too. I wouldn't ever wander around this property by myself at night. Although, I never expected Sasquatch would want to come inside. We'll need some better locks on our doors."

"So then, all of you went back to the bunkhouse together and then went right to bed?"

"The others did. I called my girlfriend first. She also works on a ranch, north of Bozeman. About two hours away from here. So we only get to see each other every few days."

"But you're sure everyone else went to sleep right away?"

Arin gave me a curious look, which meant I had probably pushed my questioning too far. "As far as I know. I mean, I don't go around and tuck everyone in."

It occurred to me that I should probably take a look at the bunkhouse, to see what the layout was. Maybe someone had snuck out and gone to the house to steal the necklace before Sasquatch had shown up. Although I still had no idea how they would have gotten past the locked door and windows of the master bedroom.

"Here it is!" Jasmine said suddenly.

She had stopped by one of the fence posts. The rest of us joined her to see what she thought was so important.

Nothing looked out of the ordinary to me. The fence was a basic barbed-wire fence; I had seen thousands of miles of it strung along the roads in central Texas. This one was newer than most. Since it was located along the main road, I presumed it needed to be replaced more than usual; half the tourists were leaning on it so they could move their phones a few inches closer to the bison. Those few inches certainly didn't make one bit of difference to their photos, but they were doing it anyhow.

The fence posts were shafts of four-by-fours, cemented into holes in the ground. Six strings of barbed wire were affixed to the posts with U-shaped nails. Every now and then, there was a small tuft of brown hair caught on one of the barbs, indicating that a bison had rubbed up against it.

Apparently, Arin and Summer didn't see what was so important about the fence post either, because both just stared at Jasmine blankly. "What should we be seeing here?" Arin asked.

"Look." Jasmine pointed to where there were two small holes in the post above and below a strand of barbed wire. "And here. And here." She pointed to similar marks on lower strands.

"I don't get it," Summer said.

Jasmine explained, "I think someone pulled these strands of barbed wire free, then nailed them back again."

I slowly grasped what she thought had happened. The sets of holes were all from the previous U-shaped nails that had held the strands in place. When I looked closer, I could spot small gouges in the wood between them, where someone had used a screwdriver to pry the nails loose. "So what do you think happened?" I asked. "They took the fence apart, stole a bison, and then patched it back up again?"

"Exactly!" Jasmine now pointed to the nails on the post. "These are newer than the nails on posts a few yards away from here. That's only the case with four posts, but that's all the thieves would have needed. The posts are ten feet apart, which means that if you remove the nails on four, then you have fifty feet of slack wire. They could have pressed that down low enough to walk a bison over it, then pulled it back up and nailed it back into place."

"That's still not proof that someone stole the bison," Arin said. "Maybe whoever was building this fence ran out of one brand of nails and needed to use different ones."

"But it looks like some of the nails have been pried out," I said.

"Maybe they were hammered in wrong in the first place," Arin countered.

Jasmine gave Arin an annoyed glance, as if she was frustrated with his arguments.

"I'm not saying you're wrong," Arin told her. "I'm only saying there are other reasons the fence could look like that."

Jasmine sighed heavily. "I know. But this is all the evidence I have that the bison were stolen."

I considered the fence post again. It was impossible to say whether someone had actually taken the fence apart or not. But if someone *had*, they had done an extremely good job of covering their tracks. The fence looked almost normal, except for the tiny holes where the U-shaped nails had gone before and the gouges from removing them. It probably never would have been noticed unless someone had been looking for signs of tampering.

"Don't you have security cameras along the fence?" Summer asked.

Jasmine laughed. "Maybe your father can afford to protect his ranch like that, but this place operates on a shoestring.

There's twenty miles of fence. We're lucky we can afford to keep it standing upright, let alone run cameras along it."

Summer turned slightly pink. She never liked to take her family's wealth for granted and always found occasions where she did to be embarrassing. Then she stiffened slightly, looking annoyed.

I followed her gaze and realized what had brought the change over her. Two college-aged boys were coming along the fence, staring at Summer with the same amount of awe the other tourists had for the bison. They had obviously recognized her.

The college boys came right up to the fence. Both had takeout cups of coffee in their hands. "You're Summer McCracken, aren't you?" one of the guys asked.

Summer deployed her usual trick to deflect attention. "Sadly, I'm not," she said, speaking with a fake deep western twang. "Although I get mistaken for her a lot."

The college guys scrutinized her carefully, as though unsure whether to believe her or not.

"I'm really not her," Summer told them. "My name's Jolene Turpin and I live right here on this ranch, not some fancy mansion in Texas."

"Could we take a selfie with you anyhow?" the second guy asked. "Then we could just tell people that you *were* her."

Summer frowned at the thought of this, then forced a

smile onto her face. "Oh, I don't think that'd be right," she said. "I don't want the *real* Summer McCracken getting angry at me for pretending to be her. I hope you understand."

She said it in a charming enough way that the guys had to agree with her, but they were obviously both disappointed. "I guess so," one said. They headed back to their car. On the way, one polished off his coffee, then crumpled the cup and simply dropped it on the shoulder of the road.

"Hey!" Summer shouted after him. "You dropped something!"

"So?" the guy asked.

"If the real Summer McCracken was here, she'd hate you for being a litterbug!" Summer shouted after him.

The guys didn't respond, even though they were obviously within earshot.

I realized, to my dismay, that they weren't the first people to have behaved like this. The swath of grass between the fence and the road was strewn with trash from people who had stopped to watch the bison: fast-food containers, candy wrappers, shards of broken beer bottles. There was even some litter on our side of the fence; as I looked at my feet, I spotted quite a few bottle caps and cigarette butts.

It struck me as bizarre that anyone could have stopped to see the bison, indicating that they had at least some appreciation of nature—and then dropped their garbage.

But it had obviously happened over and over again.

An idea suddenly occurred to me. If someone had recently pried the nails from the fence posts, maybe they had dropped them on the ground as well. I started kicking through the tall grass along the fence, trying to see if I could spot anything.

Instead of a nail, I noticed something else. It was a thin piece of blue plastic, and it had landed sideways in a tuft of tall grass, so that it was almost invisible when seen from directly above. If I hadn't been carefully searching the ground, I might never have seen it. I reached down and picked it up.

"What's that?" Summer asked me curiously.

"I think it's proof that the bison were stolen after all," I said.

9

THE TAG

"It's an ear tag," I continued, holding up the piece of plastic. "From one of the bison here."

The tag was blue and had the number 823 in large print over the words "Oy Vey." It narrowed toward the top, where it would have been attached to the bison's ear with a stud, but someone had sliced through the plastic with scissors or a knife.

Jasmine gave a small gasp and started toward me.

"I know these don't come off easily," I continued. "I've seen them on my friends' ranches. Someone must have cut this off when they were stealing the bison. To hide the fact that it was from this ranch."

Jasmine took the tag from me, looking concerned. "This is not good," she said.

"Why not?" Summer asked. "You aren't excited to have evidence?"

"I am, but . . ." Jasmine held up the tag. "This is from one of our purebred bison."

Now Arin made a gasp of concern as well.

"What's wrong?" Summer asked.

Jasmine said, "After the bison in this country nearly went extinct, various attempts were made to increase their populations. A lot of ranchers bred them with cattle."

"Oh," I said. Breeding members of two different species is common in captivity. It's how all the different breeds of dog on earth were created—as well as cats, chickens, cattle, and every other domesticated animal. Occasionally, people introduce wild species into the mix, as when breeders arrange for wolves to mate with dogs, although this is often frowned upon by conservationists. "Do you have an issue with that?"

"Not really," Jasmine told me. She started for the horses. Now that we had our evidence, she apparently wanted to get back to the ranch house quickly.

Arin, Summer, and I hurried after her.

Jasmine continued, "Most bison only have small amounts of cattle genes in them—and obviously, the crossbreeding was important in bringing the population back to sustainable levels. But now there's interest in keeping those bison that have no cattle genes at all, pure. The herds in Yellowstone are mostly uncontaminated, and they're large enough that the park service has been lending bison out to some ranches to help us purify our stocks."

"And this bison that was taken was one of the pure ones?" Summer asked.

"Yes. We tagged all the purebreds with blue tags." Jasmine reached her horse and swung herself into the saddle with one graceful movement. "Dark blue for males, and light blue for females."

"So the one that was stolen was a male," Arin added, hopping onto his horse.

Summer followed suit. I did my best, but I wasn't nearly as practiced. Molasses began moving as I tried to mount him, forcing me to awkwardly hop alongside him with one foot in the stirrup and the other on the ground.

Jasmine said, "The *real* problem here is that we don't own that bison. He was on loan from the park service. And now I'm going to have to call them and tell them we let it get stolen. Which they won't be happy about. Although there is one good piece of news."

"What's that?" I made a valiant attempt to mount Molasses, kicking hard off the ground. I swung up into the saddle—and nearly toppled right off the other side of the horse. I had to throw myself forward and wrap my arms around his neck to prevent this from happening, which was not very suave.

I caught a glimpse of Summer giggling at my failure.

If Jasmine had noticed any of this, she didn't show it. "We use the tag numbers to keep tabs on all the bison. So I might be able to pinpoint when 823 was stolen." She took out her phone and began to scroll through it. Unlike someone who was driving a car, she didn't have to keep her eyes on the road; she could trust Dynamite to do that for her.

I finally managed to get myself upright in the saddle on Molasses.

"Nice form," Summer teased.

"Stuff it," I told her, but gave her a smile to let her know I wasn't really mad.

"Here we go." Jasmine squinted at her phone in the light of the rising sun, then made a sound of surprise. "Hmmm. According to our records, 823 was only born a year ago in May. We bred him here."

Summer asked, "Then does that mean he doesn't belong to the park service?"

"No. Any purebreds we breed are technically theirs. What interests me is his age. A yearling would be considerably easier to steal than a full grown male. They're still pretty big, but not *that* big. Also, no one has logged a sighting of 823 since May twenty-ninth."

"So that's when he was stolen?" I asked.

"Not necessarily," Jasmine replied. "Since there's so many

bison, we can't log them all every day. But we log a good number of them. It's possible we randomly missed 823 over and over again, but we do try to note the purebreds when we see them."

Arin said, "So we can't guarantee 823 was taken on May twenty-ninth. But there's a good chance it was around that time."

"That was six weeks ago," I observed.

"Which means the trail has gone awfully cold," Summer added. She looked to Jasmine. "Is there any reason someone would want to steal a purebred bison over one that wasn't?"

"Purebreds are worth a bit more," Jasmine answered. "Though I suspect this might have been an accident. You can't tell a purebred by looking at it—and I doubt many people know that we even have any of them—except us and the park service. They would have known it was a male, though. That's easy to tell."

Summer said, "It'd be helpful to know if the other bison that was stolen was a purebred too."

Jasmine sighed. "Yes. But we won't know which one that was until we can do a full census. I doubt we'll get lucky enough to find another ear tag."

"Maybe not," I said. "Chances are, they stole both bison the same way. Maybe even at the same time. So perhaps there's another tag in the grass over there."

Arin laughed dismissively. "Oh? All we have to do is comb through an acre of grassland looking for a tiny piece of plastic that might not even be there? That's literally hunting for a needle in a haystack. You're welcome to do that if you want, but I'll pass."

I looked back toward the fence. We were now far enough away that all the people were only specks on the horizon. "Are there always tourists along that fence?"

"Most of the time," Jasmine said. "People come here from all over the world to see wildlife, and those are often the first bison they come across. They don't care that they're on a ranch. Or maybe they don't realize it. So they stop to take pictures. As long as there's daylight, they're there."

"Then whoever stole the bison probably did it at night," I concluded. "You couldn't take down fifty feet of fence and make off with a bison in front of a crowd."

"It'd still be awfully hard to do in the dark," Summer surmised. "How do you steal a living thing that big?"

"The same way you rustle a normal cow," Jasmine said. "Though maybe you'd have to be a bit more careful, because bison are less docile than cattle. You'd also need a good-size truck to load the bison into. It'd take some time to coax it along, but someone who knew what they were doing could manage it."

"And what kind of person would know that?" I asked.

"It'd have to be someone who knows how to handle cattle," Jasmine answered. "Someone with ranching experience. Someone who can throw a lasso. Wrangling a bison into a truck wouldn't be easy. An amateur probably wouldn't be able to do it."

"Maybe it was someone from the park service who took it, then," Summer suggested.

"Why would someone from the park service steal a bison?" Arin wanted to know.

Summer shrugged. "Same reasons as anyone. Maybe they needed money. How much is a bison worth?"

"Anywhere from two to five thousand dollars," Jasmine said.

"That's a good amount of cash," Summer observed. "And the bison wasn't locked up, like a piece of art might be. Or a piece of jewelry . . ." She trailed off, probably thinking about her mother's necklace.

"It's a lot harder to move a bison than a piece of jewelry, though," I reminded her. "And if you were stealing it for the money, you'd still have to sell it."

"There are other reasons someone might want a bison," Jasmine said.

"Like what?" I asked.

Only, Jasmine didn't answer me. Instead, she reined Dynamite to a stop and cocked her head, listening.

The rest of us stopped to listen too. Or, I *tried* to stop and listen. Molasses refused to follow my orders and kept going. I tugged tighter on the reins, but he stubbornly continued onward.

However, I could still hear what had grabbed Jasmine's attention. A whirring noise cut through the quiet of the morning. A helicopter was heading toward the ranch from the direction of town.

It was coming in low, only a few hundred feet above the ground.

We were now amid a much larger portion of the Krautheimers' bison herd. Hundreds of them were grazing in the open field all around us. The bison hadn't taken any notice of our group as we rode past, but now they stirred at the sound of the incoming copter, lifting their great heads from the ground and grunting in what sounded to me like agitation.

"What's that idiot doing?" Jasmine asked, focused on the aircraft as it came closer and closer.

It was quickly upon us, roaring over the herd about fifty yards to our right. It was a small copter, built for only two people, and it was low enough that we could see both of them inside the glass bubble of the cockpit.

They could obviously see who we were too, because one of them waved to us.

Summer groaned. "That idiot is my father."

Karina was at the controls with J.J. McCracken beside her. I quickly realized what they were up to—and why they had been in such a hurry that morning. "They must be looking for Sasquatch!" I yelled to the others.

"Well, they need to stop it!" Jasmine yelled back. "Or they're going to spook the herd!"

I quit trying to make Molasses stay and tried to make him move faster. If the herd started to run, I didn't want to be anywhere near it.

Unfortunately, Molasses was being ornery. Now that I wanted him to move, he decided to stop. "Oh, come on," I groaned. I nudged him lightly with my stirrups, trying to be as nice about it as possible.

Molasses didn't budge. Instead, he lifted his tail and deposited several pounds of horse patoot on the ground.

To my dismay, the helicopter banked around over the river and started back toward us.

Close by, Summer had taken out her phone and called her father. He must have answered on the first ring, because she started talking right away. "Daddy! You guys need to stop flying over the herd! . . . Yes, I know you're looking for Sasquatch, but I don't think he's here. If he was with the bison, we would know it. . . . Well, of course you saw a big brown animal in the middle of the herd! They're *all* big brown animals!"

The helicopter roared and came back over the herd again, even lower this time, so close that Jasmine and Arin both had to hold on to their cowboy hats to keep them from blowing off their heads. Through the windows of the chopper, I could see J.J. and Karina were both looking down, closely studying the ground below them. But while they were busily searching for a giant bear, neither seemed to realize the effect they were having on the bison.

The herd was spooked. A few started running away from the helicopter. In doing this, they jostled other bison, who began to run as well.

And once a good number of bison were running, a literal herd mentality set in. Innate behavior that had evolved over thousands of years kicked into gear. All the bison started to run at once, creating a great stampede.

And unfortunately, they were stampeding right toward us.

10

THE STAMPEDE

This was not the first time I had been caught in a stampede. I had once been surrounded by panicked antelope in the Asian Plains at FunJungle, but those were all significantly smaller than bison. Getting hit by a bison would be like getting run over by a truck. (I had also witnessed an elephant stampede from behind, but watching elephants run away from you is far less dangerous than watching bison stampede *toward* you.)

My big concern now was that I was on a horse. I wasn't good on a horse when everything was calm and controlled. So it was terrifying to be astride one with a herd of bison thundering toward me.

However, the stampede managed to do what I couldn't: convince Molasses to move. My horse stopped stubbornly grazing, looked toward the approaching herd, then whinnied in terror and galloped across the plains.

Until that moment, I'd had no idea that Molasses could gallop. It was quite possible that Molasses himself hadn't known. It had probably been years since he had last done it. He took off so suddenly that I nearly fell backward off the saddle into the pile of fresh horse patootie. I had to grab on to his mane to keep that from happening.

Jasmine, Summer, and Arin took off on their horses as well. Summer was adept enough to ride one-handed while holding her phone as she desperately tried to get her father to understand what was going on. "Dad! I know the bison are stampeding!" she yelled as we galloped away. "They're stampeding because of *you*! Get away from here! Oh crud!" She cried out as her phone slipped from her grasp and tumbled to the ground, only to be trampled by the horse that was following her.

That horse was mine. Despite the fact that Molasses was running with every ounce of strength he had, he still wasn't as fast as the other horses. He was old and out of shape, the horse equivalent of a couch potato. He was wheezing like an asthmatic and stumbling quite a lot, as though, after years of not running, he was trying to remember how to do it.

I certainly wasn't helping the situation. There was probably a proper way to ride a horse at a full gallop, but I had no idea what that was. Instead, I was clinging to Molasses's mane for dear life while I bounced up and down in the saddle like a dribbled basketball. I was also screaming a lot.

Molasses didn't seem to appreciate any of this. (But then, if I had been running for my life with a smaller creature yanking my hair, bouncing up and down on my back, and screaming, I probably wouldn't have appreciated it either.) I couldn't be sure, but it seemed to me that as Molasses ran, he was trying to shake me, juking from side to side in the hopes that I would tumble off and lessen his load.

The helicopter had stopped buzzing back and forth over the herd and was now following it. I figured that J.J. either hadn't heard Summer telling him he was responsible for the stampede—or he had gravely misunderstood her. The sound of the rotors was deafening, spurring the herd onward.

Behind me, the bison were gaining. I had heard tales of how bison could get blindly caught up in their stampedes. For centuries, several Native American tribes had used this to their advantage, funneling herds over the edges of cliffs. In the heat of the stampede, the bison wouldn't even notice the cliff coming and would then plummet to their death. These cliffs were known as buffalo jumps; one of the most famous was unsettlingly named Head-Smashed-In.

I figured that if bison in the midst of a stampede couldn't even turn to avoid running off of a cliff, then they certainly weren't going to avoid trampling a young human on a slow-moving horse that was in their way. Ideally, I needed to get myself and Molasses as far from them as possible before Molasses collapsed from exhaustion and we both got stomped into goulash.

Unfortunately, I didn't have many options. The land ahead of me was only flat, open plain, all the way back to the ranch house. The closest tree for me to climb was down by the river, a quarter mile away. We were coming alongside the dirt road, but that was separated from us by a barbed-wire fence that Molasses probably couldn't jump—and even if he could, the bison would simply flatten it.

There was no chance of safely pulling over and letting the herd run past us. The bison had fanned out on both sides, so there was now a line of them charging behind us, and we were smack in the middle of it. It felt oddly as though I was surfing a big, shaggy brown wave that was threatening to break on top of me.

I had no choice but to keep clinging to Molasses as tightly as I could and hope the old horse had enough stamina left in him.

On their faster steeds, Jasmine and Arin were pulling well ahead of me. Summer probably could have too, but she kept glancing back my way nervously, as though afraid of what might happen if she left me behind.

I signaled for her to keep going. "Don't wait for me!" I yelled. "I'll be fine!"

Summer either couldn't hear this over all the noise—or she chose not to listen. She somehow managed to get Powder Keg to slow down so that she could pull alongside me.

Even though we were right next to each other, she had to shout to be heard over the bison, the helicopter, and the hoofbeats of our own horses. "Jump onto my horse!"

"No way!" I shouted back. "Your horse can't carry both of us!"

"This horse is young and strong and we don't weigh that much! Your horse is old and about to collapse!"

I quickly assessed the situation. Powder Keg did seem to have energy to spare; her stride was still smooth and easy, and she looked as though she wasn't even trying that hard. Meanwhile, Molasses was definitely struggling. If he was a car, he would have been belching steam and blowing gaskets. His skin was slicked with sweat and his breath was ragged.

However, moving from one horse to another at a full gallop was dangerous on normal occasions. With the bison stampede right behind us, I couldn't afford to make a mistake.

I locked eyes with Summer. Even that wasn't easy to do on separate horses.

Her gaze was strong and confident. If she was concerned

about the bison, she wasn't showing it. She reached her arm out to me. "Come on! I know you can do this!"

I worriedly glanced back at the stampede.

"Don't look at them!" Summer yelled. "Look at *me*!"

I shifted my attention back to her, then slowly reached for her arm.

Summer and I had been in enough tight spots to know that, in a situation like this, you didn't grab hands. Each of you grabbed the other's wrist, so if one of you lost your grip, the other still had a solid hold.

Summer grabbed my wrist and I grabbed hers.

"Jump!" Summer yelled. "I've got you!"

I sprang off Molasses and onto Powder Keg.

My intention was to throw one leg across the horse and gracefully slide into the saddle behind Summer. Instead, I belly flopped onto Powder Keg's rear end. There was just enough room between the back of the saddle and the tail of the horse for me to fit on. I ended up draped over her backside like a blanket, with my head pointing one direction and my legs pointing the other. Powder Keg handled the sudden addition of my weight with surprising calm and even picked up speed, while Molasses, now freed of me, seemed to get a burst of energy as well.

I had no idea how to straighten myself up and get into

the saddle. All I could do was grab the saddle's straps as tightly as possible and try not to get thrown off the horse as she galloped across the plains. I was now being bounced even more violently than I had when astride Molasses, when my legs could at least help cushion the blows. It felt as though my teeth might shake loose and my brain might vibrate out of my ears. Plus, my face was disturbingly close to the smelliest parts of the horse.

But when I cocked my head tailward, I could see that the bison herd was falling behind us.

However, they were still stampeding.

It finally seemed to have occurred to J.J. and Karina that they were part of the problem. The helicopter had pulled back and was landing in the field far behind the bison. A few bison even stopped running, mostly young ones that had grown tired. But most of the herd kept on coming after us.

I shifted my gaze in the other direction and saw that we were finally coming up to the ranch house. Some people were gathered on the upstairs balconies. I couldn't make out who they were, given that I was bouncing so hard the whole world was blurry.

Up ahead, Jasmine and Arin were heading directly toward the house. Summer followed them and Molasses dropped in behind us, wild-eyed with panic and foaming at the mouth.

The house was big enough that even the bison seemed to recognize it as an impenetrable obstacle. The herd began to split, like a river that had encountered a rock, with most veering to the east of the house, while a smaller stream went west.

We galloped past the porch where we had all dined the night before. A few of the teenage bison stayed close behind us, knocking the patio furniture aside like bumper cars. I saw Heidi Krautheimer watch in dismay as a chaise lounge was crushed to a pulp.

All of us on horseback made a tight turn just beyond the house . . . and came to a sudden stop beside the wall.

The bison kept on running. After all, they weren't *trying* to flatten us. They were simply stampeding in fear and we had happened to be in their way. With the house blocking us from them, they continued right on by.

Although they didn't run far. The helicopter was no longer hovering over them, and they were wearing out from their run. The stampede quickly fizzled, like a wave that had come into shallow water. First, the bison in the back stopped running, and eventually the ones in the front stopped too, although the rambunctious teens kept on going for a bit. Soon the house was surrounded by exhausted bison. A few of them lay on the ground, panting, but most went right back to grazing, as though nothing out of the ordinary had happened.

I slid off Powder Keg and dropped to the ground, clutching my chest. It felt as though I had bruised every one of my ribs. Powder Keg seemed completely fine; she went right back to grazing as well.

Meanwhile, Molasses was puffing like a freight train and slick with sweat. He was so exhausted, he lay down on the ground. But he looked as though he would be all right, once he got some rest.

Thankfully, none of the bison seemed to have been hurt—although many of the red dogs had been separated from their mothers. Now they bleated dolefully, moving about the herd in search of their family. In short order, I saw many reunions, where the youngsters immediately went to their mothers' sides and began nursing.

Jasmine and Arin came over to check on Summer and me. "That was some nice riding back there," Jasmine told Summer.

Arin patted me on the back. "I have no idea what *you* were doing, but I guess it worked."

My parents came around the back of the house, along with Kandace, filled with relief to see that Summer and I were okay. Mom threw her arms around me, hugging me tightly—which was the *last* thing my sore ribs needed. "Thank goodness you're all right," she said.

"You're hurting me," I said. "My sides are in pain."

Mom quickly released me, looking mortified. "I'm so sorry, Teddy!"

"What do you need?" Dad asked.

I considered that, then said, "Believe it or not, I'm starving. Is breakfast ready yet?"

THE STARGAZER

It was hard to believe it was only slightly after seven in the morning. So much had happened already, it felt as though I should be eating dinner, not breakfast.

Daisy Creek had put together yet another amazing spread, with platters full of bacon, sausage, scrambled eggs, and homemade cinnamon rolls. We had to eat inside, in the dining room, because all the patio furniture had been destroyed by the stampede. The search party wasn't back from tracking Sasquatch yet, but everyone else eagerly piled their plates high and gathered around the table.

The dining room table was a great, long slab of wood, hewn from a redwood tree. Of course, an elk-horn chandelier hung above it.

Heidi sat beside J.J. McCracken, giving him an earful.

"It's not bad enough that we had a bear in the house? Now you had to spook all my bison and cause a stampede? I'll be lucky to have any furniture left by the end of the week."

"I'm sorry," J.J. told her, and he seemed to really mean it. He was obviously greatly embarrassed by the trouble he had caused. "I was only trying to find Sasquatch. . . ."

"Sid, Evan, and the others are taking care of that."

"I thought it'd help to have some eyes in the air."

J.J. and Karina had rented the helicopter at the Yellowstone Airport from a company that normally used it for giving aerial tours. Wary of starting another stampede, they had left the aircraft parked in the field near the house. Karina was also embarrassed; she hadn't said much, besides apologizing profusely.

Meanwhile, I had sat next to Pete and Ray, wanting to question them about the night before. Ray was the only person I hadn't seen during the incident with Sasquatch, as he claimed to have slept through everything. Although I was having trouble getting a word in. Ray couldn't stop talking.

"I can't believe you got to ride in front of a stampede!" he exclaimed. "That must have been the rush of a lifetime! I mean, I ran with the bulls in Pamplona once, but this sounds way more exciting. In Pamplona, there's only six bulls. You had, like, a thousand bison chasing you! How'd you feel?"

"Terrified," I said.

"But also exhilarated, right?"

"Er . . . no. Really just terrified."

"You're a lucky kid," Ray told me. "Do you know how few people on earth have seen a bison stampede from so close by? Less than a dozen, I'll bet. *And* you got to see a grizzly bear this morning! That must have been amazing!"

"That was also really scary," I reminded him.

"I can't believe I slept right through it," Ray said, sounding disappointed. He turned to Pete. "Why didn't you wake me up?"

"That was one of the most horrible experiences of my life!" Pete exclaimed. "You were *lucky* to sleep through it."

"Lucky to miss an up-close encounter with a grizzly?" Ray asked doubtfully. "You know how much I love wildlife."

"You wouldn't have liked this, trust me." Pete sneezed into a monogrammed handkerchief. His allergies had him stuffed up like a clogged drain. He had made an attempt to dress casually, donning shorts and a polo shirt for the day, although both had been freshly ironed.

I took advantage of the break in the conversation to finally ask Ray a question. "You didn't hear a single thing last night? Even though your room was right across the hall from the one with the bear?"

"Ray sleeps like a rock." Pete blew his nose wetly into the handkerchief. "He can sleep through *anything*. Once, we were on a plane to Paris that experienced the worst turbulence I've ever been through in my life. All around us, everyone was vomiting and screaming. And this guy was out cold the entire time."

Ray shrugged. "It's a gift."

"Although, he's not great at *going* to sleep," Pete added. "It takes him hours sometimes. But once he's out, he's out."

"Hours?" I repeated.

"I'm really a night owl," Ray said. "It's usually hard for me to get to bed before one or two in the morning."

"Was that the case last night?"

"Definitely," Pete said. "He was restless as could be." He looked to Ray. "What time did you ultimately turn in?"

"It wasn't until around two," Ray admitted.

Which meant that Ray had been up long after Pete—and everyone else—had gone to bed. In theory, he could have stolen the necklace *before* Sasquatch showed up. Although I still had no idea how he would have gotten in and out of the locked bedroom.

"So what did you do until then?" I asked.

"I read, mostly," Ray said. "Although I also went outside for a bit. I've never seen so many stars in my life! It was incredible." He launched into a whole discourse about what he'd seen: the Milky Way, Venus, Mars, and a dozen meteors.

I started to point out that the stars at home were equally as amazing, but then caught myself. My parents and I lived on the edge of the wilderness behind FunJungle, which was far from the closest city, whereas Ray and Pete lived in Austin, which was well over an hour away. (Pete griped about the length of his commute all the time, but then, he would have loathed living in the trailer park.) Instead, I was struck by a thought. I waited until Ray finally took a break in his story, then said, "Which door did you go out through?"

Ray looked at me curiously. "Why do you ask?"

"Sasquatch came in through the front door last night," I explained. "It was wide open. I was trying to figure out how that happened."

A worried look crossed Ray's face. "I *did* go out through that door. I went to the front yard to look at the stars. I remember noting that it wasn't locked—because we would *never* leave our door unlocked in the city. But I'm sure I shut it when I came back inside. At least, I *think* I did."

"You must have," Pete said supportively. "You're not the kind of person who would leave a door wide open in the middle of the night."

"I certainly wouldn't have forgotten to shut it." Ray nervously poked at his eggs with his fork. "But what if I didn't close it all the way? Then it'd be *my* fault that the bear got in here!"

Pete put a calming hand on Ray's arm. "That bear was coming in no matter what." He turned to me and spoke in the self-assured voice he used for all public relations events.

"Ray was in no way responsible for that bear's intrusion into this house. Yes, he went out to see the stars, but he is a responsible adult and he was sound asleep throughout the entire time the bear was indoors."

I asked Ray, "After you looked at the stars, you went right to bed?"

"Yes. The next thing I knew, Pete was waking me up, hysterical, and telling me that a bear had been inside."

Pete sneezed into his hankie again. "I wasn't *hysterical*."

"You were awfully close."

I considered pressing Ray further, to see if he could remember whether he had fully closed the front door or not, but before I could, the hunting party returned.

Sidney, Evan, Melissa, Zach, and Gavin came in through the kitchen door, as it was the closest entrance to the stables, looking tired, dusty, and frustrated.

"No luck?" Heidi asked, reading their mood.

"Not enough." Sidney sagged into a chair, then looked to J.J. apologetically. "Sorry. We gave it our all. But the trail went cold."

J.J. didn't bother trying to hide his frustration. He dropped his fork onto his plate with a loud crack. "So you're just giving up?"

"What do you expect me to do?" Sidney asked. "I'm not a wizard. I can't wave a magic wand and make the bear appear."

"You had dogs, though. Couldn't they follow his scent?"

"They're herding dogs, not hunters. They got confused. Sasquatch has been going back and forth through those woods by the river for weeks. His scent is everywhere. The dogs ended up running in circles."

"Then why didn't you bring some *real* hunting dogs?"

"This is what I've got! What was I supposed to do, run into town and get some hunting dogs at five in the morning?"

"Yes! And what happened with your son? I thought you said he was the best tracker around."

"He is. But he can't work miracles. A bear doesn't get to be as big as Sasquatch without learning to shake a hunting party."

J.J. angrily smacked his hand on the table. "So what are you saying here, Sidney? That the bear's smarter than you are? If I'd known you were gonna quit so easily, I would've stayed up in the helicopter."

"So you could start another stampede?" Sidney asked tartly. "We're lucky someone didn't get hurt, thanks to that stunt. And all my patio furniture's ruined."

"Patio furniture?" J.J. repeated. "You're upset because you lost a few chaise lounges? That stupid bear of yours may have eaten a necklace that's worth more than this entire ranch!"

A silence fell over the table. The argument had already

grabbed everyone's attention, but now the whole room seemed shocked by J.J.'s statement.

"Exactly how much is that necklace worth?" Melissa asked.

J.J. was obviously upset at himself for letting that slip. "Plenty," he said.

"What's 'plenty'?" Heidi pressed. "Thousands of dollars? Hundreds of thousands?"

"Plenty," J.J. replied in a brusque tone that indicated he wasn't going to say any more.

Another silence followed that, as everyone tried to guess what "plenty" meant to a man like J.J. McCracken.

Finally Evan spoke. "I think Sasquatch might be in the mine."

Everyone turned to him at once.

"What mine?" J.J. asked, intrigued.

"There's an abandoned gold mine on the property," Sidney replied. "But there's no way Sasquatch is in there."

"His paw prints were around the entrance," Evan said.

"Hold on now," J.J. said. "Are you telling me you tracked the bear to this mine but then didn't go in after him?"

"That mine is a death trap," Sidney said. "We boarded it up years ago, but it looks like some of the wood planks rotted away. Going in there would be *meshuge*."

"What's that mean?" Summer asked.

"Crazy," Melissa translated.

"And there's no point anyhow," Sidney said. "Bears don't go into old mines."

"They're not supposed to go into houses, either," J.J. reminded him. "Or eat jewelry. But this one did." He looked to the table. "We are running out of time to find that bear before he poops out my necklace. If it's that dangerous to go into the mine, I'm willing to pay whoever's willing to risk it, for their troubles."

Zach and Arin turned to him, suddenly intrigued.

"I'll go," Zach said without a moment's hesitation.

"Me too," Arin volunteered.

"And me!" Evan shouted excitedly.

"No," Sidney told him firmly. "I don't want you going into that mine. It's way too dangerous."

"But they can go?" Evan asked, pointing to Zach and Arin.

"They're adults," Heidi said. "They can make their own decisions. . . ."

"No matter how thoughtless," Sidney added under his breath.

Evan shoved his breakfast plate away angrily. "This sucks. You're always telling me I need to get outside more—and now, when I finally want to do something, you tell me I can't do it."

"We don't want you to end up in danger," Heidi said.

Evan glowered sullenly. "I never get to do anything exciting."

Everyone else resumed their conversations, filling the room with noise again. While they were all occupied, I turned to Evan and said, "If you want excitement, I could use some help."

Evan looked at me warily. "Doing what?"

"Solving a mystery."

THE BUNKHOUSE

Even though J.J. had asked me not to tell anyone what I was doing, I couldn't figure out how to investigate the disappearance of the necklace without getting the help of at least one of the Krautheimers. I didn't know the property or the staff well enough, and I had only a limited amount of time. It had already been a few hours since the necklace vanished, and I had made little progress.

Evan was the most obvious choice. To begin with, he was another boy my age. It made sense that the two of us would be hanging out together; in fact, our parents had been hoping that we would. I had noticed both sets looking disappointed each time Evan opted to play video games rather than spend time with me.

However, once Evan learned that I was looking for a

possible thief, he was excited to help. He also felt there was something strange about Sasquatch's entry into the house that morning. After all, he had lived in that house his entire life, and a bear had never broken in before. The fact that Kandace's jewels had gone missing afterward seemed suspicious to him as well.

The first thing I wanted to do was see the bunkhouse, and after breakfast, it was empty. Jasmine and Gavin were busy making sure that none of the bison herd had been hurt during the stampede, while Arin and Zach had eagerly gone off with J.J. to see if Sasquatch was really in the abandoned gold mine.

I wasn't sure if visiting the bunkhouse would be allowed or not, but it turned out to be no big deal. Since the Krautheimers owned the building, it wasn't unusual for one of them to enter it. "When we were kids, Melissa and I were over there all the time," Evan explained as we walked to it. "It was kind of like our playhouse. And Jasmine would watch us there when our parents went out. Although, it's been a while since I was last over there." He grew a little wistful as he said this.

"How long?" I asked.

Evan shrugged. "A year maybe. We used to have two other hands who lived there, up until last year. Tom and Grady. They were always cool to Melissa and me. But they each got foreman jobs on other ranches, so they took off . . .

and Melissa and I don't need anyone looking after us anymore. So I just stopped going. Times change."

The bunkhouse was a one-story building situated a short walk from the ranch house, in the midst of the same great meadow of grass, next to a series of holding pens for the bison. The path to it was easy to follow, a mostly straight line where the grass had been worn away by the constant stream of people moving back and forth over the years.

The bunkhouse wasn't even locked. The front door led into a common room, where there was a kitchenette, a dining table with six chairs, and a couch facing a TV with a video game system. From there, a hallway led back to the private apartments. Unlike the ranch house, there were no animal heads on the walls or elk-horn chandeliers. In fact, little attention had been paid to decor at all; it looked as though all the furniture had been found at yard sales. None of the chairs at the dining table matched. Still, the building appeared to have been remodeled somewhat recently; the fixtures, the carpet, and the paint job all looked relatively new.

"Originally, this was all one big room," Evan explained. "There were just bunks in here, and a common shower down that way." He pointed in the direction of the apartments. "Although, obviously, that wouldn't work for us now. Not with Jasmine here. But women didn't work on ranches back when this was first built."

"Is it very common now?" I asked.

"More and more. Though I can't think of many other ranches with a woman as foreman."

"Do the guys working here have a problem with it?"

Evan paused. "I don't know. I never really thought about it. Want to see their rooms?"

"Sure."

We passed through the common room to the apartments. There were six, although of course only four were being used. The door to each could be locked, although four hung open. Two were for the empty apartments, while two were for ranch hands who apparently weren't very concerned about anyone getting into their room.

Evan led me to the first open door. "This is Gavin's room," he said.

The apartment was small, with only enough space for a twin bed, a desk, a chair, and a dresser. There was a bathroom with a toilet, a sink, and a stall shower. The room was cramped, but then, I figured it was still much better than communal bunk beds and showers would have been.

Gavin's apartment was extremely tidy. The bed was made with military precision. There were almost no personal possessions, save for a surprising number of cowboy boots. Gavin owned twelve different pairs, and each was buffed free of dirt, then lined up against the wall. Three library books were on the desk: two Zane Grey westerns and a nonfiction book about building the transcontinental railroad.

"Are all the apartments the exact same as this?" I asked.

"Exactly. Should we go through Gavin's stuff? To see if the necklace is in here somewhere?"

I hesitated before answering. It certainly made sense to search the rooms while we could, although it also seemed somewhat wrong to me, like we were violating the trust of the ranch hands. "I don't know."

"C'mon," Evan prodded. "If the necklace is here, this is our best chance to find it."

"I guess," I said.

We made a quick search of the room. It didn't take long, as Gavin had so few belongings. We just had to do a cursory search of the dresser and turn each boot over to see if anything fell out. We even checked the water tank of the toilet. But we came up empty.

The room had a narrow window over the bed. If Gavin—or any of the other hands—had wanted to slip out in the middle of the night to run off to the ranch house and steal Kandace's necklace, they could have come and gone that way without passing through the common room. Except for Zach, possibly. I wasn't sure the former linebacker could have fit through such a narrow window.

Although, it probably would have been easy to just walk

out through the common room without being noticed. Arin had said everyone went to bed right when they got back, which meant that no one would have been sitting up in the common room anyhow. Assuming Arin was telling the truth.

"How well does your family know your ranch hands?" I asked Evan as we left Gavin's room.

Evan shrugged. "It depends who you're asking about. My parents have known Jasmine her whole life. She's like an older sister to me and Melissa. But the other guys . . . not so much."

"Even though Gavin's been working for you even longer than Jasmine?"

"I don't know if you've noticed, but Gavin's not exactly what you'd call friendly. And Zach and Arin only started here this summer." He led the way into the other open apartment. "This is Zach's room here."

I froze in the doorway. The room was a disaster area. The desk chair was knocked over and dirty clothes were strewn everywhere.

"Looks like a bear got in here," I said, concerned.

"Nah," Evan told me. "Jasmine says Zach's room *always* looks like this. He's a slob."

I didn't keep my own room particularly clean, but even I was shocked by how messy Zach's room was. The chimpanzees at FunJungle kept their living space tidier. I could barely see the floor through all the dirty clothes; garbage was everywhere—except in the garbage can; and there were dozens of partially eaten food items on the desk, some of which had entire colonies of mold and fungus growing on them. The room reeked of spoiled food and body odor.

"I guess we should search this room too?" Evan asked, sounding slightly frightened by the idea, as if spending too long in there could give us an infection.

"Yeah," I agreed.

We did our best to search the room without touching anything, kicking aside the dirty clothes and garbage. It wasn't as though we had to worry about leaving everything the way we'd found it; I doubted Zach would notice a difference in the mess. I came across one pair of socks so encrusted with dirt that they had hardened into a piece of sculpture, but no necklace. I also noticed that Zach didn't have a single book in his room.

"What do you think of Zach?" I asked.

Evan grunted noncommittally. "He's okay, I guess. He doesn't spend that much time here when he's not working. He was really popular in high school, so most nights, he still goes to town to see his friends. The other hands are here a lot more. They even eat with us a lot."

"What's Arin like?"

"He's nice enough. His room's right over here." Evan

quickly led the way out of Zach's room and took a big gulp of fresh air.

Arin's apartment was one of the locked ones, but Evan had brought a master key from his house. He unlocked the door and opened it.

Entering an apartment that had been locked felt like an even bigger violation of trust than searching the apartments that had been left open. I hesitated uncomfortably in the doorway for a bit.

Arin's room wasn't as shipshape as Gavin's, but not as messy as Zach's. (Although, I had seen garbage dumps that were less messy than Zach's room.) The walls were adorned with posters of cricket teams while framed photos sat atop the dresser: group shots of what must have been his family and portraits of a pretty blond woman who I assumed was his girlfriend. Manuals about ranching lay on the desk, alongside yellow pads where Arin had taken detailed notes. There were also several very thick engineering textbooks.

"Is Arin an engineer?" I asked.

"That was what his family *wanted* him to do," Evan explained. This time, he didn't even ask if we should search the room. He just started going through it. "That was why they sent him all the way to Montana State from Bangalore. But when he told them he wanted to be a ranch hand instead . . . I don't think they were happy. He's had a tough time with it. Plus, I don't think people around here have been that nice to him."

"Why not?"

"'Cause he's from India. The ranch hand community is pretty tight and mostly local. So they haven't let him forget he's different."

I nodded understanding. I knew from experience how hard it could be to come into a community as an outsider. When I had first moved to Texas, my school had been in a small town where everyone already knew one another. Most of the other kids hadn't been interested in making new friends—and a lot of them had been pretty cold to me.

"I mean, *my* family's pretty different too," Evan went on. "There aren't many Jews around here. But no one can tell I'm Jewish by looking at me. Arin can't hide the fact that he's Indian."

"Do your other ranch hands treat him differently?" I asked.

Evan thought about that for a bit. "I have no idea what Gavin thinks. And Jasmine's used to being an outsider too. Obviously, there's a lot more Native Americans around here than Indians, but still, it can be tough. And she's a woman, while most of the ranch hands are men. So I think she's been nice to Arin. As for Zach . . . I'd doubt it."

"You think he's racist?"

"Not exactly. Just . . ." Evan took some time to pick his

words. "When Zach goes to hang out with his friends in town, he never takes Arin along. I don't think it's ever even occurred to Zach to invite him. Doesn't look like the necklace is in here, either." Evan finished rifling through Arin's dresser and shoved the final drawer closed.

I hadn't found anything either. Since the apartments were so small and the ranch hands didn't have many belongings, it didn't take much time to go through everything.

Evan led me out of the room and locked it behind him. Then he moved to the door to Jasmine's apartment, key in hand, but hesitated before unlocking it.

"Is something wrong?" I asked.

"I just don't think Jasmine would have stolen the necklace. Like I said, she's like a big sister to me. And she's nicer than my *real* sister. . . ."

"We don't have to go in if you don't want."

Evan stood there awhile, considering this, then put the key in the lock. "We'll do a quick search. To prove that Jasmine wasn't behind it."

Jasmine's room was almost as clean as Gavin's, but not quite. She had more things than anyone else: jewelry boxes, makeup, a rack full of scarves, framed family photos, a collection of snow globes from all over America, and lots more books than any of the others. The walls were adorned with black-and-white photos of stark landscapes. Even though

I was supposed to be quickly searching the room, I found myself drawn to them.

"Those are Jasmine's photos," Evan said, poking through her drawers.

"They're really good."

"Yeah? I like color photos myself."

One photo in particular was really arresting. It was an older Native American couple, standing in front of a clapboard shack on a desolate plain. It looked as though it might have been taken in the 1880s—except that the couple's clothes seemed relatively new. "Do you know where this is?"

"Sure. That's Jasmine's grandparents. Daisy's mother and father. That's their house."

"They live *there*?" I asked before I could catch myself. I failed to keep the shock out of my voice.

Living in Africa, I had seen plenty of people who lived in shacks like this. Sadly, in the shantytowns around major cities like Nairobi and Johannesburg, millions of people lived that way. But I had never seen a home like that in America.

"That's on the reservation," Evan explained, sounding upset himself. "I know. It's a shack. Daisy grew up there with five brothers and sisters. Some of them are still living on the res, in places not much bigger than that."

I peered closer at the photo. "Do they even have electricity?"

"No," said a voice from the doorway.

Evan and I turned, startled, to see Arturo Creek standing there.

"There's no running water or sewers, either," Arturo continued. "The government promised the tribe they would build them, but never delivered on that. And that's not unusual. Nearly fifteen percent of homes on reservations in this country don't have electricity."

Evan had turned bright red, embarrassed to have been caught in Jasmine's room. "We came in here looking for Jasmine," he said.

"Oh, I know exactly what you're doing in here," Arturo said. Then he stepped aside so we had room to leave. He didn't tell us to get out, but it was clear that's what he wanted us to do.

Evan and I filed back into the hall. As we passed Arturo, he held his hand out.

Once again, Evan knew exactly what he expected. He set the master key in Arturo's palm.

Arturo locked Jasmine's door, then ushered us into the common room. "Life isn't easy on a lot of reservations. Poverty is high. Crime is high. Alcohol and drug abuse is high too. Lots of folks act like that's the fault of the Native Americans, but the deck was stacked against us from the beginning. We got kicked off our homeland and forced onto land we didn't have any connection to. We were told we couldn't practice our traditional ways of life. Our populations were decimated by disease. And we never got half the things white folks take for granted: water, power, roads, hospitals. The Indian Health Service operates on a shoestring, and our schools have the lowest funding of any in Montana. The only way you can get a leg up in a place like that is to leave it. And even doing that costs money that most people don't have."

Evan led the way outside. In the short time that we had been in the bunkhouse, it felt as though the temperature had shot up twenty degrees. It was turning into a hot day.

Arturo locked the bunkhouse door, then pocketed the master key. "Why don't you boys find something more productive to do today than invading people's private space?" he asked, then started up the trail toward the ranch house.

Evan and I dropped in behind him, though we kept our distance. Once Arturo was too far away to hear us, Evan asked me, "So, is that it for our investigation?"

"Not at all," I told him. "We're just getting started."

13

THE BAIT

Thirty minutes later, Evan and I were standing in the middle of the dirt road that ran between the Oy Vey Corral and the Spooner Ranch, hunting for bear prints.

One of the main reasons I had asked Evan to help me with the investigation was his tracking ability. While he had spent much of the morning looking for where Sasquatch had gone after coming into the house, I was interested in where Sasquatch had been *before* breaking in.

I wanted to figure out why Sasquatch had come into the house at all the night before, given that it had never happened before—and why the bear had been so intent on getting into the McCrackens' room rather than any other. It seemed to me that learning where Sasquatch had been earlier in the evening might help explain that.

"Bears can be much harder to track than a lot of other animals," Evan told me, squinting at the ground. "People think it should be easy, because they're so big. They assume that a big animal is going to leave giant footprints all over the place, but that's not true. Bears walk on the soles of their feet, like we do, and the soles are soft. So unless a bear is walking over loose dirt or mud, it won't leave a track at all."

Evan had quickly determined that Sasquatch had come down the front path to the house from the dirt road, but tracking him down the road was proving difficult. The road was mostly hard-packed dirt, baked by the sun, so not ideal for finding tracks. We were moving along it slowly, pausing often for Evan to inspect something closely. Usually, it was a mark on the ground that didn't look like much of anything to me.

"Now, a deer or an antelope really walks on its toes," he explained. "A hoof is basically a giant toenail. Or sometimes two big toenails. All the weight is focused on that one point. So even though a deer is much smaller than a bear, it's far more likely to leave a track. Plus, deer poop like crazy. So it's not hard to see where they've been." Evan pointed to the road ahead. Sure enough, there were little black pellets of deer poop everywhere. But I could also see a few hoofprints. They were pairs of lopsided triangles, like someone had pressed two carrots into the ground.

"Is it weird that Sasquatch was walking down the road?" I asked.

"Not really. Bears use the roads a lot around here. For the same reason humans do. They're easy to travel on and they're usually the shortest route from point A to point B. That's why you get so many bear jams in Yellowstone. The problem is, the bears sometimes walk along the roads for miles, so it can be tough to find when they got on or off. And cars mess up the tracks." He pointed to some tread marks in what little loose dirt there was. "This road isn't busy, but there's already been a few vehicles on it this morning. Looks like a few pickups and an RV."

I gaped at him, impressed. "You can even tell what kind of cars have been down here?"

"Sometimes. Pickups tend to have different tires than regular cars, because around here, they're often going off-road. Those tracks are wider, with thick tread marks. As for RVs, they weigh so much they make deeper tracks. Plus, the tires tend to have less tread because people drive them for hundreds of thousands of miles."

I looked back and forth down the road. Because it served so few people, there was almost no traffic on it. We hadn't seen a single car all morning. "If this road only goes to you and the Spooner Ranch, why would there be an RV on it?"

"Because RV drivers get lost. All the time. Even with

GPS. Plus, cell service can be spotty out here. At least once a week we have someone show up at our door asking if we know how to get to Yellowstone. Or thinking that our house is their hotel." Evan suddenly let out a gasp of surprise and pointed to the side of the road. "Hey! Look!"

I followed his command but couldn't tell what had gotten him so excited. "What?"

"Sasquatch left some tracks!" Evan dragged me to the roadside. There, in the soft dirt of the shoulder, were a few roundish, flattened areas, each with a few smaller divots in front of it. Bear tracks.

The roundish areas were from the soles of the bear's feet, while the smaller divots were from the pads of the toes. Each rounded part was the size of a salad plate, indicating an enormous bear. "Sasquatch?" I asked.

"It has to be. There couldn't be two bears that big around here. They'd kill each other."

The tracks were clear enough that even I could read them. Given the toe divots, it was easy to determine the orientation of the feet and, thus, what direction Sasquatch had been going. The bear had approached the ranch house from the south.

Sasquatch had walked along the edge of the road by the Spooner Ranch for a while, which made the job of following his trail much easier. Evan and I followed it, moving far more quickly than we had before.

The Spooner Ranch sloped uphill away from the road. They were raising bison too, although their herd looked to be smaller than the Krautheimers'. Every now and then, a bison would be grazing so close to the fence that I could have reached over and touched it. The young calves were skittish as we passed, but the older bison were nonplussed by our presence. They didn't even look up from their grazing.

"Sorry we didn't get to finish searching Jasmine's room today," Evan said. "I don't think we'll be able to get back in there. Arturo held on to that master key."

"That's all right," I said. "I just needed to see the bunkhouse. I don't think there's much point to searching the rooms anyhow."

"Why not?"

"Well, if you'd gone through all the trouble to steal a necklace like that, would you just leave it in your room?"

Evan scratched his head. "I guess not. That'd be the first place anyone would look for it."

"Exactly. I mean, there must be a million places to hide a necklace on your ranch. You could bury it and mark it with a rock, or hide it in a hollow in a tree. . . ."

"So then, the fact that we didn't find the necklace in any of the ranch hands' rooms doesn't mean they didn't take it."

"Right."

"Is there any point to searching the rooms of the other guests, then? Like Pete and Ray? Or Karina?"

"Probably not."

"We should still search my sister's room, though," Evan said. "She's evil."

"She seems perfectly fine to me."

"You don't live with her. Trust me, you're lucky to be an only child."

The sound of hoofbeats rang through the still air.

"Speak of the devil," Evan grumbled.

Melissa and Summer came trotting down the road. Summer was astride Powder Keg once again—the horse had fully recovered from our action that morning—while Melissa was riding Sassafras.

Evan glowered, although I suspected it was really an act. I figured having an older sister wasn't nearly as bad as he claimed. As an only child, I often felt it would have been nice to have a sibling.

"What are you guys doing all the way out here?" Melissa asked.

"Nothing," Evan said a little too quickly.

Both girls narrowed their eyes suspiciously.

"I haven't seen you this far from a video game since summer vacation began," Melissa told her brother.

"You're investigating something, aren't you?" Summer asked me.

"No," I said, trying to make it sound like it was the truth.

"Don't lie to me, Teddy," Summer said. "It's not cool to lie to your girlfriend. You've been questioning the adults all morning about what they were up to last night, and now you're out here poking around on the edge of the road when there's a million other things you could be doing. What are you trying to figure out?"

I weighed whether or not to keep lying to Summer. The fact was, I didn't want to. I knew that J.J. might be upset at me for telling her the truth, but I hated the idea of keeping a secret from her. So I decided to split the difference and just leave J.J. out of it. "I'm trying to figure out what happened to your mother's necklace."

"We *know* what happened to it," Melissa said. "Sasquatch ate it."

"Maybe not." I quickly laid out my questions about the case as we continued down the road, and explained why Evan and I were following Sasquatch's tracks.

While I talked, the girls dismounted their horses and walked with us, leading the horses by their reins. When I finished, Summer said, "Well, I don't know who took Mom's necklace, but I think I know *how* they did it."

"How?" Evan asked.

"They came through the secret underground room," Summer said. "It goes right under our bedroom."

"But there's no way to get from the secret room to the bedroom," Melissa said.

"Are you sure?" Summer asked. "The entrance you came through was pretty well hidden. So maybe there's another doorway you don't know about."

Melissa and Evan considered that as we followed the tracks.

"Maybe," Melissa finally conceded.

"No," Evan said confidently. "There's no way. We've lived in that house our whole lives. If there was another access to that room, we'd know about it."

"Would we?" Melissa asked. "If no one had ever told us about the secret room under the kitchen, do you think we would have ever figured out it was there?"

"*I* would have," Evan said defiantly, although I could hear a hint of doubt in his voice.

Summer gasped as something occurred to her. "I think the thief might have even been down there with us last night!" She turned to Melissa. "Remember when we heard that noise and you said it was probably just an animal that had gotten in? Well, maybe it was the thief! They were hiding down there, waiting for everyone to go to sleep, so they could then come up into the bedroom and steal the necklace!"

All of us considered that as we walked down the road.

"If someone *did* go through there to access your room," I said, "how would they get back out through the kitchen again? Jasmine closed the trapdoor after we all came out. It was so heavy, it took three of us to lift it. And there was a table on top of it."

Melissa and Evan both chimed agreement with this, but Summer was undaunted. "Maybe the thief was a lot stronger than us. Like Zach. I bet that guy could have lifted the trapdoor if a car was parked on top of it."

"But it couldn't have been Zach," Melissa argued. "He was in the living room with everyone else when we came back out."

"Well, someone as big as Zach, then," Summer said, undeterred. "Was anyone missing last night when we came out of the cellar?"

"Gavin," Evan said.

All of us looked to him, trying to recall if this was true or not.

"No," Melissa said finally. "He was in the living room with everyone else."

"Was he?" Evan challenged. "The guy says, like, three words a month. If he'd left the room, would anyone really have noticed?"

"We've known Gavin most of our lives," Melissa countered. "He would never have stolen that necklace."

"So your only proof is a gut instinct?" Evan asked snidely. "We *don't* know Gavin. Not really. He's never exactly been friendly."

"He's just quiet," Melissa said.

Evan shrugged. "For all we know, the guy could be a drug dealer or a bank robber."

"No way." Melissa kicked a rock down the road. "He's been working for Mom and Dad our whole lives. If he was a bank robber, don't you think we'd have noticed?"

"Not if he was a really good bank robber," Evan said. "Maybe he's been robbing people blind the whole time and we've never suspected a thing."

I said, "If he's been robbing banks, he hasn't been spending much money. He doesn't have many possessions."

"How do you know that?" Summer asked suspiciously.

"Evan told me," I said quickly, not ready to admit that I'd been snooping around the bunkhouse.

"I did," Evan agreed, backing me up. Then he said, "Although, not having stuff isn't proof that Gavin's not a criminal. A smart thief wouldn't go off and spend all their money right away. He'd hide it somewhere." His face suddenly lit up with excitement. "Like in the old gold mine! That'd be the perfect place! No one's been in there in years!"

"That's ridiculous," Melissa told him. "Gavin is not a bank robber. Or a criminal of any kind."

"Well, *someone* here must be," Evan said. "Because Summer's mom's necklace got stolen last night."

We arrived at the driveway for the Spooner Ranch. It had a much fancier entrance than the Oy Vey Corral. Two iron gates were set into stone pillars, with an SR logo on each of them. It looked as though it had been built recently. The barbed-wire fence that stretched out on both sides of the gate also looked newer than the one around the Krautheimers' property. A surveillance camera was situated atop the stone pillar on the right. Despite all the money that had been put into the gate and the fence, the driveway to the house was still unpaved.

The dirt road between the ranches continued on into the distance.

"Does anyone else live on this road?" I asked.

"No," Melissa replied.

"Then where does this even go?" Summer inquired.

Melissa said, "It dead-ends about three miles away, right around the Idaho border. There's a backcountry trailhead. Some of the most incredible hiking in the area, and barely anyone visits it. All the tourists just go right into the park."

Evan stopped walking suddenly, noticing something ahead. "Holy cow," he gasped. "Look at their garbage shed."

At first glance, the shed looked virtually the same as the Krautheimers'. It was a simple wooden structure designed to protect their garbage cans from bears. It was set alongside the road, close to the gate, where the garbage trucks could access it. For garbage day, the trash would have to be brought down from the house and placed there. The wooden doors had four separate latches on them to confound the bears.

But a bear had definitely tried to get in anyhow. There were dozens of claw marks furrowing the doors.

Evan hurried over to examine them. The rest of us followed him.

The furrows were a half inch deep in the wood, all in sets of four parallel lines, one for each of the bear's claws. One of the latches had been ripped off, although the others had held. It also looked as though the front left corner of the shed had been gnawed on.

"These marks look like they were made last night," Evan observed, then pointed to the ground. There were multiple, overlapping salad-plate-size paw prints in the loose dirt. "And that's definitely Sasquatch."

Summer sniffed the air. "Do you guys smell cupcakes?" she asked.

The moment she said it, I realized that I smelled it as well.

So did the others. "It's vanilla," Melissa said.

"Uh-oh," Evan said. He started undoing the latches on the garbage shed.

"What's wrong?" Summer asked him. "Is there something bad about vanilla?"

"Maybe." Evan unlocked all the latches and swung open the shed doors.

There were four garbage bins inside, two black for regular garbage and two blue for recycling. The smell of vanilla was coming from one of the black ones. A dozen bees were buzzing around it, lured by the scent. Evan flipped up the lid.

A thick cloud of flies swarmed out. Evan peered into the bin and said, "Yeah. That's not good."

The rest of us joined him. The bin was mostly empty, except for some items lying at the bottom. There were several plastic wrappers for bulk hamburger meat, each having held five pounds. A few chunks of meat were still on the wrappers, which was what had drawn the flies.

There were also two empty one-gallon jugs of vanilla extract, which had attracted the bees. With the lid open, the smell of even the residual vanilla extract was extremely pungent.

"That's a *lot* of vanilla extract," Summer said. "I bake sometimes, and it'd take me *years* to use all that. What would anyone need that much for?"

"Bear baiting," Melissa said, concerned.

I frowned at the very thought. Baiting is a trick, often used by hunters, to lure animals out so they can shoot them. It isn't considered very sportsmanlike, so it's illegal in most states.

Summer turned to Melissa, surprised. "You mean, your neighbors were *trying* to lure bears here?"

"Looks that way," Evan said. "Bears *love* the smell of vanilla. They can detect it from miles away, so this would lure them from all over the county. And then, obviously, the meat would be to feed them."

"Back away from the garbage," said an angry voice behind us.

Evan and Melissa stiffened, as though they recognized the voice—and feared it. Evan dropped the lid shut and we slowly turned around.

One of the biggest men I had ever seen in my life stood on the other side of the fence on the Spooner Ranch. He looked to be in his forties. His shoulders were as broad as an ox's, his muscles bulged beneath his shirt, and he had an angry scowl on his face.

But the thing that *really* concerned me was that he was aiming a shotgun at us.

NUISANCE BEARS

"You kids are trespassing on Spooner property," the man with the gun said. "It's within my legal rights to shoot you."

Melissa spoke in a voice that was surprisingly calm, given the circumstances. "We were only looking in the garbage, Jericho. On this side of the fence. We didn't set foot on the Spooners' property."

"The garbage shed *is* the property," said Jericho. He then pursed his lips as a question occurred to him. "What are you poking around in the garbage for?"

"Sasquatch got into our house last night . . . ," Melissa began.

"Yeah, I heard that," Jericho told her. "What's that have to do with us?"

"Sasquatch also tried to get into your garbage last night." Evan's voice was much shakier than his sister's, betraying how nervous he was. "Because there's bear bait in it."

Jericho's gaze grew even angrier. "No there's not."

"Come and see for yourself," Summer told him. "There's wrappers from hamburger meat and empty jugs of vanilla extract in there."

"It's not ours." Jericho made no attempt to confirm whether or not what Summer had told him was even true. He stayed right where he was, the shotgun still trained on us. "Someone else must've dumped it there. Maybe *you*."

"Us?" Evan asked, surprised.

"Yeah," Jericho said menacingly. "Maybe that's what all of you were doing right now, messing around with the garbage. Dumping your trash in our bins."

"It was already here," I tried to explain. "In fact, it was definitely here last night. Because Sasquatch tried to get into your shed last night. Come see if you want."

Since Jericho was on the ranch, he was looking at the opposite side of the garbage shed than we were, so he couldn't see the damage that Sasquatch had done. And yet, he still didn't move. Instead, he fixed his angry stare on me. "I haven't seen you before. You look like trouble to me. And I don't like trouble."

The tone of his voice, along with his accusing stare, unsettled me. I noticed that Summer was uneasy as well.

Thankfully, at that moment, a black SUV came down the driveway, diverting Jericho's attention. The SUV looked brand new and appeared to have been freshly washed, even though it was impossible to go ten feet on the dirt roads without getting dusty.

Jericho lowered his shotgun as the SUV approached but didn't stow it. Instead, he kept it cradled in his hands, ready to use it at a moment's notice.

The SUV stopped close to Jericho, on the other side of the gates, and the driver and passenger hopped out. They appeared to be in their thirties, and were dressed in the same sort of clothes that everyone in the area wore—jeans, boots, and cowboy hats—although theirs looked much newer, like they had just bought them the day before. Their hats matched the color of their cowboy boots; the man, who had been driving, wore black, while his wife, who had been in the passenger seat, wore baby blue. They looked less like ranchers than people who were pretending to be ranchers.

Still, both were a lot friendlier than Jericho, which was a relief. They flashed big, cordial smiles and waved to us.

"Hey, Melissa!" the woman called out. "Hey, Evan!"

"Hey, Mrs. Spooner," both said.

"What's going on here?" Mr. Spooner asked Jericho.

"These kids were messing around with your garbage," Jericho reported.

"I don't know if that's any reason to turn a gun on them," Mrs. Spooner said.

"You can never be too vigilant where trespassing is concerned," Jericho replied.

"We weren't trying to cause any trouble," Melissa told the Spooners. "We just found evidence that Sasquatch was trying to get into your garbage before he came to our place last night. There's meat wrappers and vanilla extract in there."

The Spooners' friendly smiles faded and were replaced with looks of concern. Mr. Spooner clicked a fob on his car keys and the big iron gates slowly swung open. The Spooners came out through them to examine their garbage shed.

Jericho stayed put. He hadn't taken a single step since we first saw him.

The Spooners both gaped in astonishment when they saw the damage to their shed.

"Jeez Louise," Mrs. Spooner said. "He really went to town on this."

Mr. Spooner hurried over to look inside the garbage cans. He saw the evidence, then called out to Jericho. "Do you know anything about this?"

"No," Jericho answered. "Though maybe you should ask the kids about it. They were poking around in the garbage when I got here."

"I'm sure they didn't mean any harm." Mrs. Spooner

started to look embarrassed about Jericho's behavior. She shifted her attention to Summer and me. "We haven't met yet. I'm Taffy Spooner. And this is Ike."

"Hey," Ike said, extending his hand.

I shook it. "I'm Teddy."

"And I'm Summer." Summer flashed a pleasant smile.

Recognition flashed across Taffy's face. I could see her trying to decide if she should admit she knew who Summer was or try to pretend like she didn't. She ultimately chose the second option—and then lowered her voice so that Jericho wouldn't hear her. "Sorry about Jericho. He runs the ranch for us, and, well . . . he can be a little overzealous when it comes to protecting the place."

"We bought this property about a year ago," Ike said. "I'd been working in Los Angeles for the past fifteen years. Hedge funds. Investments. That kind of stuff. But Taffy and I had always loved it here, so one day, we heard this place was up for grabs and decided to take the plunge. And just like that, we were ranchers! Only, neither of us really knew what we were doing. While Jericho kind of came with the property."

"Ike!" Taffy exclaimed. "You're making it sound like Jericho was an appliance!" She looked to us. "He worked for the old owners. So it made sense to keep him on."

Ike asked Melissa and Evan, "How's everything going at your place after this morning?"

"All right, I guess," Melissa replied.

"It's a miracle no one got hurt," Taffy said. "I hope Sasquatch didn't come to your home because of what was in our garbage, but I swear to you, we didn't know anything about this. Someone else must've dumped it there."

"Taffy's right," Ike agreed. "We never even bring our garbage down here until trash day—and that's three days from now. All our stuff is locked up by the house."

I understood why that would be. The Krautheimers had the same setup. No one wanted to run the garbage all the way out to the main road every time they had some, so they had another bear-proof shed closer to their house. Then, on trash days, they would bring everything to the road at once so that the garbage trucks could pick it up. In the meantime, it would be easy for anyone passing by to drop the bear bait into their garbage bins. While the sheds had latches, they weren't locked; the garbage collectors needed to be able to open them.

I said, "Since this road leads to public land, maybe someone's been baiting bears down there. And they dumped the garbage on the way out."

Everyone considered that. "Could be," Ike admitted.

"We should alert the police," Taffy said. "Or the park service. Or Fish and Wildlife. Whoever's responsible for protecting the bears around here. If someone's baiting, that could cause a whole lot of trouble."

"It's *already* caused trouble," Evan reminded her. "Last night."

Ike nodded. "Has there been any talk at your place about relocating Sasquatch?"

"Relocating?" Summer asked. "You mean, like, moving the bear?"

"Right," Melissa agreed. "Every now and then, a bear gets habituated to humans, usually because people keep leaving garbage where the bear can get to it. And that can obviously be dangerous, so sometimes the government tries to relocate the bears. They dart them, then drive them a couple hundred miles away and release them into the wild."

"But a lot of the time, it doesn't work," Evan added. "We've had a couple habituated bears in West Yellowstone. The Forest Service will take them a hundred miles away and the bears will come right back. A couple days later they're right back in town. They call those nuisance bears."

"So what happens to them?" Summer asked.

"Sometimes they end up in captivity," Melissa said. "There's a place in West Yellowstone that has some nuisance bears for tourists to see—and others have been sent to zoos. But if they can't find a place for them, well . . ." She trailed off ominously.

"They kill them?" Summer gasped.

"No one wants to do that," Taffy said. "But sometimes,

there's no choice. What happens if a bear as big as Sasquatch becomes a nuisance? He's already broken into the Krautheimers' home. What if he starts breaking into others? I love the bears, but I don't want to find Sasquatch in *my* bedroom."

"So you haven't had any incidents with Sasquatch?" I asked. "He hasn't been on *your* property?"

"Not that I know of," Ike said. "Except for this." He pointed at the garbage shed, then called to Jericho. "You haven't seen him, have you?"

Jericho shook his head. He still hadn't moved and his face was locked in a scowl, which made me think that maybe he wasn't being honest.

Taffy looked at her watch and made a little gasp. "Ike, we're gonna be late," she said.

Ike looked at his watch as well, then returned his attention to us. "It was nice meeting you kids. You guys need a ride back to your place?"

"We're okay, thanks," Evan said.

"All right then." Ike started back through the gate toward his SUV.

Taffy said, "I hope the rest of your vacation is less eventful than last night."

Before they got back in the SUV, Ike stopped to speak to Jericho. They were too far for us to hear them, but it looked like maybe Ike was telling Jericho he shouldn't be aiming his gun at the neighbors' kids. Or maybe they were more concerned about him aiming it at Summer, given that she was famous and had thousands of followers on social media. Whatever the case, Jericho didn't seem pleased. He gave them a curt nod, then turned and stalked back up the driveway.

The Spooners got into their SUV and drove off, giving us a good-bye honk and wave before they headed down the dirt road toward town.

"They seemed nice," Summer said.

"They are," Melissa said, although Evan gave a noncommittal grunt. Melissa looked to him. "What's your problem with the Spooners?"

"They're so LA," he said. "They made a whole bunch of money there, then think they can just move out here and start ranching, like it's easy. They don't know anything about this business at all."

"And you do?" Melissa asked pointedly. "At least they're *trying* to ranch. They could have carved up this whole property into subdivisions, and then we'd have thousands of people living right next door to us. That'd be a million times worse."

"I guess," Evan said begrudgingly. Then he looked off into the distance and said, "Taffy wasn't really telling the truth when she said no one wants to kill the nuisance bears.

Lots of people do. In fact, lots of people would be happy to kill off *all* the bears. And the wolves, too."

I realized he was watching Jericho as he said this. Jericho was heading off across the ranch, pausing now and then to glance back at us.

"You think Jericho is one of those people?" Summer asked.

"I *know* he is," Evan said.

Melissa added, "There are a lot of members of the ranching community who don't like the bears. Or the wolves. Because the bears and wolves sometimes kill their cattle. Even though it doesn't happen very often."

"But the bears and the wolves were here first," Summer said angrily. "If you're going to raise cattle on their hunting grounds, what do you expect will happen?"

"They don't see it that way," Melissa replied. "There are community meetings every now and then where people discuss issues with bears and wolves and other carnivores. So it's no secret who's on which side of the issue. Jericho's as antibear as they come."

"Him and Mr. Purdue," Evan said, which made Melissa look uncomfortable.

"Who's Mr. Purdue?" I asked.

"Zach's father," Evan said. "He's the biggest antibear guy around."

"That doesn't mean Zach's antibear," Melissa said quickly.

"I never said it did," Evan replied. "I'm just saying his father doesn't like the bears."

On the Spooner Ranch, Jericho had stopped walking. He was standing atop a small hill, looking back at us. I couldn't see his face from that distance, but I assumed he was scowling.

A phone rang, shattering the silence. Melissa took hers from her pocket, glanced at the caller ID, then answered it. "Hey," she said. "What's up?" Then after a few seconds, she glanced at me and said, "Yes, I'm with him right now." There was a bit more back-and-forth, and then she said, "Okay, I'll tell him." She hung up and looked over at me. "That was Jasmine. She has someone she wants you to talk to."

"About what?" I asked.

"Seems like we're not the only ones who've had a pure-bred bison stolen lately," Melissa reported.

"Who else did?" Evan asked.

"Yellowstone National Park."

THE GEYSER BASIN

The person who'd called Jasmine about the bison was a Yellowstone ranger named Linda Oh. Jasmine drove Summer and me into the park so that we could talk to her in person, but it took a while. Yellowstone is bigger than the states of Delaware and Rhode Island combined, and the roads were narrow and twisting. Daisy Creek had to pack all of us lunch for the trip.

However, before we had left, Melissa, Evan, Summer, and I had carefully inspected the floor of the McCrackens' bedroom, looking for any secret doors to the room hidden beneath. It was only carpeted with area rugs, which we easily rolled out of the way, but sadly, we couldn't find anything. There didn't appear to be a single route from the bedroom to the basement. Summer was so annoyed that her theory hadn't panned out, she was silent for the whole drive into the park, staring sullenly out at the scenery.

On that day, Ranger Oh was working in the Upper Geyser Basin near Old Faithful. The bison were free to range wherever they wanted in the park, and a few dozen had decided to graze in the most popular section, as though they were tourists. Ranger Oh was assigned to talk to interested visitors about the bison—and make sure no tourons did anything stupid around them.

Old Faithful was named for the fact that it erupts somewhat predictably; it goes off around twenty times a day, blasting thousands of gallons of two-hundred-degree water up to 180 feet into the air. It is amazing to witness, and thus attracts so many visitors that the parking lot is nearly the size of FunJungle's. There's one section solely for enormous RVs, which feels more like being at a bus depot than a national park.

Just north of Old Faithful, a network of paved trails and boardwalks wind around dozens of lesser known—but still really fascinating—geothermal features: smaller geysers, pools of steaming iridescent water, slicks of bubbling mud and hissing steam vents. Due to the fact that the gasses released by these features are somewhat toxic, the area is relatively free of trees, so if you stand at any point, you can see a great panorama of strange geologic formations, with occasional clouds of noxious steam drifting across it. It's like being on another planet.

The bison were grazing on a patch of grass near Castle Geyser, indifferent to the occasional eruptions or the hundreds of gawking tourists around them. Ranger Oh was posted on the pathway closest to them. She was small of stature, but she had an extremely commanding voice when she needed it—which was quite often. She was dressed in the standard ranger uniform: a gray button-down shirt, green pants, and a wide-brimmed Smokey Bear hat.

"Most people don't realize it, but Yellowstone sits directly over the largest supervolcano in North America," Ranger Oh told us. "That's why there's so much geothermal activity here. The last time it blew, it ejected almost two hundred forty cubic miles of debris, leaving a caldera that's over forty miles across. We're smack in the middle of it right now. Beneath our feet, there's a magma chamber twice the size of the country of Luxembourg, holding enough molten rock to fill the Grand Canyon ten times." She noticed our concern and added, "But don't worry. The last eruption was six hundred forty thousand years ago."

"Doesn't that mean we're due for another one?" Summer asked.

"Probably not," Ranger Oh said, not quite as reassuringly as I would have hoped. Then she suddenly turned and shouted at a group of tourons, "PLEASE DON'T ATTEMPT TO TOUCH THE BISON! THEY'RE DANGEROUS!"

The visitors, who had left the clearly marked path to try to pet a young bison, scurried back to safety.

"How many bison have been stolen?" I asked Ranger Oh.

"To be honest, I can't be one hundred percent sure that a theft has happened," she conceded. "We don't even know exactly how many bison are in the park. There's at least five thousand, and they have thousands of square miles to roam, much of which is inaccessible, so it's impossible to keep track of them all. PLEASE DON'T FEED THE CHIPMUNKS! IT ISN'T HEATHY FOR THEM!"

A family of tourons who were giving Fritos to a chipmunk shrank back in fear.

"Then why do you think the bison were stolen?" Summer inquired.

"It was only a hunch until a few hours ago," Ranger Oh replied. "I'm with this herd a lot. There's a group of yearlings in it. There were twenty-six in early June, and now there's twenty-four. I figured we might have lost them naturally. Maybe they got killed by predators. Or drowned in a river. Or fell into a thermal pool and got boiled alive. That's not so common, but it's been known to happen. Meanwhile, some other rangers reported that other groups of yearlings were thinning out at an unusually high rate. Which, again, is completely conceivable. Sometimes there's just a harsh year and not as many yearlings survive. But then Jasmine called me to say that a yearling had been stolen from her . . ."

"Maybe two," Jasmine added. "Or even more."

". . . and I realized that might be what was going on here, too. PLEASE GET AWAY FROM THAT GEYSER! IF IT GOES OFF, THE STEAM WILL SCALD THE FLESH RIGHT OFF OF YOUR BONES!"

Two teenage tourons scampered away from the geyser they had gone off trail to see.

Ranger Oh gave us a sheepish grin. "Actually, the steam isn't quite that hot. But if I don't scare the pants off these idiots, they'll just go right back when they think I'm not watching."

Down on the edge of the Firehole River, which wound through the basin, a geyser began coughing and spurting, like a lawn sprinkler that was ready to start spewing water. "Look!" Ranger Oh exclaimed. "I think we're going to get lucky! Riverside Geyser is about to go off!"

She immediately started leading us to a viewpoint closer to the geyser.

I asked, "Do you have any idea who might want to be stealing the bison?"

Ranger Oh sighed. "If it was only one juvenile, I'd think that maybe a tourist had taken it. We regularly come across them trying to catch smaller animals, like chipmunks and rabbits, so I can imagine someone out there might actually be dumb enough to try to take a young bison home. But multiple bison . . . that's a concerted effort. PLEASE DO NOT PICK THE FLOWERS! THOSE ARE PART OF THE NATURAL HABITAT AND THEY DO NOT BELONG TO YOU!" She paused to make sure that the tourons she had yelled at actually listened to her, then resumed speaking in her normal voice. "So maybe it's one of the antibison groups."

"Antibison groups?" Summer repeated, surprised. "Who has a problem with bison? They don't cause any trouble."

Jasmine laughed at this, despite herself. "There are plenty of local cattle ranchers who would disagree with you on that. They claim that bison can spread a disease called brucellosis to domestic cattle. Even though the evidence shows that, if anything, bison caught it from the cattle."

Ranger Oh added, "Plus, our studies show that it's probably the elk spreading brucellosis, not the bison. We still do our best to test the park bison anyhow. If we find any with brucellosis, we put them down—"

Summer gasped, interrupting her. "You *kill* them? But they're endangered wildlife!"

Ranger Oh frowned, indicating that this upset her as well. "That's just what we have to do. And while we try our best to keep the herd inside the park, we can't fully control it. They're not domestic animals. Sometimes bison migrate outside the park, and these ranchers consider that a threat to their herds. WOULD YOU PLEASE PICK UP THAT LITTER YOU JUST DROPPED? THIS IS A NATIONAL PARK, NOT A TRASH DUMP!"

A touron who had just tossed an empty potato chip bag into the bushes made no attempt to pick it up again. Even though there was a trash can five feet away.

So Ranger Oh shouted at him in German. Then Arabic. Then Italian.

That did the trick. The touron reluctantly grabbed the chip bag and carried it to the trash can.

Ranger Oh said to us, "Sadly, in this job, you have to be able to speak to morons in twelve different languages."

I asked, "Why do you think these ranchers would try to steal your bison?"

"To make a point," Jasmine answered. "Some of them *really* hate the bison—and they're angry. We've gotten death threats at the ranch because we're raising them instead of cattle."

"Death threats?" Summer echoed. "Really?"

"Really," Jasmine said sadly. "Chances are, it's just people trying to scare us—but we still have to take them seriously."

"Do you know who you've gotten those threats from?" I asked. "Because maybe that'd be a lead as to who stole your bison too."

"The threats have all been anonymous," Jasmine replied. "We showed them to the police and they couldn't tell us anything. But I'm pretty sure it's George Wiley."

Ranger Oh groaned at the mention of the name.

"You know him?" Summer asked.

"George Wiley is a constant thorn in our side at Yellowstone," Ranger Oh said. "He's the biggest cattle rancher in the area. As other ranchers have gone bankrupt over the years, he's swept in and bought their properties. He owns land on the northern, eastern, and western sides of the park. And he fights us on every single thing we try to do for the welfare of our wildlife. He's been filing one lawsuit after another against us for years. He wants us to fence the buffalo, hunt down all the bears, and stop reintroducing wolves. If he had his way, the National Park Service would be shut down for good. THE RIVER IS NOT SAFE TO SWIM IN! PLEASE GET BACK TO THE TRAIL RIGHT NOW OR I WILL HAVE YOU ARRESTED!"

Three young tourons who had been stripping down to their bathing suits meekly grabbed their clothes and left the riverbank.

We reached a good vantage point for viewing Riverside Geyser. Our timing was perfect. As we arrived, it began to erupt. Riverside is an unusual geyser, because it doesn't shoot straight up. Due to its location on the riverbank, it is tilted, so it fires its great spout of hot water at a sixty-degree angle, arcing over the Firehole River. Ranger Oh had led us to the perfect place to watch it. The sunlight refracted through the spray of water and clouds of steam, creating multiple rainbows over the river.

Hundreds of tourists gathered to witness the spectacle around us.

We fell silent for a few minutes, enjoying the show. Even Ranger Oh, who had probably witnessed a thousand eruptions, observed it with awe. Eventually, it died out, gasping and spurting. The crowds remained a bit longer, as if hoping for an encore, and then quickly dispersed.

We stayed right where we were, looking out over the Firehole River.

"What people like George Wiley fail to realize," Ranger Oh said sadly, "is that all these species they think they can just get rid of are integral to this landscape—often in ways that are hard to predict."

"Tell them about what happened when the wolves came back," Jasmine urged.

"Back in the early days of the park, wolves were regarded as a nuisance," Ranger Oh told us. "They were eradicated by the 1920s. No one realized it at the time, but this set off what is known as a trophic cascade. It had incredibly deleterious consequences on the entire ecosystem. Without wolves to hunt them, the elk populations exploded, and by the 1980s, they had severely overgrazed many of the willow and aspen forests along the rivers. The depletion of those forests had serious effects on all the animals that relied on them."

As Ranger Oh spoke, tourists began stopping to listen, so she raised her voice for everyone to hear.

"When wolves were finally reintroduced in the mid-1990s, after being gone for seventy years, the effects rippled through the ecosystem in ways almost no one had imagined. The wolves immediately resumed hunting the elk, lowering their numbers, which allowed the forests the elk had over-grazed to rebound with surprising speed. When the forests grew back, songbirds and beavers returned to them—and as the beavers built more dams, that created better habitats for muskrats and otters and a host of reptiles and amphibians.

"Meanwhile, the wolf kills provided more carrion, which was beneficial for species that scavenge, like grizzlies, coyotes, and foxes—and even birds like ravens and bald eagles. Nowadays, elk populations are steady, while the numbers of endangered carnivores like wolves, bears, and mountain lions have increased. The entire ecosystem is much healthier than it was only a few decades ago. We were able to see firsthand what the catastrophic repercussions of removing just one species of animal had been. So imagine what might happen if George Wiley got his way and *several* species were removed from the park. This entire ecosystem might collapse. And Wiley's ranchlands would go with it. If anything, he should be thankful that Yellowstone is here. His livelihood wouldn't exist without it. DO NOT TRY TO CATCH THE RABBITS! THEY ARE WILD ANIMALS!"

The gathered crowd turned at once to face a touron father who was chasing after a rabbit for his daughter. He immediately shrank under their collective gaze.

Despite all the tourons we had seen, most of the visitors to the park had behaved well and were genuinely interested in learning more and doing the right thing. The crowd that had gathered to listen to Ranger Oh speak stayed put, peppering her with questions about the reintroduction of the wolves and the Yellowstone ecosystem in general—although one dimwit did ask her where in the park he could find the presidents' heads carved into the mountain.

Ranger Oh didn't want to ignore the tourists, so she turned to us and said, "I can put together a list of ranchers besides George Wiley who've been outspoken against the bison herds. Maybe that will give you some leads."

"That'd be great," Jasmine said.

"Thanks for your time," I told Ranger Oh.

"Thanks for coming by," she replied pleasantly, then suddenly glared off into the distance and shouted, "DO NOT THROW GARBAGE INTO THE GEYSERS! THEY ARE NOT TRASH RECEPTACLES! THEY ARE NATURAL GEOLOGICAL FORMATIONS, AND YOU ARE GOING

TO DESTROY THEM WITH YOUR BAD BEHAVIOR!"

The tourons she had caught doing this were the very same ones who she had chased off from swimming in the river. Now they had been about to drop some empty soda cans into a geyser for no good reason. They sheepishly backed away once again, but I could only imagine that it wouldn't be long before they tried to do something else moronic.

Jasmine, Summer, and I started back toward Old Faithful. Our route took us along the bank of the Firehole River, which had obviously been named for the numerous thermal features along its banks. At multiple points, scalding water flowed into it, creating clouds of steam that billowed across the surface.

"It's so beautiful," Summer observed, then asked Jasmine, "Since you live close by, do you come here a lot?"

Jasmine frowned, as though the question made her uneasy. "Not so much. I have mixed feelings about this park."

"Because it's built on Tukudika land?" I asked.

"Yes," Jasmine said. "Although the Tukudika didn't really think of this as *our* land. We weren't the only ones the park service stole it from. Twenty-six different tribes shared this area, and there's evidence of Native American activity here going back at least eleven thousand years."

I gaped at her in surprise. "That long?"

"Back to the time when there were still mammoths and mastodons," Jasmine said. "But when the government took the land, they didn't only kick us out—they also lied about us ever having been here at all. To encourage tourism, they rewrote history, claiming that Native Americans had actually avoided this place because we were afraid of the geysers. Like we were children. I mean, who would be afraid of that?" She pointed across the river, where a small geyser was ejecting a thin jet of steaming water into the air.

"In truth, many tribes thought the geysers had spiritual power," Jasmine continued. "But that was inconvenient for the park service, who wanted to sell the idea that this land was immaculate. For decades, every visitor to Yellowstone got a brochure saying that this park showed the natural world the way it was before humans, as though my people had never existed. Thankfully, that's changing; the park service is finally taking steps to educate tourists about Native American life here, but there's still a long way to go." She waved a hand toward the hundreds of tourists roaming about the geyser basin. "These people might be learning a lot about geology and wild animals, but I'll bet only a tiny fraction of them have ever even heard of the Tukudika."

I nodded sadly, realizing that my own knowledge of Native American history was spotty at best. My middle school American history class had spent far less time on the thousands of years of Native American history than the few hundred years since settlers had arrived. I looked around the geyser basin, seeing it slightly differently now, imagining what it might have been like with the Tukudika, rather than tourists.

I would have liked to spend another few hours exploring the area, but I was feeling a bit daunted. It was already well into the afternoon, and if anything, both mysteries I was investigating had gotten even more complicated. The number of potential suspects in each had exploded, rather than shrinking down.

Still, I was hoping that we had time to watch Old Faithful erupt. The park rangers couldn't predict exactly when it would go off, but after years of practice, they were able to give extremely good estimates, which were then posted for tourists. Given the size of the crowd gathered around the geyser, it was obviously close to time for the next eruption.

However, as we neared it, Jasmine's phone and mine started ringing at once. That seemed like a bad sign to me.

My father was calling me. I didn't know who was calling Jasmine. We both answered at the same time.

"Hey, Dad," I said. "What's going on?"

"Are you with Summer?" he asked.

Summer overheard her name and looked to me, concerned. She didn't have a phone, as hers had been trampled by my horse earlier in the day.

"She's right next to me," I said.

"You both need to get back here right away," Dad told me. "J.J.'s in trouble."

THE RESCUE

We learned the full story as we were hurrying out of the geyser basin.

As we knew, J.J. had recruited Zach and Arin to go look for Sasquatch in the abandoned gold mine on the Oy Vey Corral. When Kandace hadn't heard back from J.J. after lunch, Sidney and Gavin had ridden out to see if anything had gone wrong—and their worst fears had been confirmed. There had been a cave-in at the mine. The Krautheimers had called the local fire department to organize a rescue, but Summer understandably wanted to get back to the ranch as quickly as possible so she could help out in any way. I would have done the same if my own parents had been in trouble— and I was concerned about J.J. too.

We walked right past Old Faithful and headed for the

parking lot. We were the only people going that way. The geyser began erupting as we left, so crowds were racing in from the lot to see it before it finished, forcing us to weave through them like salmon swimming upstream. I was frustrated to miss the eruption—all I could see of it was a glimpse of the great, steaming column of water in the distance—but this enabled us to get out of the parking lot faster. Once the eruption was over, hundreds of tourists would be heading for their cars at once.

However, we still had to get through many miles of crowded roads to reach the park exit. (We got stuck in one traffic jam for fifteen minutes, which turned out to have been caused by tourons stopping in the middle of the road to see a common white-tailed deer.) Then, once we got to the ranch, we had to get horses and ride out to the mine, so it was nearly two hours from the time we had heard about the accident until the time we arrived on the scene. Jasmine led us there. I had to use a different horse than Molasses, because Molasses was still recuperating from that morning's ride. I was given a feistier horse named Starbuck who was a handful to control. Since I wasn't that talented a rider, I got bounced around a lot more than either Jasmine or Summer did, and so after our ride to the mine, my ribs—which had been sore since the morning—were aching once again.

I didn't realize it until we arrived, but my entire knowledge of what a mine looked like was based on the movies. I had expected a large tunnel through the mountain, wide enough for railroad tracks and tramcars, but what I found instead was much less impressive. The passage that led into the mountain was a narrow, rough-hewn gap, not much wider or taller than an adult human. There were no railroad tracks, although some ancient mining equipment that had been abandoned a century earlier was strewn outside the entrance. The metal was so rusted that it had fallen apart, so it was hard to tell what anything had originally been. The mine looked more like a cave, which was why it might have appealed to a bear to hide inside.

It had been boarded over until recently. Now the rotted wood and warning signs had been pulled off and piled near the entrance.

The fire department's rescue squad was already there. They, along with all the other adults, Evan, and Melissa, had formed a line heading into the mine. Given the mine's remoteness and narrowness, the system to remove the landslide inside was decidedly primitive: Everyone was simply lifting the rocks out by hand and passing them from one person to another. They all looked tired and sweaty. Evan, who was at the end of the line, was tossing the rocks aside. There was a pile three feet tall, indicating they had been at this awhile.

"They're here!" Evan called out when he saw us, and word quickly passed up the line.

Then, to my surprise, word quickly came back from inside. "See if Teddy can come in."

"Why me?" I asked.

"It's pretty tight in there," Evan explained. "And you're the smallest guy."

"I'm smaller than he is," Summer said angrily. "Why don't they want me? Don't they think a girl can do this?"

Jasmine placed a hand on her shoulder, giving her the message that now wasn't the time to start an argument. "I'm sure you can help your father out here," she said. "I'll bet they could use some more people on the rock line."

"That's right," Evan agreed, although he had a look on his face that indicated that maybe the idea was to prevent Summer from seeing how dire the situation was. He tossed me a hard hat with a headlamp attached.

I put it on and hurried into the mine.

Inside, it was even narrower, which made sense; the easiest place to excavate would have been the entrance. The inner tunnel appeared to have been hacked by hand with pickaxes through almost solid rock. The walls were jagged and irregular, with plenty of sharp corners. At many points, the tunnel was no wider than a few feet, and the ceiling repeatedly dropped low enough that adults had to stoop. Cold water dripped steadily from above and pooled on the floor. Back in the day, it would have been incredibly dark inside, lit only by gas lamps. It seemed like a nightmarish place to work.

The adults all flattened themselves along the rough-hewn walls so that I could pass, and even then, there were times when I could barely fit. Melissa, Heidi, and Kandace were stationed right inside the entrance, although Kandace immediately hurried out to talk to Summer. Then came Pete, Ray, Karina, Arturo, Gavin, Mom, Dad, and Sidney. Everyone wore hard hats with headlamps.

Mom and Dad happened to be in a junction in the mine, where two other dank, narrow tunnels split off, so they had a bit more space. Mom clutched my shoulder as I passed, stopping me briefly. "Just so you know, you don't have to do this if it scares you too much," she said.

"Do what?" I asked.

"You'll see," Dad said.

Beyond them were seven big, brawny firefighters—and one older firefighter who seemed to be in charge. He was positioned near the front of the line.

Not far ahead, the tunnel had caved in. A jumble of broken rocks and dirt completely blocked the mine, although the firefighters had made some progress in excavating it. They had been working from the top and had dug a narrow passage back into the rockfall. It was still too small and tight for the firefighters to get inside—so Daisy Creek was doing it. She would stick her entire torso in the passage, pry out a big rock, and then pass it down the line. It was obviously hard work, and even in the dim light, I could see that Daisy was sweaty and coated with dirt.

I realized what everyone needed me to do.

The older firefighter stepped out of the line to greet me. "Teddy, I'm Chief Hogan. Has anyone explained the situation to you?"

"No," I replied. "But I'm guessing you need me to take over for Daisy."

"That's right. She's been at this for over an hour. As you can see, we're trying to clear an opening through this blockage as fast as we can. If we can do that, they'll be able to get fresh air, and we'll be able to pass them food and water. Once that's taken care of, it'll buy us some time to get the rest of these rocks out. The problem is, this blockage goes farther back than we expected—and all the adults except Daisy are too big to fit in that opening. I hate to ask a kid to go in there, but . . ."

"I'll do it," I said.

"You don't have to." Daisy Creek emerged from the narrow passage clutching a rock the size of her head and passed it on. She looked to Chief Hogan. "I can keep going. There's no need to ask Teddy to put his life at risk—"

"You've done more than your fair share," Chief Hogan told her. "It's time for you to take a break."

"I don't need one," Daisy replied. "I can keep going. . . ."

"Maybe so," the chief said. "But I'm ordering you to stop. The last thing I need right now is another emergency. So go take five and get yourself some water—or I'll have my men drag your stubborn rear end out."

Daisy cracked a slight smile, then nodded agreement. "All right, Chief. But I'll be ready to go again if you need me." Before she left, she grabbed my hands and gave me a heartfelt look. "Be careful, Teddy."

I noticed that, despite Daisy's insistence that she could go on, she appeared exhausted. There was a weariness in her eyes, and her fingertips were raw and bloodied from dragging out rocks.

"I will," I said.

"Good." Daisy headed back down the tunnel toward daylight.

Chief Hogan added, "She's right. You need to exercise caution. It's going to be really tight in there. And if we tell you to get out right away, then you get out right away, okay? Don't be a hero. We don't want another cave-in."

"All right," I said, then asked, "How are they doing?"

"We don't know," Chief Hogan said gravely, and in that moment, I understood why Summer hadn't been asked to do this. There was a chance that her father wasn't alive on the other side of the cave-in.

I climbed up the rockfall and peered into the narrow passage.

Daisy had managed to excavate about three feet back. I had thought that the main tunnels of the mine were claustrophobic, but this was far worse. It was dank and muddy and full of weird cave insects and broken stones that scratched at me as I reached inside. There wasn't even enough room for me to wear my hard hat; I had to set a flashlight inside so I could see what I was doing. Above me, there was a new ceiling of stones that had wedged in the hole after the other ones had fallen, but if they went, a whole new cave-in would come down right on top of me.

I figured I had better work quickly.

I started pulling out rocks as fast as I could. Sometimes they came out easily; sometimes it took me a while to figure out how to work them free. At the same time, the firefighters were taking apart the wall of rocks, pulling away bigger stones to give me more room to get in and out. Still, the passage I was in remained disturbingly small. I kept banging my head on the low ceiling and scraping my knuckles on rocks. There was dirt and mud everywhere, in my nose and my eyes and my mouth. But I still kept digging, because three people's lives depended on it.

Every now and then, Chief Hogan would shout for J.J. or Zach or Arin. But no shouts ever came back.

The passage was getting deeper. I had cleared another foot of rock away and was wondering how much farther the blockage could go when I heard something.

It was a muffled noise, from behind the rocks. It seemed to have a slight Texan twang.

"J.J.?" I yelled.

"Teddy?" the voice was faint but unmistakable.

"Yes!" I cried.

That was followed by the sounds of three different people whooping on the other side. People who sounded like they were all okay and thrilled to hear help was on the way. Even so, I figured I should check. "Is everyone all right?"

"Yes!" J.J. yelled back. "Though the faster you can get through here, the better we'll be!"

I retreated from the passage and gave everyone the good news. "They're alive!"

Word quickly passed down the line, accompanied by whoops of joy.

I returned my attention to clearing the passage with new vigor. But I instantly discovered a problem: A rock the size of a watermelon was wedged ahead of me, blocking my access to them. I couldn't possibly move it. Not without getting all the other rocks out of the way first.

I reported this to Chief Hogan. He frowned for a moment, then said, "Is there any room around it? Or is it blocking the entire passage?"

"I think there's room around it."

"Then that's all we need to get air through, which is the priority." He handed me a large chisel. "Tell them to start pulling out stuff on their end as fast as they can, then you work the areas around the rock with this."

I forwarded his directions. J.J. responded that he understood, and then I heard the sounds of rocks being removed on the far side. I aimed the flashlight at the blockage, then chipped away at the rocks and dirt around the big rock with the chisel, wedging out what I could. I ended up focusing my attention on one three-inch-wide gap at the base of the big rock, excavating an even smaller passage, driving the chisel deeper and deeper into it. Although after a while, I had pushed it as far as it could go. It was being blocked by dirt and rock. . . .

And then it wasn't.

Something fell away at the tip of the chisel, and air began flowing around me, as though it, too, had been stuck in the passage and now could suddenly move.

"You're through!" J.J. yelled, and this time, there was nothing muffling his voice.

I pulled back and aimed the flashlight through the tiny passage. I saw an eyeball at the other end.

J.J. whooped with excitement. I could hear Zach and Arin behind him.

I backed out of the passage and told the others, "We're through! I can see them!"

A chorus of elated cheers echoed through the mine.

"Nice work, Teddy," Chief Hogan said. "You're done here. Move out."

I remembered what he had said and stepped aside. "Are you sure?"

"We've got this now. They're gonna live, thanks to you. But this will be tricky work, getting those rocks out and making sure we don't have another collapse. The best thing you can do is go home, get yourself cleaned up, and bandage those knuckles."

I looked down at my hands. Beneath the mud caked on them, my knuckles were scraped and bleeding.

"Tell me y'all brought some water for us!" Zach called through the passage. "I'm so dry, I'm worried nothing's gonna come out when I pee except sand."

"It's on the way!" Chief Hogan yelled back.

Sure enough, a device was being passed up the line, a water tank with a hand pump and some long, thin plastic tubes attached. The idea, I realized, was to snake the tubes through the tiny gap in the rocks and then pump water through.

I was in the way. So I slipped back past the firemen to head out.

Mom and Dad hugged me happily when I got to them. "Good work," Dad said proudly.

"We need everyone to clear out of here!" a firefighter yelled. "Now that we can get them air and water, we're gonna take it slow and make sure we do this as safely as possible. I know all of you want to help, but the best thing you can do right now is give us room to do our jobs!"

Everyone filed back outside. When I emerged into the sunlight, it was almost blinding.

While my eyes were adjusting, someone locked their arms around me so hard it almost squeezed the air out of me, then peppered my face with kisses.

"I hope that's Summer," I said.

"You taste like mud," she replied. "I don't think I've ever seen such a dirty person in my entire life."

My vision returned enough to find her face right in front of mine. Now that she knew her father was alive, she was beaming with excitement.

The rest of our group was gathered around, looking extremely relieved. Despite her exhaustion, Daisy was doing a jig of happiness with Jasmine. Everyone looked ready to celebrate.

Except Kandace. She was chewing a fingernail nervously. "Are we *sure* they're going to be okay?"

"They'll be fine," Heidi told her reassuringly. "Now that they can breathe, the worst is over. Chief Hogan can afford to take his time and be careful now, which is what he'll do. He's gotten people out of far worse scrapes than this."

"How long do you think that'll be?" Kandace asked.

"Could be a few hours," Sidney told her. "Or maybe even longer."

Kandace groaned. "And we're just supposed to sit here and wait?"

"No," Heidi said. "The fire department has this under control. We can trust them. In the meantime, maybe we should find something to take your mind off this."

"Like what?" Kandace asked.

"How do you folks feel about a rodeo?" Melissa asked.

THE RIDE BACK

Almost every night in the summer, there was a rodeo in West Yellowstone. This was a big tourist attraction—as well as the main sporting event in the community. (West Yellowstone was located farther from a professional baseball, football, basketball, soccer, or hockey team than almost any other point in the United States.) Local kids grew up training for the rodeo in the same way that kids in central Texas grew up playing football.

Melissa was competing in the barrel racing competition that night. We had all been planning to attend, but with the excitement of the past day, everyone had forgotten about it. Even her parents.

There was a brief discussion as to whether or not it made sense to go, given everything else that had happened. But everyone seemed eager for a diversion, even though we were concerned about giving up the hunt for Sasquatch. After all, it had been nearly twelve hours since the bear had broken into the house, so if he really had consumed the necklace, it was getting close to time for him to poop it back out again. If we didn't locate him soon, the jewels might be lost forever.

Everyone deferred to Kandace for an answer, seeing as they were *her* jewels.

Kandace graciously conceded that the hunt for Sasquatch should end. "You've all done more than enough, looking for him," she said, then glanced toward the abandoned mine, where her husband was trapped. "And besides, this hunt has caused a great deal of trouble. I don't want to cause any more."

"But if the necklace is important to you . . . ," Heidi began.

"It's not so important that people should die to get it back," Kandace said. "I don't want people chasing down a grizzly bear in the dark. Jewelry can be replaced. People can't."

Thus, the hunt came to an end. Melissa and her parents needed to be at the rodeo early for her to practice—and they needed to bring her horse, too—so the three of them rode off ahead, racing back to the house. The rest of us returned far more slowly. I was awfully banged up and sore, while

Karina and Pete were even less adept on horseback than I was. Karina had never ridden a horse before—although, as an ex–fighter pilot, she was handling it capably—while Pete's natural distrust of animals made him nervous and skittish. He clutched the pommel of his saddle tightly with both hands as he rode, as though expecting the horse to try to buck him off the moment he dropped his guard.

Everyone was feeling down about our failure to find Sasquatch and worried for J.J., Zach, and Arin, but despite that, it was a beautiful ride. There hadn't been much time to focus on the scenery on the way to the mine. Now we returned via a path close to the river, passing through a gorgeous forest of towering pines. Along the way, there were many small cataracts and beaver ponds, and the trees were alive with birdsong.

Personally, I wasn't upset that we had given up looking for Sasquatch. By now, I was quite sure that someone besides the bear had taken the jewels. Although that caused me a different kind of angst. J.J. had asked me to figure out who had done it, and I still had no idea. In fact, there were still several suspects I hadn't had a chance to talk to yet.

However, it wasn't easy to do that on the ride. We had to proceed single file along the path, which wasn't conducive to conversation. Daisy Creek had taken the lead to ensure that no one got lost along the way, and we had all fallen in behind her. I had ended up close to the rear of the line, right behind Evan.

Despite the exquisite surroundings, it was obvious he was in a bad mood. Every time we passed a low-hanging pine branch, he would yank a cone off it and then hurl it angrily. And whenever I tried to start a conversation with him, he only gave me monosyllabic answers.

Finally I asked, "What are you so upset about?"

"Oh gee, I don't know," Evan said sarcastically. "I only blew my family's whole deal to sell our ranch. Now I'm going to be stuck in this lousy place forever."

I fought back the urge to tell him the ranch was possibly the least lousy place I had ever been. Instead, I said, "No you didn't. . . ."

"I told J.J. that I thought Sasquatch was in the mine, and so J.J. went in to look for the bear, and then he got trapped in there and nearly died. You think he'll buy the ranch after all that?"

"If J.J. thinks this ranch is a good investment, then he'll buy it no matter what."

"How could he think it's a good investment? He could be stuck in that mine all night, thanks to me." Evan tore another pinecone off a tree and heaved it into a beaver pond.

"J.J.'s predicament isn't your fault," a voice behind us said. "It's J.J.'s."

I turned around, surprised to find that it was Gavin who had spoken.

These were the first words I had heard him say, even though I'd been at the ranch for almost two days. He had been so quiet, I had even forgotten he was behind us, bringing up the rear of our train. His voice was harsh and gravelly, as though it had fallen into disrepair from disuse.

"But he never would have gone into the mine if I hadn't mentioned it," Evan said.

"You didn't force his hand," Gavin observed. "He's an adult. So are Zach and Arin. They made their decisions on their own."

I slowed my horse a tiny bit so that I could be closer to Gavin. "Do you know how much J.J. was paying Zach and Arin to help him find Sasquatch?"

"He offered us each five hundred dollars for the day. And ten times that if we recovered the necklace."

That snapped Evan out of his funk. "Five thousand dollars? Each? And you didn't take him up on it?"

"To go into an abandoned mine to corner the biggest grizzly in Montana? I don't need money that badly."

There was something in the way Gavin said "money" that struck me. His tone was disdainful, as though he didn't care much about money at all—and couldn't understand why anyone else would. Since I actually had Gavin talking, I decided to try my luck and ask the question I'd had in mind for him all along but hadn't felt comfortable to ask. "Is it true that, in your entire life, you haven't been more than a hundred miles away from here?"

Gavin shrugged. "This is the most beautiful place I could ever imagine. Why would I want to go anywhere else?"

"You're not interested in seeing anywhere else on Earth? Like the beach? Or the ocean? Or New York City?"

Gavin laughed at my last question, as though the thought of him in New York City was the most ridiculous thing he'd ever heard. But then he caught himself and said, "To be honest, there is *one* thing in New York City I'd like to see."

"What's that?"

"The subway. A train that goes underground? That must be an incredible thing."

I almost laughed at this myself, then realized it wasn't such a crazy statement. An underground train *was* fascinating. I had been amazed the first time I saw one. Most people who lived in cities probably took them for granted, forgetting what an unbelievable accomplishment a subway system was.

"You're right," I agreed. "It is."

Evan asked, "So would you go to New York to see the subways?"

"Nah," Gavin said. "I wouldn't like it there. I hear the

buildings block the sky. You can't even see the sun and the moon there. *This* is where I belong." He looked around the forest, taking in the river and the trees with delight, even though he had certainly seen them thousands of times before.

In that moment, Gavin seemed to be the most content person I had ever met. I had assumed he'd been so quiet all along because he didn't like other people that much, but now it occurred to me that he simply enjoyed being silent. The idea of him plotting to steal the necklace suddenly seemed ludicrous, because, by his earlier comment, he had no desire for the money it would bring him. His apartment at the bunkhouse wasn't sparsely furnished because he couldn't afford things—but because he didn't *want* things. Clearly, he was happy with his life exactly the way it was.

He wasn't the only one taking in the scenery. Just ahead of Evan, Karina had stopped her horse in the middle of the path and was watching a large pool in the river intently. She signaled to us to stop our horses, then pointed toward the water. "Look! A beaver!"

Sure enough, a furry brown animal was swimming through the water, its tiny head poking just above the surface.

"Actually," Gavin said, "that's a muskrat."

"A muskrat?" Karina's excitement wasn't dimmed at all. "Oh! I've never seen one of those."

I realized that I hadn't either, even though muskrats live throughout the United States. Surprisingly, while American zoos like FunJungle generally had plenty of African animals, they often lacked native animals, either because they weren't as exciting—or they didn't do well in captivity. But even if I *had* seen a muskrat in a zoo, that wasn't the same as seeing it in the wild.

So I stopped to watch it too, as did Gavin. Evan had to stop as well because Karina's horse was blocking his path, although he seemed annoyed by this, as if he'd seen more than enough muskrats in his lifetime.

The animal looked quite a bit like a beaver, only smaller, and without the beaver's famous flat tail. Instead, its tail was thinner, like that of a rat. The muskrat was dark brown, with the large buckteeth common to most rodents. We watched as it swam to the other side of the river, then climbed out onto the far bank and disappeared into the reeds.

Karina continued staring at the river.

"The muskrat's gone," Evan told her.

"It might come back," she said.

Evan sighed heavily. "I doubt it."

"There's a pool just ahead where there's a whole family of beavers," said Gavin.

"Really?" Karina asked excitedly. "Can you show me?"

Gavin nodded, then pulled his horse past hers. While we

had been stopped, my parents and the others had ridden on ahead. But we were in no rush to get back, and I still hadn't spent much time with Karina yet.

In truth, I had always been a little uneasy around Karina. I usually only saw her when she was working, and at those times, she always had a no-nonsense military demeanor. But now, off the job, she was showing a different side of herself, which was probably closer to the real her; she was relaxed, enthusiastic, and eager to see new things.

The beaver pond in question wasn't far. An exceptionally large dam had created a great, wide expanse of river. The banks were marked with the stumps of numerous saplings felled by the beavers, each gnawed to a point. As we arrived, we could see a beaver on the far side of the pond dragging a large branch into the water.

Karina gasped with excitement.

Evan sighed again. Apparently, he was also done with beavers.

I had never seen a beaver in the wild myself, so I was quite excited too. I stopped my horse right beside Karina's to watch.

"It's amazing, isn't it?" she asked me.

"Yes," I agreed. "Although, it's weird that we were so much closer to a grizzly bear yesterday."

"No kidding," Karina said. "That was insane, right? I went

to Alaska once, hoping to see bears, and the closest we got was half a mile. All they looked like was little dots on the horizon. And then we come here, and there's one in the freaking house."

The beaver arrived at its dam, then climbed out, dragging the branch along, looking for a place to put it.

The impact the beavers had on their environment was extremely evident from where we sat. Plants couldn't really grow in the faster-moving sections of the river, but the wide, calm pool behind the dam had thick stands of reeds, cattails, and lilies. These attracted lots of birds and insects, while frogs peeped and trout darted just below the surface. I spotted a few fish that were over a foot in length.

On the opposite side of the river, the forest gave way to grassland, and I could see the buffalo herd grazing en masse, with the ranch house up the hill beyond it.

"Were you awake when Sasquatch showed up last night?" I asked Karina.

"Oh no," she replied. "I was sound asleep until I heard *you*. Although, I think maybe Sasquatch might have come around earlier in the night. *Something* woke me at three ten in the morning."

I was so surprised by this information, I turned away from the beaver to face her. "Three ten?"

"Three eleven, actually. I wear a watch to sleep and I always look at it right when I wake up. Force of habit from my air force days. If something woke you on an aircraft carrier, you needed to be prepared."

"What woke you last night?"

"I don't know, exactly. Do you ever snap awake and not really know why? I'm pretty sure it was a loud noise, but after I was up, I didn't hear anything else."

"You mean, a noise outside the house, like Sasquatch poking around?"

"Exactly," Karina said, although she froze the moment she had finished the word, as if she regretted saying it. "But now that I think about it, when I first woke up, I thought the sound had come from *inside* the house."

"Where inside?" I asked.

"Evan!" my father shouted from ahead. His voice was so loud that he startled the beaver, which dove off its dam, plopped into the water, and disappeared from view. "I think we found Sasquatch's trail!"

Evan spurred his horse and galloped ahead, with Gavin right behind him. Karina followed them, so excited about the tracks that she forgot all about answering my question.

I slowly brought up the rear. My body was too sore for galloping.

I caught up to everyone a hundred yards farther along in the forest. Evan was already off his horse, looking over a pile of bear poop the size of a football.

It was off to the side of the trail, so even though it was an exceptionally large poop, most people probably wouldn't have noticed it. I wasn't surprised that my father had, though. Dad had spent plenty of time tracking animals in the wild. He might not have been as adept as Evan, but he had a talent for it.

Evan was considering the pile of poop carefully, poking it with a long stick. "It's definitely grizzly scat. It's way too big for a black bear. Big for a grizzly, too. So it's probably Sasquatch's. But it's not fresh enough to be from today. I'd bet it's from yesterday."

"Still," Arturo said, "we might as well make sure. If that *is* from today, there could be a million-dollar necklace in there."

Ray whistled. "Wow. That'd have to be the most valuable bear poop of all time."

Evan regarded the poop warily, obviously in no mood to poke through it, no matter how much money was at stake. "Anyone else want to do the honors?"

No one volunteered for a few seconds. Finally Mom said, "Oh, all right, I'll do it. It's just poop."

She climbed off her horse, took the stick from Evan's hand, and jabbed the poop with it a few times, tearing it apart.

I chose to spend this time looking around the woods in search of birds or other woodland creatures. There were thousands of other, far more attractive things to focus on than my mother dissecting the largest bear poop in history.

Finally Mom spoke again, now sounding disappointed. "There's no jewelry in here."

I turned back to confirm that she was right.

Meanwhile, Evan was kneeling over the ground not far away, having found something else. "Here's Sasquatch's tracks. He came this way after he pooped." He followed them across the dusty ground. "He stopped here, then turned a bit and . . ." He trailed off thoughtfully, as though something was bothering him.

"Is something wrong?" my mother asked.

"I smell vanilla," Evan said, sounding extremely concerned. He looked back at the last pawprint, then followed it in the direction it was pointing.

This quickly led him to another print, and then another, which took him to a bush that looked as though it had recently taken a beating. Many of the branches had been broken, and even from a distance, I could see a few clumps of bear hair on them.

Evan pulled aside the branches to reveal a spot on the ground that was surprisingly free of leaves, given that it was under a bush. Evan knelt to inspect it, picked some dirt off the ground, then held it to his nose and smelled it. He frowned angrily in response. "There's been meat here. And vanilla. Someone's been baiting bears on our property."

Daisy Creek gasped in horror. "Who would ever do such a thing?"

"I have a pretty good idea," Evan said angrily.

THE RODEO

Evan and I couldn't put Evan's theory to the test until we got to the rodeo that night, as that's where his suspects were.

My parents drove us there, along with Ray and Karina, who wanted to see the rodeo as well. Summer, Kandace, and Pete opted out. Summer and Kandace wanted to be at the house for when J.J. got back from being rescued, whenever that might be. Plus, Ranger Oh had emailed us her list of ranchers with a history of antagonism toward wildlife conservation measures, and it was quite long. Summer had volunteered to investigate the names while I went to the rodeo. Besides, she had said, she wasn't a big fan of rodeos, given how animals were treated there. (Meanwhile, Pete claimed he didn't want to go because, as he said, "I can't think of anything I'd like to do less than spending two hours watching people wrestle with animals in the mud.")

We were a little late getting to the rodeo, as it took me a very long time to get clean again. I had to shampoo my hair ten times to get every last bit of dirt out of it. By the time we arrived, the first event, bronco busting, was already well under way. Cowboys were doing their best not to get thrown off untamed horses as they bucked wildly about in the ring. It was obviously extremely difficult; earlier that day, I'd had a hard enough time staying atop a horse running in a straight line, let alone one actively trying to throw me. The longest anyone had managed to last so far was 8.6 seconds, which Evan assured me was quite good.

Once the cowboy was thrown, he had a brand-new problem: getting out of the way before the bronco accidentally stomped on him. To aid him, three rodeo clowns were stationed around the ring. Two would distract the horse, while the third would help the rider to safety. Although the clowns were dressed comically, with cartoonish clothing and painted faces, their work was quite serious and potentially deadly— especially during the bull-riding competitions, which were scheduled for later in the evening.

This was not my first rodeo. I had been to the annual one in San Antonio, but that had been held in a giant indoor arena and thus felt more like a professional sporting event.

The West Yellowstone rodeo was a down-home affair. While a few journeyman riders were participating, most of the competitors were locals. In fact, many weren't much older than me.

The rodeo took place in a large field on the western outskirts of town. The arena was a great oval of dirt, surrounded by a metal fence bedecked with advertisements for local businesses: horseback riding stables, mom-and-pop restaurants, and white-water rafting guides. One side of the arena was flanked by the stands, which were the same sort of metal bleachers we had at our local high school football stadium. The dirt in the center was devoid of so much as a blade of grass, having been churned by thousands of hooves.

At one end of the oval were a series of metal chutes where the contestants—and the animals they were either going to ride or chase—waited before the events. Volunteers loaded them into each chute through a gate on one end, and then, at the appropriate time, a gate on the other end would fly open, releasing them into the arena. Beyond the chutes was the staging area, where dozens of horses, bulls, and calves were kept in pens, and beyond that was the dirt parking area for animal delivery, filled with hundreds of livestock trailers, each of which was hooked to the bumper of a pickup truck.

The parking lot for the fans was located at the opposite side of the arena; it was really just a large, recently mowed field. Behind the viewing stands was the food court: dozens of booths, almost every one of which was serving barbecue that claimed to be "The Best in Yellowstone"—although there was also soft-serve ice cream and homemade lemonade and one stand serving Chinese food, which seemed to be selling extremely well, given that it was the only dinner option for people who didn't want barbecue.

The biggest line of all, by far, was for beer.

And since there was so much beer being drunk, there were a great number of Porta-Potties. These were all arranged in a line at the end of the arena near the animal pens. ("They try to keep everything that stinks in the same place," Evan explained.)

It seemed that the rodeo was the main social event in town; while a good portion of the crowd was tourists, much of the local community had turned out as well. Just as many people were hanging out in the food court as were watching the rodeo itself. All around us, people were greeting friends and catching up. Evan's entire middle school appeared to be there. I spotted Jasmine, Arturo, and Daisy, who had come separately from us, socializing with their friends. There was also a large, rowdy group of locals about Zach's age, and I guessed that if Zach hadn't been trapped in the mine right then, then he probably would have been hanging out at the rodeo too.

Evan and I got pulled-pork sandwiches for dinner, which

took a while, because the lines were long and Evan had to say hi to everyone he ran into. The barrel racing was just beginning as we slid into our seats in the bleachers. Since Evan's parents had come early with Melissa, they had saved us most of a row. Evan sat next to them, while I sat between him and my parents. Ray and Karina were at the end.

A sophomore girl from the local high school was making her debut in the event. As far as I could tell, she was an excellent rider, but according to the announcer, her time wasn't that good. Still, the audience cheered for her supportively.

"Your sister's riding third," Heidi told Evan. "You almost missed her."

"You guys are baiting bears on our property, aren't you?" Evan asked.

His parents both turned to him, startled. Their reaction betrayed that they knew exactly what he was talking about, even though they tried to act like they didn't. "I don't know what you mean," Sidney said, but he wasn't a good enough actor to make it sound convincing.

"Don't lie to me," Evan snapped. "I even know *why* you did it. You wanted J.J. to see some bears. So he'd think our property would be the perfect place for a safari lodge."

Evan had explained his line of thinking to me in detail right after he'd found the bear bait on his property. The site was relatively close to the ranch house, which ruled out any hunters. If hunters were going to take all the trouble to bait bears, they would have done it someplace remote and far from humans, not in a place where they could easily be seen—and their guns would certainly be heard.

Meanwhile, Sasquatch hadn't started to show up on a regular basis at the Oy Vey Corral until only a few days before we all arrived. Evan had only seen bears that close to his home a few times in his entire life, so it had seemed suspicious that one was suddenly coming by right when a potential bidder for the property was visiting.

Thus, the Spooners and Jericho hadn't been involved at all. The garbage had simply been dumped in their trash cans to keep it away from the Krautheimer property.

Sidney glanced at me—and the rest of us on the bleacher bench. My parents were close enough to overhear their conversation, although Ray and Karina didn't seem to be aware of it; they were farther down the bench and completely focused on the rodeo.

"You told everyone?" Sidney asked Evan, obviously upset.

"We happened to be there when he found the bait," Mom explained, to take the blame off Evan. "We were all on the way back from the mine."

Now Sidney looked less shocked and more upset. "Do the McCrackens know too?"

"J.J. doesn't," Dad said. "But that's because he's still trapped in the mine."

Sidney took a deep breath. He seemed really upset with Evan—and also with himself.

In the arena below, another rider and her horse blasted out of the gate and started racing around the barrels.

Heidi spoke, more to my parents and me than Evan. "The baiting wasn't bringing any harm to the bears. It was only to give you all a show, let you see some of our amazing wildlife. We only thought it'd bring a black bear or two, not a grizzly like Sasquatch. And we certainly had no idea he'd come into the house. . . ."

"That had nothing to do with the baiting," Sidney said.

"Like heck it didn't!" Evan exclaimed. "Sasquatch would never have come anywhere *near* our house if it wasn't for the baiting. And then he obviously started to connect humans with food. Now Fish and Wildlife's probably gonna have to put him down!"

The Krautheimers looked around nervously to see if anyone else in the stands had overheard this, but everyone was focused on the rodeo, and the crowd was too loud and raucous for eavesdropping.

The rider finished up her race with a solid time and the crowd cheered.

"That's not going to happen," Heidi told Evan. "We've

learned our lesson. We're not going to set out any more bait. It won't take long for Sasquatch to realize this, and then he'll stop coming around."

"Maybe not," Evan said. "In fact, if Sasquatch stops finding food at your baiting site, he might be *more* likely to come to our house. Or someone else's. I can't believe you did something this stupid."

Both of his parents looked as though he had slapped them across the face. They certainly would have been upset by the insult under normal circumstances, but it was worse to have Evan say it in front of me and my parents. However, before they could respond, the rodeo announcer's voice rang out over the public-address system.

"Our next rider is a local favorite!" he said. "She's been competing here since she was only fourteen years old—and now she's one of our shining stars! Give it up for Melissa Krautheimer!"

The crowd went wild. Lots of people in the stands seemed to know the Krautheimers, and many shouted words of support to Heidi and Sidney.

"Watch your sister ride," Heidi told Evan. "Then we'll talk."

We all turned our attention to the arena. Melissa was astride Sassafras in one of the loading chutes. While the crowd cheered, she waved her cowboy hat and smiled brightly, then looked into the stands, toward her parents.

They gamely waved back at her. "Go Melissa!" Sidney yelled.

"We love you!" Heidi called.

Many tourists in the crowd near us grew excited, being in the presence of local celebrities.

Melissa put her cowboy hat back on, clutched her reins tightly, then prepared herself to ride.

The gate of the chute flew open and she and Sassafras took off like a shot. They tore around the barrels at a much faster pace than the previous competitors.

My phone buzzed with a text. It's was from Kandace's phone: It's Summer. Call me when you can.

Obviously, Summer had borrowed her mother's phone, since her own phone had been trampled that morning.

I returned my attention to the arena. Even in the brief moments that the text had distracted me, Melissa had covered a lot of ground.

Despite the tension about the bear baiting, Evan and his parents were all enthusiastically rooting Melissa on.

Melissa finished up, galloping at full speed across the finish line, then reining Sassafras to a stop near the chute where she had begun.

"Fourteen-point-two seconds!" the announcer exclaimed. "That's a course record!"

The crowd went wild. The Krautheimers all leaped to

their feet to applaud Melissa, and most of the people in the stands did too.

The rodeo clowns opened a gate that led out of the arena. Melissa rode through it, waving her hat to the crowd once again.

The Krautheimers turned to us, looking proud of Melissa and embarrassed about the bear baiting all at once. "We need to go down there to congratulate her," Sidney said.

"Of course," Dad said. "We'll save your seats."

Heidi gave Evan a pointed look. "You ought to come down too." I had no doubts that she really wanted him to show his support for his sister, but I assumed she was hoping to continue their conversation away from us as well.

Evan nodded agreement, and all three Krautheimers moved to the nearest aisle. Locals slapped Sidney on the back and shook his hand as they headed out.

I told my parents, "I need to go call Summer. It's too loud here."

"Any word about J.J.?" Mom asked.

"We'll see." I got up and headed out as well.

The next barrel racer came out of the chute while I was heading through the stands. The crowd was so loud, I had to get far away to call Summer back. I ended up heading out toward the end of the arena, close to where the animal pens were.

The barrel racing was coming to an end and the bull

riding was about to begin. This was the marquee event at the rodeo, similar to bronco busting, except that now the riders would be atop a 1,500-pound bull, bred solely for a bad temperament. The riders didn't even get a saddle, only a thick rope tied around the bull's chest, and they could only hold on with one hand. They had to stay on at least eight seconds for the ride to count, and even that happened rarely. Serious injuries were possible, from being either thrown, gored, or trampled. The event was known as "the most dangerous eight seconds in sports."

The bulls were kept in separate pens in preparation for the event, each with its name marked in chalk on a small slate. Most were obviously named to be imposing—Howitzer, Blockhead, Death on a Rope—although I spotted an ironically named Tinker Bell as well. A few cowboys were delicately maneuvering an ornery, snorting behemoth named Grievous Bodily Harm out of his pen and into the bucking chute.

There were far more contestants than tourists in this area, although a few visitors had come to see the livestock in the pens. The bull riders were easily recognizable because they wore specialized vests to protect their chest from falls, goring, or trampling. Plus, they tended to be extremely muscular and were very quiet—almost meditative—as they prepared for their event.

Meanwhile, some other cowboys and cowgirls were practicing for the team roping competition, which was far less dangerous—although still very difficult. In that event, two riders on horseback would go after a steer at the same time; one would throw a lasso around its horns, and then the other would try to rope both its back legs. Whichever team did it the fastest won. A few of the contestants were practicing throwing their lassos at fake steers, getting the noose over their horns time and time again. Unlike the bull riders, they were relaxed and having fun, good-naturedly talking trash to one another.

I suddenly recalled something that Jasmine had suggested that morning: Whoever had stolen the bison from the Oy Vey Corral probably needed ranching experience and the ability to throw a lasso. It occurred to me that perhaps one— or maybe several—of those steer-roping specialists had been involved in the crime. And then I found myself thinking that Zach probably had the connections in the community to recruit them—as well as a working knowledge of the ranch.

However, at the moment, my priority was calling Summer back. I finally found the quietest spot at the rodeo, a stretch of dirt between the animal pens and the Porta-Potties. It was probably also the worst-smelling spot in the county, which explained why no one else was hanging out there. I was just about to dial Kandace's number when I heard a familiar voice. "Look at the size of those bulls, kids! Give me your phone, hon. I'm going to get a picture!"

It was Morton, the touron who had been gored by the elk the day before. He was on crutches and had a large piece of padding in his shorts around his right buttock, which made it look as though the right half of his rear end was five times larger than the left. Other than that, he seemed none the worse for wear. In fact, he didn't seem to have learned anything from his experience, because he hobbled right over to the pen of a bull named Buzz Saw and promptly climbed up the fence around it, despite numerous signs warning him not to.

His wife didn't see anything wrong with this. His kids didn't even notice; despite all the activity around them, both were glued to their phones.

It was a struggle for Morton to scale the fence with an injured buttock, but he managed. His presence agitated Buzz Saw, who snorted angrily, but Morton paid the bull no mind, lifting his wife's phone up for a selfie.

"Hey!" a cowboy shouted at him. "Can't you read? You're upsetting Buzz Saw!"

Morton ignored him and snapped his photo anyhow.

"That bull's not a prop!" the cowboy yelled. "It's a living animal!"

"I'm not bothering him!" Morton yelled back, staggeringly unaware that he was doing exactly that. He finally clambered back down off the fence, then grabbed his crutches and limped back to his wife. "Jeez," he said, handing her phone back. "That cowboy's a real jerk. But I got some great photos!"

I had to fight the urge to kick him in the rear end right where he'd been gored. But I called Summer instead. Even though I dialed Kandace's phone, Summer answered.

"How's your dad?" I asked.

"He's out of the mine," she reported. It sounded as though she was walking. "And so are the others. But they're still on their way back here. Mom and I are going to the stables to meet them. They're okay, but pretty wiped out."

"That's great news," I said.

"I didn't make much progress with those names Ranger Oh gave us, though. I mean, I found some information on a lot of them, but . . . I have no idea how to tell if any of these people would steal a bison. They all sound like normal ranchers. It's not like any of them has a criminal history or anything. Although George Wiley's son did go to prison for a little bit."

"For cattle rustling?" I asked hopefully.

"No. Drug possession. I don't think that translates, really."

"It's still a criminal connection. That's something."

"But not much. Sorry. How are things there?"

"Evan was right. His parents were doing the baiting, trying to lure bears to the ranch so your dad would get more excited to buy it. They were really embarrassed about everything. And they're worried about your father finding out."

"I'm not telling him. Not tonight, anyhow. He's had a rough enough day as it is."

"Really, the Krautheimers ought to be the ones to tell him. Not you."

"Yeah, they should. Okay, I can see Dad coming with the rescue squad. I've gotta go. Have fun there!"

"All right. See you when I get home." I hung up, then started back toward the stands.

But as I turned around, I noticed another familiar face. Ike Spooner was wandering through the animal pens, taking a look at the bulls, along with an older man in standard local ranching attire. Ike had the same clothes on I'd seen him in earlier—the black cowboy hat and matching boots—as though maybe he hadn't been home.

He didn't see me. He was too busy looking at the bulls. So I figured I would go over and say hello.

Ike and the other man passed close to the chute with Grievous Bodily Harm as I closed in on them. Ike peered through the metal slats and whistled appreciatively. "That's quite an animal."

"You into bucking bulls now?" the other man asked.

"Getting tired of fooling around with bison?" There was undisguised contempt in his voice, making it clear that he didn't care for the bison at all.

I decided not to interrupt. Instead, I stayed behind them, eavesdropping as they continued on.

"C'mon, George," Ike said. "Bison are the future of ranching. They're perfectly evolved for this environment; they hold up better in the winter than cattle and you don't have to pump them full of hormones."

My ears perked up at the name, and I wondered if the older man might be George Wiley himself.

"They're wild animals," George told Ike dismissively. "While cattle have been bred for domestication for five thousand years."

"You need to open your mind," Ike said. "Why don't you come on by the ranch this week and see some of my new—"

I didn't hear anything else, because at that very moment, chaos erupted.

There was a loud clang from the chute holding Grievous Bodily Harm, followed by a dozen cries of concern. I spun around to find that somehow the rear gate to the chute had come open, allowing Grievous to escape into the concourse.

The 1,500-pound, exceptionally angry beast was loose.

And he was charging right at me.

GRIEVOUS BODILY HARM

I had come face-to-face with a lot of potentially dangerous animals in my life: a tiger shark, a polar bear, an anaconda, a herd of Cape buffalo—and as of that morning, a grizzly bear. (Surprisingly, all of those encounters had taken place *after* I had moved to civilization. During the ten years that my family had lived in a tent camp in the Congo, my life had been far safer.) But even though Grievous Bodily Harm was a domesticated animal, in a weird way he was possibly the most dangerous creature I had ever confronted. Unlike all the wild animals, he had been bred to be dangerous.

Wild animals rarely attack humans unless they feel threatened, and even then, it is usually as a last resort. Although it had been terrifying to find Sasquatch in the house, it was obvious that the grizzly hadn't been the slightest bit interested in harming any of us.

But Grievous Bodily Harm, like most rodeo bulls, had been raised to be angry. He wasn't a killer, exactly, but he was big, mean, and destructive. The moment he got loose from the chute, he was going to smash everything in his path.

And unfortunately, the first thing in his path was *me*.

Even though I only had a split second to analyze the situation, a few things were evident:

The rear gate of the chute didn't appear to have been broken. It had simply swung open, as though someone had forgotten to lock it. Or possibly as though someone had opened it on purpose.

Grievous Bodily Harm wasn't barreling straight for me. Instead, he was bucking about wildly, exactly as he would have done if he'd been in the arena and a cowboy had been astride his back. But he was still coming in my direction, he was coming fast—and he was moving erratically. If he had simply charged me, I might have been able to dive to one side and let him run past. But now I couldn't seem to get out of his way. I juked left and right, but Grievous kept changing direction as well. The massive beast continued toward me, bellowing like a train whistle. His head was lowered, so his thick, sharp horns were pointed straight ahead, ready to gore anyone or fling them aside—or both.

All around me, rodeo fans and contestants were scattering like cockroaches. Even the bull riders were fleeing out of Grievous's path. Some people vaulted over the fence and dropped into the arena, while others climbed the food vending stalls. I caught a glimpse of Jasmine hoisting a young girl up to her parents atop a barbecue stand before clambering up it herself.

I made a few more feints to get out of Grievous Bodily Harm's way, but the bucking bull kept bearing down on me, so close that the ground trembled from the thud of his hooves and I could feel the breath gusting from his nose onto my back.

Someone suddenly tackled me.

They broadsided me, knocking me sideways, out of the path of the bull. We tumbled through the dirt as Grievous Bodily Harm thundered past.

However, the bull didn't keep on running. It swiveled in our direction, still bucking and kicking wildly. So now the danger wasn't getting gored so much as getting trampled.

The man who had saved my life was instantly back on his feet. He had tackled me so fast, I hadn't been able to see his face. Now all I could tell was that he was a big man—and he was a rodeo clown. He wore baggy overalls, a garishly striped shirt, and a bright green fright wig. His face was painted white, and he had a fake red nose the size of an apple.

He was now distracting the bull from me, the same way he would have for a thrown rider in the rodeo ring. He waved for the bull's attention, giving me a chance to scramble for safety, then led it in the opposite direction.

Grievous Bodily Harm bellowed and charged the clown. For a second, it looked as though the bull was going to run him through with his horns, but the clown scampered up the arena fence with surprising agility for a man so big. The bull glanced off the fence just below him and then raged onward.

As the clown perched atop the fence, his fake nose fell off, allowing me to finally determine the identity of the person who had saved me.

It was Jericho.

Grievous Bodily Harm continued his rampage. By now all of the tourists had cleared the area and the only people around were a few other rodeo clowns and cowboys who were trying to contain the bull. Grievous veered away from them toward the Porta-Potties.

Only fifteen seconds earlier, there had been lines for all of them, but now everyone had fled, realizing there were other things more important than going to the bathroom. (Although it was possible that some people, in their fright, had relieved themselves on the run.) So the area in front of the outhouses was wide open.

Morton stepped out of the stall on the end.

It was evident that he'd been completely unaware of what was happening outside the Porta-Potty until that moment. He was simply trying to get out of the foul-smelling cubicle as quickly as possible and made it two steps before he even noticed that there was an enormous, ornery bull on the loose.

Grievous Bodily Harm responded to the sudden movement and turned his way.

Morton gaped with horror and then moved with incredible speed for a wounded man. He flung his crutches aside and raced back into the portable outhouse.

No sooner had the door slammed shut behind him than Grievous Bodily Harm rammed into it. The bull hit the cubicle with the force of an oncoming truck. The Porta-Potty rocked backward and then toppled.

From inside came the sound of a large amount of human waste sloshing out of the holding tank, followed by a scream of abject horror and disgust from Morton.

Grievous continued onward, although he was now slowing down. Either he had worn himself out, or his foul temper was fading. He was no longer bucking as wildly.

Near the Porta-Potties, a few dozen people had climbed atop a cotton candy and snow cone booth, which was groaning under their weight. One dim employee balled up some snow cone ice into a snowball and flung it at the bull, mistakenly thinking that would fend Grievous off. Instead, it provoked a last burst of rage from the bull, which gave the stand a cursory butt with his head. The makeshift structure, already strained by the weight of the people hanging on it, buckled and collapsed. Thankfully, no one was hurt, but the cotton candy machine was mortally wounded. The barrel that spun the sugar was violently ejected and clanged off Grievous Bodily Harm's head, leaving the bull with streams of bright pink spun sugar dangling from his horns.

The cowboys and rodeo clown had now surrounded Grievous on three sides.

The bull stopped bucking, considered them, then turned and quickly trotted away in the one direction that no one was covering—the direction of the Porta-Potties.

Morton had just managed to force the door open from the inside and was clambering out. He was smeared from head to toe with human waste and reeked so badly that I could smell him from thirty feet away. Now, upon seeing the bull returning, he shrieked in terror, slipped, and fell right back into the muck-filled outhouse again.

Grievous ran past him and into the parking area beyond. The cowboys and rodeo clowns chased after him.

Jericho joined them, even though he had already put his life at risk once. He paused momentarily as he passed me to glance in my direction.

"Thanks," I said.

Jericho nodded, then ran on.

Now that Grievous Bodily Harm was a safe distance away, I brushed myself off and took a look around. Ike Spooner was gone. So was the man who might have been George Wiley. The two of them had run off with the rest of the crowd once Grievous had gotten loose.

I was annoyed that their conversation had been interrupted and that I had missed what had sounded like a promising clue. But there was something else that concerned me even more:

When Grievous Bodily Harm had first escaped, I had caught a glimpse of something.

Someone had been behind the open gate of the bull chute, as though they had swung it open and were keeping it between themself and Grievous as protection. Their face was hidden behind the metal slats, but I had seen their cowboy hat.

It was baby blue.

The exact same color as the one Taffy Spooner had been wearing earlier that day.

Which made me think that maybe Grievous Bodily Harm escaping his chute hadn't been an accident at all.

THE NECKLACE

When we got home from the rodeo, J.J. McCracken was asleep on the living room couch again.

He must have been worn out after his brush with death that day, because he slept right through our entrance. He was wrapped in a bison-hide blanket, snoring loud enough to rattle the chandelier.

This time, he had decided to wear pajamas to bed, just in case.

"Think he and Kandace had another fight?" Heidi asked.

"We'll ask him in the morning." Sidney locked the front door with the deadbolt, then assured us, "Sasquatch won't get through that, I promise you."

The Krautheimers hurried upstairs for bed. The whole family had been acting uneasy around us all evening, obviously embarrassed about the bear baiting and worried about what J.J. would say when he found out.

The rest of us headed toward the guest bedrooms. It had been a very long day, and that night had ultimately been frustrating as well. I had been unable to get anyone at the rodeo to believe that Taffy Spooner might have let Grievous Bodily Harm out of his chute. In fact, I had a hard time even getting anyone to listen to me—besides my own parents. And no one would listen to *them*, either.

Despite the bull's escape, the rodeo staff was determined to get the show back on as quickly as possible. The announcer downplayed the events, saying there had been "a slight mishap in the handling area" and that all fans should stay in their seats. The cowboys in charge of the animals acted like nothing serious had happened and went right back to loading bulls into the chutes. (Grievous Bodily Harm, exhausted from his rampage, was wrangled and placed back in his pen with relative ease.) After only fifteen minutes, the rodeo was up and running again.

Even the local police wouldn't take my parents and me seriously. There were quite a few of them on duty at the rodeo; the sheriff was even one of the clowns. They refused to entertain the idea that Taffy Spooner might have tried to harm me, insisting that Taffy and Ike were good people and big sponsors of the rodeo. Instead, they—and everyone on the rodeo staff—were operating under the idea that Grievous

Bodily Harm had escaped by accident. It turned out that mishaps were rather common at the rodeo, especially ones where animals escaped, although the animals in question had always been smaller, usually calves from the calf-roping competition. They had never had a bull escape before, and it seemed that everyone wanted to sweep the incident under the rug and pretend that it hadn't happened. When we kept pressing him, the sheriff firmly told us to stop trying to do his job and go watch the rest of the rodeo; he was obviously quite annoyed at us when he said it, although it was still kind of hard to take him seriously, since he was wearing an enormous clown nose at the time.

My parents and I reluctantly returned to our seats and tried to enjoy the remaining events. I couldn't concentrate, though. I kept searching the stands for the Spooners, who shouldn't have been hard to find with Taffy's distinctively colored cowboy hat. But I never saw them again. They must have left.

However, I *did* see the other people I knew. Jasmine had joined her parents in the stands for the bull-riding competition, and they all appeared just as eager for the show to go on as the police had been. Zach had shown up as well. He seemed completely unaffected by his ordeal that day and was surrounded by friends, many of whom had competed in the rodeo. Everyone was riveted to him as he spoke; I assumed he was telling the story of his adventure in the mine. Three young women were blatantly vying for his attention, batting their eyelashes and hanging on his every word, but Zach didn't seem to care. He kept stealing glances at Jasmine instead.

Given the events of the day, my parents and I would have been fine with leaving the rodeo early, but everyone we had come with wanted to stay until the end. For the Krautheimers, it was a social event, Ray and Karina were enjoying themselves, and Melissa was a minor celebrity; kids lined up to get their picture taken with her and have her sign their programs. So it was almost ten thirty by the time we got back to the house. Seeing as we had all been up since four in the morning, we were exhausted.

The door had been replaced on the McCrackens' room, the hinges screwed back into the jamb. A light shone underneath it, indicating someone was awake on the other side.

"I want to say good night to Summer," I told my parents.

"Don't be long," Mom said. "You need your sleep. And I'm sure Summer does too." She and Dad slipped into our room.

Ray and Karina continued down the hall to their rooms. As they did, something occurred to me: Since Karina's room shared a wall with the McCrackens', then the loud noise she had heard in the house at 3:10 a.m. might have come from the McCrackens' room.

I knocked softly on the McCrackens' door.

"Hello?" Kandace replied softly.

"It's Teddy," I said. "Can I come in?"

"Of course."

I entered the room. Kandace was sitting in bed, wrapped in a large robe. She had a book in her lap, but her eyes were red and swollen, as though she'd been crying.

Summer was asleep on the sofa bed.

"Oh," I said, feeling embarrassed. "I just wanted to say good night to Summer. I didn't mean to disturb you."

"You're not," Kandace said in a way that indicated she wasn't just being polite. I got the sense that she wanted to talk. "I was having trouble sleeping again. You'd think it'd be easier, without J.J. here. That man snores like a freight train."

"Is that why he's on the couch tonight?" I asked.

"No. That was Summer's doing. He really upset her."

"How?"

"When he got back from the mine with Zach and Arin, she noticed that they only had shotguns with them."

"Not dart guns?"

"No."

"Oh." I immediately understood why Summer was angry. No dart guns meant that J.J. and the others hadn't planned to sedate Sasquatch if they found him. Their only plan had been to kill him.

"J.J. tried to explain it to her," Kandace said. "If they ran into Sasquatch inside the mine, their lives would be in serious danger. A dart gun wouldn't do them any good. They'd be in a confined space and the dart would take too long to work . . . so they'd have to shoot to kill. But that just upset Summer even more. She told J.J. that if he was so worried for his safety, then he shouldn't have been going after the bear in the mine in the first place. And that no bear was worth killing just for a necklace. Especially when there was a good chance the bear didn't eat the necklace at all." Kandace gave me a searching look, as though she was hoping for my thoughts on this.

"She has a good point."

"I understand J.J. asked you to investigate that possibility."

"Yes."

"And . . . ?"

"I don't have much," I admitted sadly. "I can't even figure out *how* anyone could have stolen your necklace. Let alone *who*." I took in the room again as I said this. There was no place for anyone to hide, besides under the master bed, and Summer and I had found that area was full of boxes of winter blankets, which were stored there over the summer.

Someone had removed the stuffed pronghorn that had caught fire. It had been replaced by a stuffed bighorn sheep from some other part of the house, as though no bedroom would be complete without some dead local wildlife.

I looked back at the door. While it had been put back in place, the latch to lock it hadn't, because the place where it had ripped free from the jamb was too damaged.

Kandace was obviously upset with my lack of information. She tried to keep herself composed but then broke into tears. Which she immediately grew embarrassed about. "Sorry. I know you're just a kid, but you've solved so many other crimes, I was hoping . . . I thought that you'd maybe . . . Oh, I've made such a mess of things! I felt it'd be a special surprise for J.J., wearing the necklace for him here. But it's only led to one disaster after another."

Her choice of words struck me. "Why did you think it would be special?"

Kandace blew her nose in a tissue and tried to compose herself. "Because this is where J.J. proposed to me."

"I didn't know that."

"Yes." Kandace smiled, thinking back, pleased by the memory. "It was sixteen years ago this summer. We came to visit the Krautheimers. It was my first time here. J.J. has always loved this place and he wanted me to see it. Originally, he was planning to propose to me a few weeks later, in New York City. He was going to buy a diamond from a merchant there, and he thought he would pop the question afterward. But then he ended up buying that sapphire instead. It kind of fell into his lap and he couldn't resist. So he bought it and proposed that night instead. We went on a moonlight horseback ride to a meadow where Heidi had arranged to have a blanket and some champagne set up for us. I know it might seem hard to believe, but J.J. can be a very romantic person."

That *did* seem hard to believe, but there was another part of the story that was much more interesting to me. "What do you mean, the sapphire 'kind of fell into his lap'?"

"Oh. He was at a bar in town with Sidney, and some local kid came in with the sapphire, looking to sell it. He'd found it out on one of the reservations in the area. It didn't look like much at the time. It was just a big, ugly lump of rock. But J.J. realized that the right jeweler could turn it into something beautiful. So he bought it off the kid and gave it to me that night. I have to admit, I wasn't thrilled that J.J. was just giving me a rock instead of a ring. But as usual, J.J.'s instincts were spot on. In fact, the sapphire turned out to be worth far more than even J.J. suspected. He likes to say it's the best investment he ever made."

"Not because of the money, though," Summer said, surprising us. She was still lying in the sofa bed but had apparently been awake and listening. "Because you agreed to marry him."

"How long have you been eavesdropping on us?" Kandace asked. It sounded stern, but she was obviously teasing.

She looked much happier than she had when I had first come into the room.

"It doesn't count as eavesdropping when people are talking right in front of you. How was I supposed to sleep through all that?"

"Sorry," I said. "We were trying to be quiet."

"Teddy came in to say good night to you," Kandace explained, "and I made him stay and listen to my boring engagement story."

"It wasn't boring at all," I told her.

Kandace said, "I think I've talked enough. It's way too late for you kids to be up. We'll see you in the morning, Teddy."

"All right," I said. "Good night, Summer. Sleep well."

"You too. Is the front door locked tonight?"

"Yes. No bears are getting in. I hope."

"Oh, Teddy!" Kandace said. "Would you mind putting this back on the bookshelf for me?" She tossed me the book she had been reading. It was a field guide to local wildlife. "It goes right by the door."

I turned to the shelves, which ran along the wall only a few feet from the entrance to the room. Sure enough, there was an entire shelf full of field guides. I tucked the book back in place, then turned back to Kandace, having one last question after her story. "Do you have any idea what J.J. actually paid for that sapphire?"

"Not exactly, but J.J. always said it was a fair price. More than the kid was even asking. Good night, Teddy."

"Good night," Summer echoed.

I slipped out the door into the hallway. The moment I closed it behind me, the lights went out in the McCrackens' room.

Down the hall, in the living room, J.J. was still snoring loudly.

The lights appeared to be out in Pete and Ray's room, and Karina's room too. Although the light shone under the door to my room, indicating that my parents were up, waiting for me to return.

Still, I stood in the hall for a moment, wanting to be alone, thinking.

I had the sense that I had missed something important, although I had no idea what it could be. It was a nagging feeling that I had been close to figuring out a piece to the mystery but then let the solution slip away.

I yawned. I was exhausted and my mind was fuzzy. That wasn't the best condition to be in to solve anything. I figured that I should go to bed, get a good night's sleep for once, and maybe, when I was nice and rested, I could calmly figure everything out in the morning.

Only, the next morning wasn't calm at all.

INSPIRATION

I didn't have any trouble falling asleep. I was so tired, it felt like I was out before my head even hit the pillow.

But then I woke up in the middle of the night, needing to go to the bathroom, and I couldn't get back to sleep.

My mind, having had some rest, was now full of questions. Starting with: Was it actually safe to go to the bathroom?

The night before, I had run into a grizzly bear. And even though I had witnessed the front door being locked, that didn't mean that someone couldn't have *unlocked* it again. Either a careless stargazer like Ray—or someone looking to lure Sasquatch back into the house once more.

I proceeded to the bathroom with caution, alert for any strange sounds or large animals emerging from the shadows.

The house was surprisingly quiet, save for J.J.'s snoring, and I made the trip to the bathroom and back safely.

Then I lay in bed, thinking about both of the mysteries.

Although I had no proof, I was relatively sure that Sasquatch hadn't eaten the necklace. But if it had been stolen, who had done it? The reason for stealing it seemed pretty simple: It was worth a great deal of money. J.J. had managed to keep the actual price a secret from almost everyone else— but anyone who saw the jewel-encrusted necklace could tell it was expensive. Even me, and I hardly knew anything about jewelry.

I ran through all the potential suspects, starting with the Krautheimers.

Sidney and Heidi seemed pretty desperate to sell their ranch to J.J. Maybe they were in serious financial trouble. They had already stooped to the crime of bear baiting to make the ranch look more appealing. They also knew their house better than anyone; if there was a secret route from the McCrackens' bedroom to the underground liquor room, they would probably know about it. And if Sidney had been there when J.J. originally bought the sapphire, perhaps he felt he had some claim to it. Maybe Sidney had also wanted to purchase the stone, but J.J. had outbid him for it and Sidney had been resentful ever since.

But if the Krautheimers were that desperate for money,

why would they steal from the very person they intended to sell their ranch to? Wouldn't that sour the deal?

So maybe it was one of the Krautheimer kids who had stolen the necklace, trying to help the family out. They knew the hidden parts of the house too, maybe better than their parents. Perhaps they were just trying to help the family weather its financial difficulties. Or maybe they wanted the money for themselves. It was also possible that one of the kids didn't want to sell the house at all. Stealing the necklace would serve two purposes: ruining the deal to sell the ranch, while giving their family the money they needed to keep it. Melissa was the one who really seemed to love the Oy Vey Corral, but Evan could have lied about his dislike for the place in order to deflect attention from himself.

Then there were Pete, Ray, and Karina. All of them had been in the house the previous night, in rooms very close to the McCrackens'. If any of them were in financial trouble, stealing the sapphire might have seemed like a quick solution.

Karina was ex-military, so she maybe she knew how to unlatch the bedroom door from the other side and let herself in. Although latching it again once she had stolen the necklace didn't seem easy. And what would be the point of doing that?

Meanwhile, I had no idea how Pete or Ray would have

gotten into the room with the door and windows locked.

I also had to consider the ranch hands: Jasmine, Zach, Arin, and Gavin. As I had observed, it wouldn't have been hard for any of them to slip out of their apartments at the bunkhouse and slink over to the ranch house at night. Perhaps one of them knew a secret way into the McCrackens' room. And someone from the outside entering the ranch house would explain the open front door; maybe the thief had forgotten to shut it tightly behind them while they were racing back to the bunkhouse.

The thought occurred to me that even if someone had stolen the necklace, that didn't necessarily guarantee them millions of dollars. The necklace was really just a bunch of rocks: a lot of tiny diamonds and a great blue sapphire. Except for being pretty to look at, they were useless if you couldn't find someone willing to pay for them. And unloading a famous giant sapphire certainly wouldn't be easy. Conceivably, there would be shady people willing to buy it, but the thief would have to know who they were and how to reach them.

As I lay in bed, I could hear the bison herd outside, making noise even in the middle of the night. Which made me think about the other mystery at hand.

Despite the size of a year-old bison, stealing one didn't seem to be nearly as complex a crime as stealing a necklace from a locked room. The bison were always outdoors and rarely under close watch. Yellowstone was never closed; tourists were free to range around the park at all hours—and the bison were free ranging. No one would have to dismantle a fence to get to get them there—although the Krautheimers' fence hadn't been much of an impediment. It wasn't electrified or monitored with security cameras, and it could have been taken apart and reassembled relatively quickly with only a screwdriver, a hammer, and a few U-shaped nails. True, year-old bison wouldn't have been as easy to make off with as, say, a koala—but a person, or more likely, a small team of rustlers, could have done it without too much trouble.

Unfortunately, the ease of the theft made the list of potential suspects quite large. Any cattle rustler for hundreds of miles could have taken the bison. Or one of the many antibison local ranchers might have committed the crime—although what they stood to gain was questionable. Certainly, stealing a year-old bison now and then wasn't going to stop the rise of bison ranching, was it?

I then found myself wondering why the thieves had changed tactics. Why steal one or two bison from the Krautheimers and then start stealing them from Yellowstone? Had the thieves simply decided that it was easier to get them from Yellowstone, where there weren't any fences to take apart? Or was it possible that they had been stealing from Yellowstone all along and only been noticed now? And how were they getting the bison out of the park? Wouldn't a truck with a young bison in the back of it be noticeable? Perhaps there weren't many rangers on duty late at night, but still, there were only a few roads in and out of the park, and there must have been *some* security at them. It seemed unlikely that someone wouldn't have noticed. So did that mean there was a crooked park ranger involved, getting bribed to look the other way—or maybe even directly involved in the thefts?

Something creaked in the house, interrupting my thoughts. I lay quiet and listened.

The creaking came again. It appeared to be coming from upstairs, so it was probably one of the Krautheimers going to the bathroom in the middle of the night, just as I had done. But even after coming to that conclusion, I couldn't shake the fear that perhaps the creaking was Sasquatch getting back into the house. I knew it was irrational—and yet it had happened once already. It could always happen again.

I got out of bed and locked the door to our room, just in case.

And the main question at the center of the stolen-necklace mystery came back to me:

Why had Sasquatch come into the house at all?

The Krautheimers had lived in that house for generations without ever having a bear get in. And now one happened to invade their home on the very night that the necklace vanished? That seemed too great a coincidence to be unconnected.

Had the thief lured the bear inside to help cover their tracks? If so, how? And why had Sasquatch gone through all the trouble to break into the McCrackens' bedroom, while ignoring all the dirty plates in the kitchen? Had something lured the bear to the McCrackens' room? Something besides the single dirty plate of dessert Kandace had left behind?

A memory suddenly came to me. In the midst of all the chaos, after Sasquatch had licked Kandace's dessert plate clean, he had still been sniffing the air, like he was trying to find something. As though the leftover dessert had only been a brief distraction from what the bear was *really* searching for.

A bear didn't see the world the same way humans did, by using its eyes. In a way, it saw the world with its nose. And its nose worked far better than our eyes did. A human would be lucky to see something a hundred feet away in the dark, whereas a bear could smell something from miles away. In addition, it could detect smells that humans wouldn't even be able to sense. It was quite likely that Sasquatch had been lured by the smell of something that seemed powerful to him, but not to any of us humans in the house.

The bear had been sniffing in the direction of the bookcase.

I looked around my room. There was no bookcase in our room, while the McCrackens' had a whole wall lined with them.

I unlocked our room and stepped out into the hallway.

The door to the McCrackens' room was directly across the hall from ours. Karina's room was farther down, on the same side of the hall. The door to her room hung slightly open.

I walked down to it. I hadn't been in Karina's room yet. I peered through the slight gap.

It was dark in the room, but my eyes had adjusted to the night over the time I had been lying awake. Karina was asleep in the bed, snoring softly. The room was quite small, about the same size as the apartments in the bunkhouse, with only the twin bed, a dresser, a nightstand, and a closet. One person didn't really need a big room, but still . . .

The room seemed smaller than it should have.

I was suddenly struck by an idea, a big one that could explain how the previous night's crime had been committed.

The problem was, I needed to get into the McCrackens' room to see if I was right. And it was after four in the morning. I really should have been going back to bed.

Only, I knew that I wouldn't be able to fall asleep again. I was too excited now.

And while it was really bad manners to wake the

McCrackens, I figured that they might not be upset when I explained why I was waking them.

So I went back down to their door. I knew it wasn't locked because the lock hadn't been replaced.

I slipped inside, then crossed over to Summer's bed and gently shook her.

"Hey," I said softly. "I'm sorry to wake you. But it's important."

Summer slowly opened her eyes, then groaned when she saw it was still dark. "It's the middle of the night. Can't this wait until morning?"

"No."

In the bed, Kandace snapped awake, startled. In her drowsiness, she forgot that she still had her sleep shades strapped over her eyes. "What's going on?" she demanded. "Where is everyone?"

"We're right here, Mom," Summer said calmly. "You still have your sleep shades on."

"Oh. Right." Kandace pulled the shade off her eyes, flicked on the lights, then gave me an imposing stare. "Teddy Fitzroy, what are you doing by my daughter's bed?"

"Asking for her help," I said. "I think I know what happened to your necklace."

THE TELLTALE SMELL

Kandace quickly changed her attitude. She instantly stopped being suspicious of me and became as eager to solve the case as I was. She hopped out of bed and slung a robe over her pajamas. "Don't just lie there," she told Summer. "Get out of bed and help Teddy!"

"Okay." Summer didn't seem quite as awake as her mother, but she was still intrigued. She climbed out of the sofa bed. "What are we looking for?"

"A hidden room," I replied.

"But we already found that," Summer argued sleepily. "It's under us. And there's no connection to it from here."

"Who says there can only be one hidden room in a house?" I left Summer's side and crossed the bedroom to the bookshelf. "I mean, if this house was built to hide illegal

alcohol, maybe they weren't hiding *all* of it in the basement."
I pointed to the bookshelf. "Karina's room is on the other
side of this. But her room is a lot smaller than it ought to be.
Some of the space between your rooms is missing."

"And you think there's a secret room behind the book-
shelf?" Summer was now wide awake, stirred by excitement.
"Awesome! I always wanted something like that in my room.
But Mom said no."

"A girl shouldn't have a secret hiding place in her bedroom." Kandace came over to the bookshelf as well. "How
do you think this opens?"

"One of the books is the switch, obviously," Summer
said. "That's how these things always work. Aha!" She yanked
dramatically on the largest book on the shelf, an old copy of
War and Peace.

It wasn't a secret switch. It was merely a book. When
Summer yanked on it, it flew off the shelf and thudded on
the floor.

"Okay, it wasn't that one," Summer said, then gamely
started pulling on other books.

So did Kandace and I. The bookshelf was divided into
three sections and we each took one.

Kandace asked me, "So, you think that someone was
hiding in here all night? And then they slipped out at some
point and took the necklace?"

"Yes. Karina said that she heard a loud noise at three ten a.m., coming from the house. This shelf is on the opposite side of the wall from her room. So maybe what she heard was the secret door opening. Or closing again, once the thief had slipped back into the hidden space."

Kandace paused in the midst of yanking on books. "That means the thief would have still been in here when Sasquatch showed up. Because the windows and doors were all locked. But when Sasquatch broke in, everyone else was outside. We saw them all."

"Not everyone," I said. "We never saw Ray."

"Because he was asleep in his room the whole time," Summer said. "That's what Pete said."

"But we don't have any proof of that," I argued. "Only Pete's word."

"So you think that Pete and Ray plotted this together?" Kandace asked. "I can't imagine them stealing my necklace. They're so nice."

"That doesn't mean they can't be thieves," I replied, but then frowned, thinking of something. "Only, I *did* see Ray before he went to bed. He was having a drink with everyone in the living room, while you were already in here, Kandace."

"Maybe it's not just a secret room, then." Summer was quickly working her way through the books and had already done three of the five shelves. "Maybe it's a secret access to the room below us. Or a secret way in and out of the house. And if that's the case, then someone could have come from outside to steal the necklace. Like one of the ranch hands. We didn't see any of them until after Sasquatch had run off. One of them could have snuck in, stolen the necklace, then gone back to the bunkhouse and pretended to have been there all along."

I continued pulling on books, but I was losing steam. The more I thought about my hidden-room theory, the less sense it made. I had figured that someone—or something— had been behind the bookshelf when Sasquatch showed up. That was what had attracted his attention. But that didn't make sense if there was only a secret passage behind the shelf, because the thief wouldn't have had to stay put. And a secret room only made sense if the thief could access it, which wasn't possible, because Kandace had been in the room all night.

"What's going on in here?" my father asked.

We all turned around to find my parents standing in the doorway to the room, bleary eyed.

"Sorry," I said. "Did we wake you?"

"People banging around and dropping books on the floor in the middle of the night tends to do that," Mom said.

J.J. shoved between them and stormed into the room, looking very upset. "It is four thirty in the a.m.! What in the holy heck is happening?" He pointed a finger at me. "And what are you doing in my daughter's room at this hour?"

"Teddy's trying to find the necklace," Summer said.

"By yanking books off the shelves?" J.J. asked suspiciously.

"He thinks there might be a hidden room behind here," Kandace told him. "Although we can't find the switch to open it."

"Did anyone try this?" Dad pointed to an elk-horn sconce that jutted from the wall between the door and the bookcase. "If I were building a secret switch, I'd put it here." He yanked on the sconce.

It also wasn't the switch. It was just a sconce. And when Dad yanked on it, it tore out of the wall.

"Oops," Dad said.

I sighed, now thinking that I had been completely wrong.

And then an item on the shelf caught my eye.

In addition to all the books, there was a single bookend: a heavy iron square. When I stepped back, I realized it was the only bookend on the entire expanse of shelves. Everything else was just books.

I yanked on the bookend.

It shifted slightly and then there was a click from behind the bookshelf. With a loud creak, the entire section of the shelves I was facing popped slightly ajar.

It was a hidden door.

Everyone in the room gasped.

I pulled the door open, revealing a room behind it.

It wasn't very big, nor was it very cozy. It was really only a narrow gap between the McCrackens' room and Karina's, merely two feet across, although a person could have easily fit inside it. It would have been tight and claustrophobic, but doable.

There was a handle on the back side of the bookcase. So that anyone who was shut inside the hidden room could get back out again.

Summer turned to me, beaming. "You were right, Teddy! It's another secret storage room for alcohol!"

J.J. stepped forward to have a better look. "Actually, I'll bet it was for storing weapons. In case the Feds decided to storm the house." He pointed to the rear wall of the hidden room, which had what looked like an empty shotgun rack built into it. "Those rumrunners were always ready for a fight. . . ." He paused and sniffed the air. "Does anyone else smell cookies?"

The moment he said it, I noticed the smell as well. I stepped into the hidden room and took a whiff. The smell was much stronger in there. The same smell I had come across twice already that day. "It's not cookies. It's vanilla."

"Yes!" Mom exclaimed. "I knew it smelled familiar!"

Suddenly, things started to click into place. Everything that had confused me about the mystery began to make sense. But there was one more piece of evidence I needed to find before I could be sure of exactly what had happened.

I stepped back out of the closet and started out of the room.

"Where are you going now?" Summer asked.

"To look for one last clue," I replied. "Come with me!"

We reentered the hall to the bedrooms. All of our talk had roused the other guests. Karina and Pete were both exiting their rooms—although Ray, unsurprisingly, seemed to be sleeping through all the excitement once again.

I went the other way, toward the rest of the house. Everyone else fell in behind me.

As I entered the living room, the Krautheimers were all coming down the stairs, also having been wakened. They seemed startled by the parade of guests in their pajamas. "Is something wrong?" Heidi asked worriedly. "Please don't tell me another animal got in."

"No," I assured her. "Did any of you know there was a secret room behind the bookshelf in the McCrackens' bedroom?"

All of the Krautheimers looked surprised. And it appeared genuine. Which I had suspected might be the case.

"No way!" Melissa exclaimed. "Show us!"

"In a bit," I said. "I need Evan's expertise first." I looked to him as he reached the bottom of the stairs with his family. "Can you look for some tracks for me?"

"Now?" he asked. "What kind? Bear?"

"No. Human," I said. "We'll need a flashlight."

The Krautheimers kept one in the closet right by the front door. I led Evan outside, with everyone else tailing us at a distance. In our rush, no one bothered to put on shoes or slippers. We headed barefoot along the side of the house toward the McCrackens' bedroom window. Light from the room shone through it into the predawn darkness.

"Summer escaped out this window yesterday morning," I explained. "But up until that point, it had been locked. What I need to know is, did anyone else come out this way *after* Summer did?"

Evan looked at me curiously but then directed his attention to the ground. I shone the flashlight at the area under the window while Evan knelt and scrutinized the dirt. After a while, he said, "Summer, were you barefoot when you went out the window?"

"Yes," she said. "I didn't have any way to get to my shoes. And then I went to meet Teddy at the front door."

"So these are *your* footprints." Evan pointed to some faint indentations in the dirt. Then he pointed to some others. "And *these* are someone else's. Someone who was wearing shoes."

In the darkness, I couldn't really see what Evan was talking about, but that didn't matter. The point was that *he* could see the evidence. And it was backing up my theory.

"Whoever it was came out after Summer," Evan continued. "Because their prints overlap Summer's. And then they went that way, away from the front door." He pointed toward the far end of the house.

I checked my watch. It was now four thirty in the morning, about the same time that Sasquatch had caused all the trouble yesterday. It was so dark out that it was hard to even see the far corner of the house, where Karina's bedroom was. Someone heading that way would have quickly vanished into the shadows.

"Why would someone else have come out the window?" Pete asked, confused.

"I think I know," I said, then turned to the Krautheimers. "You weren't completely honest with us about the bear baiting, were you? You weren't the ones who actually did it. You had help?"

"Yes," Heidi admitted. And then she said the name of the person who had helped. Which was exactly who I thought it'd be.

"I know who stole the necklace," I said. "And we're running out of time to get it back. Can we borrow your car? I'll explain everything on the way."

THE THIEF

The Krautheimers lent us their SUV, which seated seven people. J.J. insisted on driving and allowed Kandace and Summer to come as well. Sidney Krautheimer took the passenger seat so he could give J.J. directions. My parents and I filled out the remaining seats.

Summer and I had to wedge ourselves into the small back seat, which was barely big enough for the two of us. My parents had expressed some concern about us coming along, as we were only children, fearing that confronting the thief might be dangerous, but I was quite sure that it wouldn't be. At least, I figured it would be considerably less hazardous than my previous day had been.

The biggest danger, as far as I was concerned, was being in the car with J.J. driving. In our haste, we had forgotten what a terrible driver he was—and now he was in a great hurry to get his necklace back. He was going way too fast on the dirt road that led from the Krautheimers' ranch to town. It was still dark, the road was in bad shape, and there was plenty of wildlife out. We almost hit a pronghorn before we had even left the driveway.

Summer was obviously frightened by her father's driving as well. She was clenching the armrest tightly with one hand and my own hand with the other.

"Daisy Creek took the necklace," I said as we roared down the road.

Sidney's response was immediate and fierce. "Daisy?" he exclaimed. "Absolutely not! Daisy is the most honorable woman I've ever met in my life. I once overpaid her by five dollars—and when she realized, she drove all the way back to my house to return the extra money."

"I'm sure she's a good person," I said, "but all the evidence points to her. . . ."

"How?" Sidney demanded. "Daisy wasn't even at the house last night! She went home with Arturo while the rest of us were having dessert."

"No, she didn't," I explained. "She only tricked us into thinking that. And Arturo helped. Daisy actually went into the hidden space behind the bookshelf *before* you went to your room. Then Arturo left and claimed that they had gone together. But no one watched them leave, did they?"

The adults all looked from one to another, realizing this was true. "I guess not," Kandace conceded.

"That doesn't prove anything!" Sidney exclaimed.

He seemed so hurt by my accusation that I felt bad about pressing on with it. But I had to in order to reveal what had happened. I said, "Arturo even called Jasmine later and asked her to look for Daisy's car keys to give the impression that he was home with her, but that was all a ruse. Daisy spent the entire night in the hidden room."

"How did she even know about that place?" Mom asked. "None of the Krautheimers knew about it and they live here."

"Jasmine says her parents have been working at the house for a really long time," I replied. "So they could know things that the Krautheimers don't."

"Yes," Sidney admitted. "Arturo and Daisy worked for my parents. But I still refuse to believe she did this."

"I can't think of any alternative," I said sadly. "No one who was staying at the house could have gotten into the room, because the bedroom door and all the windows were locked. But Daisy didn't have to break into the bedroom, because she was in there all along. I *think* her plan was to take the necklace and then slip out unnoticed in the night, but Sasquatch came along and messed everything up."

"And that was a total coincidence?" Kandace asked, then suddenly screamed, "DEER!!!!"

A herd of whitetails was crossing the dirt road ahead of us. Most bounded away, but a few froze, staring into the headlights of the oncoming SUV.

J.J. pounded the brakes and twisted the wheel. The SUV swerved wildly and spun on the road.

Summer squeezed my hand so tightly that I thought she might break my fingers.

The SUV came to a stop sideways on the road, encased in a cloud of dust.

"Maybe you should let *me* drive," Sidney told J.J.

"I've got it," J.J. assured him. "It's not *my* fault a bunch of stupid deer don't have the sense to get out of the way of an oncoming car." He threw the SUV into reverse and promptly backed into one of the Spooner Ranch fence posts.

Sidney winced. But he didn't argue the point any further. He obviously felt ashamed about everything that had happened so far and seemed to be doing his best to keep J.J. happy.

"It *wasn't* a coincidence that Sasquatch showed up," I said as we started down the road again. "He came into the house *because* Daisy was there. The Krautheimers had asked her to set up bear bait to lure grizzlies while we were all here, to make the ranch seem like the perfect place for a safari lodge. I guess she'd been doing it for a couple of days?"

"Yes," Sidney answered softly, sounding uncomfortable.

"She was baiting the bears with meat," I continued, "and using vanilla to lure them. Then she was dumping all the garbage in the Spooners' trash to get rid of the evidence. It all worked pretty well. Sasquatch started coming by. Only, he started to associate the smell of vanilla—and maybe humans—with easy food. And once that happened, he became a nuisance bear.

"Vanilla is a very powerful scent, and bears can smell it from a long way off. I'm guessing that Daisy got some of it on her clothes. Or maybe she just couldn't get the smell off her hands. Which wouldn't have mattered if she had gone right home. But she didn't. When Arturo brought Kandace to the house, he and Daisy both saw that she was wearing the necklace and hatched their plan to take it. Daisy went into the hidden room—and Sasquatch came looking for her. Because she smelled like vanilla."

"Which is why Sasquatch didn't go toward the dirty plates in the kitchen!" Summer exclaimed. "And why he was sniffing around the shelves. Because he was more attracted to the smell of vanilla . . . COYOTE!"

Sure enough, a coyote was racing across the road in front of us. J.J. slammed the brakes once again, and we skidded to a stop so abruptly that everyone was flung forward against their seat belts.

The coyote scampered away into the night.

J.J. immediately hit the gas, throwing all of us backward into our seats.

"J.J., please be more careful," Kandace pleaded.

"I'm trying to get your necklace back," J.J. told her sharply.

"That necklace won't do me a bit of good if I'm dead," Kandace replied.

"Anyhow," I went on, "I'm guessing that Daisy was in the process of stealing the necklace when Sasquatch showed up. She ducked back into the hidden room right before Kandace and Summer woke up, but then she was stuck there while Sasquatch came in, looking for her. Obviously, we ran the bear off before he could find her, and once everyone had fled the room, Daisy saw her chance to escape. She went out the window, the same way that Summer had, and slipped away into the night. Those were her shoe prints Evan found outside the window."

"Then she had Arturo come and pick her up," Summer concluded. "And went home and changed. After which, they came back together in the morning to make it look like they had been together all night."

"Right," I agreed. "If they hadn't shown up in the morning, it might have seemed suspicious. But as it was, they were the only people who had seen the necklace who we *didn't* suspect. Because it looked as though neither one of them had been at the house to take it."

"Only, they didn't count on Teddy Fitzroy being on the case," Dad said proudly.

"Well," I said modestly, "this is all just a guess."

"Exactly!" Sidney exclaimed. "There's still no hard proof that Daisy stole that necklace." He looked to J.J. with desperation. "She risked her life to save you in the mine yesterday. She worked her fingers to the bone. And if Chief Hogan hadn't forced her out, she would have stayed right there, digging rocks out until you were free. That woman is a saint, not a thief. . . ."

"I don't think she took the necklace for the money," I said. "There's something else you all ought to know. . . ." I trailed off as we arrived at the junction of the road that bordered the northern end of the ranch.

It was so early that no one was even heading into Yellowstone yet. There were no cars or RVs heading east along the road.

And yet, there was an RV heading west. It struck me as odd that someone would have left the park so early in the morning. I couldn't tell for sure, since it was dark out, but the RV appeared to be the one I had seen leaving the park the previous morning, heading down this exact same road. It was about as large as a recreational vehicle could get, the size of a bus, with a blue stripe down the side.

The left-hand blinker was flashing, indicating the RV was

about to turn onto the dirt road we were on. The dirt road that only ran to the Krautheimers' ranch, the backcountry trailhead—and the Spooner Ranch.

"Stop that RV!" I exclaimed.

"Now?" J.J. asked. "We need to get to the Creeks before they take off with my necklace!"

"It's an emergency!" I yelled. "Stop it!"

J.J. ran through the stop sign and slammed on the brakes, coming to a halt right in the middle of the intersection.

That should have prevented the RV from going any farther. A vehicle that big wouldn't be easy to back up, and nearly impossible to make a U-turn with, so with our SUV blocking its path, I figured it would be stuck.

But whoever was driving it didn't stop. Instead, they bore down on the SUV, intending to bulldoze us out of their way.

"Jumping Jiminy!" J.J. exclaimed, realizing we were about to be hit. He punched the gas and we sped out of the way of the oncoming RV. . . .

Although we weren't quite fast enough. The RV caught the rear of the SUV with a crunch of metal, throwing us into a spin. The side airbags deployed instantly. We whirled through a half circle and slid off the road backward. There was a loud crack as the rear axle snapped and then the back of the SUV sagged.

The RV didn't fare much better. It lost control as well, skidded off the road, and crashed into a tree.

"Is everyone all right?" Dad asked.

We all responded that we were, and then my parents and Sidney sprang from the SUV and ran toward the RV.

Summer and I clambered out of the rear seat and exited the SUV with the McCrackens.

The driver of the RV leaped out and fled into the night. I had expected it to be Ike or Taffy Spooner, but I could tell, even in the night, that it wasn't. The driver was too big and stocky.

It was Jericho.

As I had seen at the rodeo, for a man his size, he was surprisingly fast and agile. He slipped through the barbed-wire fence of the Spooner Ranch and ran away.

In his haste to flee, Jericho had left the keys in the RV with the engine running.

J.J. considered the ruined SUV, then ran toward the RV. "Follow me!" he yelled to us. "We're taking that RV!"

"But it's not ours!" Kandace protested.

"And also—" I began.

"That idiot nearly killed us!" J.J. exclaimed, cutting me off. "So he forfeits his right to his RV! We can't wait around. We need to get to the Creeks ASAP!"

"But there's something you should know—" I said.

"Tell me on the way! Everyone else, hop in!"

"All right," Sidney agreed, "but this time, *I'm* driving."

He started for the driver's seat, but J.J. raced past him and sprang into it.

"The way you drive, the Creeks will be halfway to Canada by the time we get there," J.J. said.

Everyone else climbed into the RV through the side door. I followed them, still trying to get their attention. "Before we start driving, there's something you all should know—"

There was a yelp of surprise from Kandace. "There's a buffalo in this RV!" she screamed.

"I thought that might be the case," I said.

24

THE STOLEN BISON

I climbed into the RV to see the bison for myself.

The RV had been designed to maximize the interior space. There were two sitting areas behind the driver's seat, followed by a bathroom and a kitchenette with a small gap between them, and a pullout bed at the rear. Under normal circumstances, it might have been somewhat roomy, but with six people gathered in the sitting area, it was quite cramped.

Plus, there was a year-old American bison inside.

He looked to be somewhere around five hundred pounds and had started to develop the shaggy hump around his shoulders, so his bulk left him wedged between the bathroom door and the kitchenette, with barely an inch to spare on either side. His dark beard was still thin and patchy, which made him look vaguely like a teenage boy who had just started sprouting facial hair. He was facing us and was understandably agitated, given that he had recently been stolen, placed in an unfamiliar setting, and involved in a traffic accident.

The RV was an older model and thus had lots of wear and tear that had come with years of use: rips in the upholstery, scuffs on the tabletop, a dripping kitchen faucet. But there was also some unusual damage that indicated that more than one young bison had been transported in the RV: gashes in the linoleum floor where hooves had pawed it, a badly dented bathroom door, and a series of holes gouged in the cabinetry by horns.

It also stank, indicating that several—if not all—of the illegally obtained bison had relieved themselves on the floor. The one we were facing now definitely had. A fresh pile of bison poo sat by the pullout bed, and there was a small lake of urine as well.

A lasso lay coiled on the small table in the sitting area, attesting to how Jericho had caught the young bison. Still, I figured he must have needed every ounce of his strength to drag it into the vehicle.

There was something extremely bizarre about seeing a bison in an RV. He looked completely incongruous, jammed between the bathroom and the kitchenette, as though some alien race had beamed him there by mistake.

"We need to get him out of here," Summer said, concerned. "He looks scared."

"Or should we take him back home?" Mom asked. "He ought to be returned to his herd."

"How would we even know where that is?" Dad asked. "He could have been taken from anywhere in Yellowstone."

The door suddenly locked automatically behind me as J.J. started the RV. He put it in reverse and stomped on the gas. "Actually," he said, "our priority is still getting to the Creeks before they split with my sapphire!"

The engine whined as it strained to pull the RV back onto the road. The rear tires spun and screeched on the asphalt.

"Daddy!" Summer exclaimed. "What about the poor bison?"

"I'll take him right back after we get my jewels!" J.J. pressed down on the gas pedal with all his might.

The tires finally found purchase and the RV lurched backward violently. All of us tumbled into the various seats in the sitting areas. The bison wobbled, banging into the bathroom door, and bawled in alarm. The small lake of urine sloshed about.

The RV shot backward through the intersection, flattened a stop sign, and then smashed into the Krautheimers' SUV, knocking it onto its side.

Sidney gave a whimper of dismay.

"Don't worry," J.J. told him. "I'll get you a new one." He threw the RV into drive with a grinding of gears and we sped into West Yellowstone.

The RV hadn't been in great shape *before* the accident, but now it coughed and wheezed as though it only had a few miles left in it. The front end was crushed and the windshield was cracked from the run-in with the tree, and now smoke billowed from the engine.

All of us buckled into our seats and kept a wary eye on the bison. Not used to being in a moving vehicle, he was struggling to stay upright, his hooves skidding on the urine-slicked linoleum floor.

Mom turned to me, looking as if something I said before had suddenly sunk in. "Teddy, *how* did you know there would be a bison in here?"

"I'd been trying to figure out how someone could move bison out of Yellowstone without drawing attention," I said. "And then it occurred to me that an RV would be perfect. Hundreds of them pass through the park every day, and they're obviously big enough to hold a bison." I nodded toward the one in the back, which was wobbling unsteadily due to J.J.'s driving. "I saw this same RV leaving the park early yesterday morning, which is a strange time to be going out. And Evan found RV tire tracks on the road to the Spooners' yesterday, although he figured it was a lost tourist at the time."

"So you figured Jericho was stealing the bison?" Dad asked.

"Actually, I thought it was the Spooners. They must be paying him to do their dirty work. Last night, at the rodeo, I overheard Ike starting to tell George Wiley about a new bison he'd got. Or I *started* to overhear it, but then Taffy released Grievous Bodily Harm from the chute to try to get me out of the picture."

"Now you're accusing Taffy of murder?" Sidney exclaimed. "She's no killer!"

"I don't think she was trying to kill me," I said. "But she was right by the chute when the bull got out. She must have realized I was eavesdropping on Ike and decided to do something about it."

"I don't believe it," Sidney said, shaking his head. "That can't be true. . . ."

"Sure seems true to me!" J.J. exclaimed. "We found the foreman of their ranch driving an RV with a stolen bison in it. Case closed!" He glanced at me in the rearview mirror. "Two mysteries solved in one morning, Teddy! You earned every cent of your fee on this one!"

Summer had been beaming at me proudly up until that moment. But now her smile suddenly became a frown. "Hold on. Daddy was *paying* you to investigate this case?"

"Er . . . ," I said weakly. "Not the bison rustling. Only the stolen jewels."

"You told me you were investigating on your own!"

At the same time, J.J. also got upset with me. He wheeled around in the front seat and asked, "You told Summer about the investigation?"

"J.J.!" Kandace exclaimed. "Watch where you're going!"

J.J. returned his attention to the road ahead just in time to avoid plowing into a car from behind. He swerved around it, sideswiping a stop sign, which toppled like a felled tree.

"We're not supposed to keep secrets from each other," Summer told me angrily. "Even if other people ask us to."

"Summer," J.J. said, "it's really not his fault—"

"You keep out of this!" she snapped. "I'm already angry enough with you, bear hunter!"

We were passing straight through West Yellowstone, which had been a pleasant, peaceful little town until our arrival. It wasn't very big, but there was already a decent amount of traffic as tourists got an early start on the day. The parking lots of diners were filling up and families were leaving motels for the park. J.J. wove through all the cars while the RV's engine clanked and belched smoke. We all had to hold on to keep from being thrown from our seats.

The bison was growing more and more unsettled as the RV trembled around him. He lowered his head and gouged a groove in the kitchen cabinets with the tip of his left horn.

"J.J.," Mom said, growing concerned. "Could you drive more carefully? You're upsetting the bison."

"We're almost there!" Sidney announced. "The Creeks' place is just a few blocks ahead." He pointed out the front windshield, but I couldn't see much through the curtain of smoke.

I suddenly realized there was still some important information I hadn't shared about the necklace. I had started to say it a few minutes earlier but then been distracted by the RV. "Oh! There's something you all need to know about the Creeks!"

"Great," Summer said angrily. "There's something else you discovered without asking for my help?"

"Yes," I admitted. "I don't think they took the necklace for the money. Not exactly. I think they were trying to right a wrong."

"How's that?" J.J. took a corner too close, jumped the curb, and sent a garbage can skidding across the sidewalk.

We all jounced in our seats.

The bison lost his footing and smashed headlong into a cabinet, spearing the door with his horn.

"You bought that sapphire here in town, right?" I asked. "Off a local kid who found it on a reservation. And you kind of scammed him."

In the rearview mirror, I saw J.J.'s gaze narrow. "I paid him a fair price," he said.

"But only a fraction of what the sapphire was really worth," I said.

"Who told you that?" J.J. asked.

"*I* did," Kandace said. "It's the truth and you know it, J.J."

J.J. turned around angrily, intending to say something, but before he could, Sidney yelped, "J.J.! Look out!!!"

Some pedestrians were stepping into a crosswalk ahead of us.

J.J. pounded on the horn and veered wildly.

The RV jumped another curb and sheared a fire hydrant off the sidewalk, releasing a geyser of water. The right front tire blew out and we skidded to a stop in the parking lot of an apartment complex.

An upper kitchen cabinet burst open, releasing a cascade of pots and pans, which all clattered off the poor young bison's head. The bison reared his head back and bellowed, ripping off the cabinet door that was spiked on his horn, so the door now sat askew on his head, as though he was wearing a beret at a jaunty angle.

"We need to get out of the vehicle," Dad said. "Now!"

He led the way, forcing the side door open so the rest of us could get out.

Tourists were pouring out of diners and motels to see what had caused all the commotion. Several started taking selfies with the geyser of water erupting from the busted fire hydrant.

"Look at that, kids!" one father exclaimed happily. "Now we don't have to bother driving all the way to see Old Faithful!"

One tourist wasn't staring at the water spout. He was staring at *me*. It was Morton. He gaped in horror when he saw me. "No! Stay away from me! Whenever you show up, some crazy animal comes after me!"

"Morton," his wife chided. "Don't be ridiculous."

At which point, the young bison charged out of the RV and into the street. He was in a foul mood now. He shook his head angrily, finally dislodging the cabinet door, which sailed through the window of a souvenir shop. Then he bellowed at the top of his lungs.

"See what I mean?" Morton screamed. "Run away!" Having finally learned his lesson, he fled back into the safety of the diner.

None of the other tourists followed his lead. In fact, several of them actually *approached* the bison, even though he was obviously upset, and started taking selfies with him. One dumb college kid came within only a few feet of the angry beast.

Dad and Mom watched this behavior, aghast. "Go with J.J.," Mom told me. "We'll handle the tourons."

J.J. was running across the intersection toward a small apartment complex. Sidney was by his side, while Kandace followed them.

Summer stood between us and them, unsure what she should be doing.

I ran over to her. "I'm sorry I didn't tell you the whole truth. I didn't know what the right thing to do was."

Summer fell in behind me and we chased after her parents. "Being honest is always the right thing to do. . . ."

"But your father asked me not to. . . ."

"You could have told him no. We're a team, Teddy. We have to be straight with each other."

"Okay. I will. From now on."

Summer smiled, pleased that I had apologized, then glanced back toward my parents. "What are your folks doing?"

"Trying to talk some sense into the tourists."

There was a bellow from the bison, followed by some screams of fear. I glanced back to see a few tourons fleeing from the young bull as he charged after them.

"Doesn't look like they're having much success," Summer observed.

"No," I agreed. "It doesn't."

The young bull caught up to the college kid who had been closest to him and deftly butted him through the front window of the diner.

The RV burst into flames as its engine finally burned out.

The sound of wailing sirens filled the air. Three local

police cars screeched to a stop at the intersection. I saw my parents hurry over to them to explain what was going on.

Ahead of us, Arturo Creek emerged from the front door of a first-floor apartment. He was already dressed for a day of work, and he looked much more concerned about the bison in the street than he did about J.J. McCracken bearing down on him.

"Morning," he said calmly. "What's going on?"

He obviously meant with the bison, but J.J. didn't take it that way. He was already winded after his short run, so he was gasping for breath as he responded. "We know that your wife was hiding in the secret room two nights ago when the bear got in. Can we talk to her?"

"No," Arturo said. "Daisy left last night after work. She had some business back on the reservation."

"Business?" J.J. repeated skeptically. "Did it have to do with my sapphire?"

Arturo looked him in the eye. He stayed calm, but there was a hint of anger in his voice. "That sapphire was never yours."

J.J. now grew angry as well. "So you admit she stole it?!"

"You stole it first. From her nephew."

"Stole it? I paid that kid for it!"

"Barely. And you're right, he was just a kid. He didn't know what he had—and you took advantage of him."

J.J. started to argue, but Kandace cut him off. "J.J. Listen to what he has to say."

Behind us, the police were now trying to wrangle the bison. The RV was blazing. The fire department arrived to put it out. The crowd of gawkers was growing by the minute.

Arturo continued. "Like most people on the reservation, Daisy's nephew had a rough life. The only break he ever caught was finding that sapphire—and you took it from him."

"Daddy!" Summer exclaimed. "How could you do such a thing?"

J.J. gave her a wounded look. "I paid him *more* than he was asking. Five hundred dollars."

"And how much is that sapphire actually worth?" Summer demanded. "A million dollars?"

"More," I said. "A lot more."

Summer glared at J.J. Kandace looked ashamed. And J.J. was suddenly at a rare loss for words. "Wait," he spluttered. "I . . . well . . . you see . . ."

Arturo fixed him with a hard stare. "Daisy's nephew's name is Cade. He's a good man, but he's had a tough run. He's still living on the res, struggling to get by on what work he can find—and not a day goes by that he doesn't regret selling that rock to you. He didn't even know your name at first, just that you were some hotshot businessman who ripped him off, but over the years, Daisy and I put two and two together and realized it was you." He shifted his gaze to Kandace. "So the other night, when we saw that you'd brought the stone back here, Daisy said the time had come to make things right." He removed a large, bulky envelope from his jacket and held it out to J.J.

"What's this?" J.J. asked.

"Open it," Arturo said.

J.J. hesitated, so Kandace took the envelope herself. She opened it and smiled. Then she lifted out the contents.

It was the rest of the necklace: all the diamonds. Only the sapphire had been removed. And there was a wad of twenty-dollar bills inside.

"How much is this?" Kandace asked.

"Exactly what was paid for the stone in the first place." Arturo shifted his gaze to J.J. "See? We didn't steal it. We're just getting it back to its rightful owner. Daisy went to the res to take care of that—and I was on my way to bring this to you. Only, it looks like you figured things out on your own."

"Teddy did," Summer said proudly. "He also figured out that Jericho's been stealing bison. With that RV."

She pointed to the charred wreckage in the street behind us. The police were now chasing the young bull in circles.

"Oh," Arturo said. "I was wondering what all that was about."

J.J. didn't seem to know what to say. He still seemed upset, but he looked to Kandace for guidance.

"Keep the money," she told Arturo, handing the envelope back.

J.J. turned to her, aghast. "What?"

"We don't need it," Kandace said. "And besides, the stone already paid off for you." She smiled. "You got *me* with it."

"And me, too!" Summer chimed in. "It was the best investment you ever made!"

In the intersection, a policeman managed to get a lasso around the horns of the young bull. Only, the bull turned out to be a lot stronger than he'd expected. He took off down the street, dragging the policeman behind him like a dogsled, until the officer finally thought to let go of the rope.

Arturo now shifted his attention to Sidney. "We didn't mean to lure Sasquatch into the house. That was an accident. And we're very sorry. . . ."

"No," Sidney said, looking ashamed. "That would never have happened if it wasn't for my *meshuge* idea to lure the bear to the property. I should never have asked Daisy to do it."

"She could have said no," Arturo said.

I said, "Sometimes when your boss asks you to do something, it's hard to say no. Even if you don't agree with it."

Summer realized what I was really talking about and rolled her eyes.

In the intersection, the firemen couldn't put the blazing RV out because the fire hydrant had been knocked off. They were struggling to cap the geyser first.

The young bison was now eating the decorative flowers from the landscaping in front of the souvenir shop.

Kandace told Arturo, "If Daisy's nephew wants a fair price for that sapphire, he should call us. If we don't buy it, we can put him in touch with people who can sell it for him. At the right price."

Arturo smiled. "Thanks. I'll let Daisy know." He looked past us, toward the chaos in the intersection. "A lot of strange things have been happening since you people showed up."

"Oh, that's not us," Summer said. "That's Teddy. Chaos follows him wherever he goes."

"That's not true!" I protested.

"It darn well is," J.J. said.

"But you know what?" Summer asked me. While the RV burned and the geyser spouted and the young bison eluded yet another attempt by the police to catch him, she slipped her hand into mine and grinned. "I wouldn't have it any other way."

Epilogue

THE RELEASE

Later that day, I stood on the side of the road in Hayden Valley in Yellowstone National Park, watching a herd of bison. I had come with my parents, the McCrackens, and Jasmine to witness the return of the young bison that Jericho had stolen.

I had feared the drive there would be awkward because of the whole situation with the necklace, but Jasmine had quickly thanked the McCrackens for doing the right thing, and that had defused any tension. The trip had turned out to be very pleasant, with Jasmine pointing out lots of scenic points and wildlife. Thanks to her keen eyes, we saw three herds of elk, a moose, and a mother grizzly with two cubs on our way to the release site.

It had taken the police in West Yellowstone an hour to

capture the young bull that morning. They hadn't wanted to tranquilize him, because knocking an animal out is always risky, but wrangling him wasn't easy. Ultimately, they had to wake one of the best cattle ropers from the rodeo. In the meantime, the young bull had eaten most of the flowers in the town park and appeared in over two thousand selfies.

"Jericho used to be a champion roper, back when he was younger," Jasmine explained. "You need the skill to lasso your target, and the strength to overpower it. Jericho had both. Not many people could wrangle a year-old bison into an RV on their own. But if anyone could, it was him."

It turned out, I had made a mistake in my deductions about the bison thefts. Jericho had been acting on his own. The Spooners were innocent.

After finally wrangling the stolen bison, the police had taken our advice and gone to interview Ike and Taffy, who had been shocked by the accusation that they had stolen any bison. They said that they had only asked Jericho to purchase more bison for them. Jericho had told them that he could get better deals if he offered local ranchers cash, and the Spooners had agreed. But instead of buying bison, Jericho had been stealing them, then pocketing the thousands of dollars the Spooners paid him for each one.

He had started off by targeting the local ranches, hitting not just the Krautheimers, but also two other neighbors, before ultimately realizing that it was easier to get the bison in the national park. In Yellowstone, he didn't have to take fences down or worry about the bison being tagged—and there were a lot more bison to choose from. The RV was his own, although it had already been in bad shape when he had the idea of using it to commit his crimes. He had been driving around in the park at night, targeting young bison that were close to the road, roping them, and then dragging them into the RV. All in all, he had stolen eleven bison over the past month, ranging in age from six months to a year.

Thus, it wasn't Taffy Spooner who had opened the chute and released Grievous Bodily Harm at the rodeo. It was Jericho. He had noticed me eavesdropping on Ike Spooner's conversation and wanted to create a distraction. (At the time, he had been wearing an older one of Taffy's signature baby blue cowboy hats as part of his rodeo clown outfit, but had lost it in the commotion.) Jericho hadn't meant to put my life at risk, which was why he'd intervened when the bull nearly flattened me—although I was now less thankful to him for saving me, given that he was the one who'd put me in jeopardy in the first place.

The Spooners had been mortified to learn that they had supported a rash of thefts and quickly volunteered to return all the bison to where they had been stolen.

However, the first to be released was the one that Jericho had stolen that very morning.

Before us was a great swath of grassland, on which over five hundred bison were gathered. There was plenty for them to eat, so they were widely spread out. Calves gamboled about. Young males butted heads. The occasional adult wallowed in the dirt, playfully rolling about like a puppy that weighed half a ton.

Ranger Oh was relatively sure that the young male had been stolen from this herd, although she couldn't guarantee it. "There are almost always bison in this section of the park," she had told us. "And there's a road that goes right through the middle of it. So if anyone wanted to steal a yearling, this would be the best place to come."

Unfortunately, returning a bison to a herd isn't always easy. A few years earlier, a family of tourists had mistakenly thought a bison calf had been separated from its mother and made a well-meaning but ill-conceived attempt to rescue it. They had put it in the back of their minivan and driven it to the ranger station. Afterward, the rangers had tried to reunite it with its mother but found the mother wouldn't take it back. The young bison we had rescued that day was much older and no longer nursing, but there was still a chance that he might be ostracized from the herd. Or traumatized by his removal.

As it was the middle of the afternoon, there were dozens of cars and RVs parked along the roadside. Tourists were lined up along the shoulder, taking photos and selfies. On the road, traffic was jammed, as tourists too lazy to even get out of their cars simply slowed to a crawl to let their families take photos out the window.

Ranger Oh was walking up and down the shoulder, warning tourists to stay by their cars and not approach the bison.

Now a park service truck pulled off the road, towing a cattle trailer with the young bull in the back. A faint dirt track led into the grassland, and the truck followed that for a short distance, getting away from the main road.

"Hey!" a tourist near us shouted. "How come they can drive off-road and we can't?"

"Those are park service employees," Ranger Oh explained. "They are participating in an important bison rehabilitation project today. . . ." She then turned and shouted, "PLEASE DO NOT TRY TO TOUCH THE BISON! THIS IS NOT A PETTING ZOO!"

A few yards away, a father who had been walking directly toward a young calf returned to his family, giving Ranger Oh a dirty look. "You don't need to have such an attitude!" he yelled.

"You don't need to be such an idiot," Ranger Oh muttered under her breath. She stopped next to us to watch the truck.

"How's this going to work?" Mom asked.

"Hopefully, it will be nice and simple. They open the

gates and the bison comes right out. We'll see. . . . DO NOT TRY TO FEED THE BISON! THEY ARE PERFECTLY CAPABLE OF FEEDING THEMSELVES! AND WHEN YOU PICK PLANTS, YOU KILL THEM!"

A family who had gathered handfuls of grass to feed to the bison sheepishly returned to the roadside.

Ranger Oh looked to me. "Whether or not this works, the park service is very thankful for your help in figuring out who stole our bison. We can't give you a cash reward or anything like that, but if you'd like a personal tour of any of our attractions, let me know and we can work it out."

"Maybe you could give Teddy VIP seating at Old Faithful?" Summer asked. "He didn't get to see it erupt when we were there the other day."

Ranger Oh grinned. "I'm sure we could arrange that. Oh, for Pete's sake."

Down the road from us, a father was carrying his toddler toward an adult bison in a moronic attempt to sit her on its back for a photo.

Ranger Oh left us to intervene. "A BISON IS NOT A SHOW PONY!" she shouted. "PLEASE DO NOT ATTEMPT TO POSE YOUR CHILDREN ON THEM!"

"Speaking of rewards," J.J. said to me, "I still owe you for recovering my necklace."

"But I *didn't* recover it," I reminded him.

J.J. shrugged. "You still figured out what happened to it. Which was the mystery I asked you to solve."

"And besides," Kandace said, "things worked out better this way. We made them right."

Arturo Creek had called as we were driving into Yellowstone. He reported that Daisy's nephew was thrilled to have his sapphire returned to him. Now Cade was trying to figure out what to do with it. Arturo suggested that it would be nice if Kandace could make good on her offer to help Cade sell the sapphire at a fair price, so that Cade and the Creeks could establish a fund to provide much-needed health care and school repairs to the reservation.

Out in the midst of the grassland, two park rangers got out of the truck and walked back to the cattle trailer.

"As I recall," J.J. said to me, "you asked for a percentage of the value of the sapphire as payment. But as far as my finances are concerned, I'm actually out five hundred bucks for that thing."

"Daddy!" Summer chided. "That's not cool!"

"In fact," J.J. said teasingly, "this has been an *extremely* expensive vacation. Not only did I lose that sapphire, but I'm also out a big chunk of change for the Oy Vey Corral."

Despite everything that had happened, J.J. had decided to buy the Krautheimers' property. Although, I assumed that had probably been a done deal all along. J.J. obviously loved the place, and even though Pete Thwacker had been miserable there, he was sure he could sell the idea of a FunJungle-branded American safari—as long as they could keep grizzlies from getting into the lodges.

To that end, there had been no sign of Sasquatch since the night he broke in. Evan suspected the bear was still around, but without bait to lure him, there was a good chance we wouldn't see him again. "Even a bear that big can stay hidden if it wants to," Evan had said.

Out in Hayden Valley, the rangers opened the rear gate on the cattle trailer, then quickly stepped away to give the young bull some space.

The bull stepped out tentatively, sniffing the air.

"Anyhow, Teddy," J.J. said, "I was thinking that maybe I could put off paying you for a few years. Like, until it's time for you to go to college."

My parents were so surprised, they turned away from the bison to face J.J.

"Are you saying you'll cover my tuition?" I asked.

"Seems like a good investment," J.J. said. "That brain of yours is a national treasure. With the right support, you'll probably cure cancer someday. Or invent some kind of new green energy to stop global warming."

"Or open the world's greatest detective agency," Kandace added.

"J.J.," Mom said, "we can't accept that—"

"Like heck we can't!" Dad interrupted. "Do you have any idea how much college costs these days?"

The young bison suddenly bolted away from the trailer. He ran to where a few other young males were gathered and fell in with them. The males responded with some jostling and head-butting, but it wasn't really aggressive. It looked more like practice: teenagers readying themselves for the day when they would be adults. They circled around one another and kicked up a cloud of dust.

The tourists who were actually facing the bison, rather than trying to take selfies, oohed and aahed.

"So it's settled, then?" J.J. asked me. "Is that a fair payment?"

"Sure," I said. "If it's okay with my parents."

"Ooh!" Summer exclaimed. "Maybe we'll go to the same college, Teddy!"

I could no longer tell which of the young bison was the bull we had brought back and which were the ones that had been there all along.

Jasmine said, "Looks like that return went as well as we could have hoped for."

Kandace asked me, "Teddy, have you given any thought to what you'd like to study for a career?"

I took in the great grassy field filled with bison. In the

distance, a few pronghorn grazed as well, while in the air high above, a bald eagle glided on a thermal. It was as beautiful a sight as I had ever seen in my life.

"Zoology," I said. "What else?"

SASQUATCH IS NOT THE ONLY GRIZZLY BEAR IN DANGER!

The wildlife of the United States has not fared well over the last few hundred years. Yes, the recovery of the American bison is an incredible conservation success story—although it is tempered by the story of how humans slaughtered the bison in the first place. The history of the USA is filled with tales of abundant wildlife being hunted to extinction or near-extinction. Take the passenger pigeon, which was once the most abundant bird in North America, numbering an estimated three to five billion animals, and was wiped out by humankind within the space of a century.

The grizzly bear's story isn't quite that horrible, but it hasn't had an easy time. Grizzlies have been prized by hunters and vilified by ranchers and farmers. Our own government has, at times, participated in—or encouraged—their slaughter. Historically, they ranged through much of the western USA, getting as far east as Missouri, but now there are only about 1,500 left, clustered mostly in Northern Montana and the Yellowstone region. (Consider this: A grizzly bear is the central image of the flag of California, and yet no grizzly has been seen there since 1922.)

While there are now many people who would like grizzlies to rebuild their numbers, there are plenty of other people still fighting to have them eradicated. (And, sadly, wolves have probably fared even worse.) The fortunes of grizzlies can shift dramatically depending on who is in office as president of the United States. Under Barack Obama, the practice of baiting grizzlies by hunters was declared illegal in much of the country; under Donald Trump, it was declared legal once again.

There also remains the issue of space. We have an incredible national park system in this country, but still, that isn't enough. A large carnivore like a grizzly needs a lot of land. At a certain point, even a large area such as the Yellowstone/ Grand Teton region can only support so many bears. If there aren't protected wildlife corridors to allow the bears to get from one protected area to another, their populations won't be able to grow—and the isolated populations will lose genetic diversity.

So what can you do? (1) Support organizations that fight for conservation and wildlife protection. (2) Write to your political representatives. A lot. Unsure who to write to or what to write about? Don't worry, those conservation organizations will be happy to help you do that. I'll list a few of them at the end of this essay. But before I do . . .

There's one more really easy thing you can do to protect wildlife:

Don't be a touron.

I did not make that term up. It's quite popular because, sadly, there are an awful lot of tourons. If you doubt me, google the term.

I wholeheartedly encourage you to see animals in the wild. But if you do, treat them with respect. Don't approach them too closely. Don't feed them—or leave food where they can get to it. Don't antagonize them in an attempt to get a great selfie. Don't venture off marked trails. And for Pete's sake, don't litter. Doing any of these things degrades the environment and can endanger the animals. (It might also endanger *you*, although it is very rare for any wild animal—even a grizzly—to attack a human unless it is provoked.)

Okay. I've said my piece. Here's that list of organizations:

First off, I'm a big fan of the World Wildlife Fund, whose animal crimes division continues to advise me on these books: worldwildlife.org.

Defenders of Wildlife does a particularly good job of focusing on helping carnivores: defenders.org.

Visiting our national parks is one of the greatest vacation deals on earth. The relatively small amount it costs per car to enter doesn't even come close to covering the costs of operating them. The National Park Foundation helps cover the difference. If you want to keep our national park system going—and help it protect and study wildlife—visit nationalparks.org.

If you are looking to help protect the wildlife and ecology of Yellowstone in particular, Yellowstone Forever supports research and conservation efforts, like the Yellowstone Wolf Project: yellowstone.org.

Finally, if you want to help American bison *and* Native American culture at the same time, check out the InterTribal Buffalo Council, a collection of sixty-nine federally recognized tribes from nineteen different states whose mission is to restore buffalo to Indian Country in order to preserve their historical, cultural, traditional, and spiritual relationship for future generations. Reestablishing healthy buffalo populations on tribal lands helps reestablish hope for Indian people. Returning buffalo to tribal lands will help heal the land, the animal, and the spirit of the Indian people: itbcbuffalonation.org.

Acknowledgments

Strangely, this book might never have existed if it hadn't been for the pandemic.

I wasn't supposed to write a FunJungle novel in 2020. I was supposed to write a Charlie Thorne novel and a Spy School novel, and then do a lot of traveling: for a book tour, for author festivals—and to visit some amazing places with the intention of doing research for a FunJungle novel that I would write in 2021. And then the pandemic hit.

Suddenly, I couldn't go *anywhere*. Which left me with a lot more time to write than I had expected.

So I agreed to write a FunJungle novel for 2021. Only, I had to come up with a new idea relatively quickly, set it some place I knew well, and deal with animal issues that I was familiar with.

Yellowstone immediately came to mind.

(I know that there are a few readers out there who aren't pleased that I have begun to shift the FunJungle series away from FunJungle itself, but I was worried that keeping the series locked in that one location would make it eventually start feeling stale. And honestly, if FunJungle suffered one more major crisis, it was either going to go bankrupt or the government was going to have to shut it down.)

I had been to the Yellowstone region quite a lot, because three of my closest friends from college live there—and a fourth *used* to live there. In fact, they all live in the same city, Bozeman, Montana. So, if it hadn't been for the generous hospitality of Jeff Peachin, Katie Goodman, Soren Kisiel, and Kent Davis, this book probably wouldn't exist. Thanks to them, I have spent many lovely vacations exploring Yellowstone National Park and the national forests to the north of it.

Sadly, due to the pandemic, I couldn't get back to Yellowstone to research this book and mostly had to rely on my fond memories of the place. However, I needed some expertise as well. So I am incredibly thankful to Dennis Jorgenson, the Bison & Tribal Program lead for the World Wildlife Fund's Northern Great Plains Program, for his help—as well as Giavanna Grein, the senior program officer for TRAFFIC at the WWF, for making the connection. Also, thanks to Daniel Stahler, a wildlife biologist at Yellowstone who works as a project biologist for the Yellowstone Wolf Project.

And while I'm at it, I suppose I should thank all the

rangers at the Yellowstone and Grand Teton National Parks who have given me such great information and advice over the years.

I am also extremely thankful to Mary Gibson, an Eastern Shoshone librarian and land protector, for advising me on how to present the Tukudika people in this book and address the continued mistreatment of Native Americans in the United States. Mary did ask me to point out that although reservation life can be very grim, there are still positive tribal activities and programs, such as the Eastern Shoshone Buffalo Program at the Wind River Reservation.

In addition, I drew much of my discussion about Native American history at Yellowstone from Richard Grant's fascinating article "The Lost History of Yellowstone," which appeared in *Smithsonian* magazine in January 2021.

Next, thanks to my summer intern, Caroline Curran, for all her help. It was a bummer that the pandemic prevented us from ever being able to actually meet in person, but she did an amazing job remotely. And thanks once again to Mingo Reynolds, R.J. Bernocco, and everyone at the Kelly Writers House at the University of Pennsylvania for finding me such great interns every year.

Then there's my incredible team at Simon & Schuster, starting with my editor, Krista Vitola, who spearheaded the fast-tracking of this book, and also Justin Chanda, Lucy

Cummins, Kendra Levin, Dainese Santos, Anne Zafian, Milena Giunco, Audrey Gibbons, Lisa Moraleda, Jenica Nasworthy, Chrissy Noh, Anna Jarzab, Brian Murray, Devin MacDonald, Christina Pecorale, Victor Iannone, Emily Hutton, Emily Ritter, and Theresa Pang. And massive thanks to my incredible agent, Jennifer Joel, for making all this possible.

Thanks to my amazing fellow writers (and support group) James Ponti, Sarah Mlynowski, Julie Buxbaum, Christina Soontornvat, Karina Yan Glaser, Max Brallier, Gordon Korman, Julia Devillers, Leslie Margolis, Elizabeth Eulberg, and Rose Brock.

Thanks to all the school librarians and parent associations who have arranged for me to visit, all the bookstore owners and employees who have shilled my books, and all the amazingly tireless festival organizers and volunteers who have invited me to participate.

Thanks to the home team: Ronald and Jane Gibbs; Suz, Darragh, and Ciara Howard; Barry and Carole Patmore; Andrea Lee Gomez; Megan Vicente; and Georgia Simon.

And last but not least, thanks to my favorite research assistants, Dashiell and Violet. It's been a while since we last made it to Yellowstone, but I hope to get you guys back there again sometime soon—as well as many other amazing places. I love you both more than words can say.

A Reading Group Guide to
Bear Bottom
by Stuart Gibbs

About the Book

In the seventh novel in the *New York Times* bestselling FunJungle series by Stuart Gibbs, Teddy Fitzroy returns as FunJungle's resident sleuth to solve the disappearances of endangered bison and an irreplaceable necklace. Teddy, his family, and some other FunJungle employees have been invited to visit a bison ranch just outside Yellowstone National Park that FunJungle's owner, J.J. McCracken, is considering purchasing. But as usual, trouble isn't far behind. The ranch's endangered bison have been mysteriously disappearing. Then a massive local grizzly bear named Sasquatch breaks into the house, causing chaos. In the aftermath, Kandace McCracken discovers that her exceptionally expensive sapphire necklace has vanished. With over a dozen suspects, it's up to Teddy to detangle this hairy situation, before his family or friends—or any more expensive objects—become dinner.

Discussion Questions

The following questions may be utilized throughout the study of *Bear Bottom* as reflective writing prompts, or alternatively, they can be used as targeted questions for group discussion and reflection.

1. Pause after reading the book's opening and learning that Teddy and his family have finally left FunJungle for a vacation. What do you predict will be the most exciting part of this change of scenery for Teddy? What challenges would a mystery in this new location present?

2. Teddy tells readers, "I always thought that FunJungle attracted an unusual number of dumb tourists. But at Yellowstone, I discovered that there were dumb tourists *everywhere*." Does learning this surprise you? What makes such behavior so disappointing? Do you think social media is to blame? Why does getting attention online sometimes make people behave poorly? Explain your answers using examples from the book and your own life.

3. For Teddy and Summer, the trip to Yellowstone is their first excursion outside of FunJungle as a couple. Are there any ways that traveling with both of their families could be a challenge? If so, what might those be?

4. When a girl visiting with her family recognizes Summer, her brother tells her, "'It's obviously not her. Do you really think Summer McCracken would be driving around Yellowstone in that car?'" Do you think Summer's trick to hide her identity proves to be a clever one? Are there ways in which having to deny who you are becomes a burden? Are there any possible benefits?

5. When Summer and Teddy's father attempt to get Morton, a Yellowstone tourist, to leave the elk alone, he tells them, "'I saw people getting way closer than this to plenty of animals today!'" In what ways does Morton demonstrate he is behaving like a classic "touron"? In your opinion, does Morton get what he deserves? Explain your answer.

6. After spending so much time in the scenic Texas hill country, Teddy still finds himself in awe of the West Yellowstone landscape. Why do you think he finds it so striking? What's the most visually beautiful place you've visited? What did you enjoy about it?

7. From what you learned in your reading of *Bear Bottom*, what makes American bison so unique and special? Were you aware that there are ranches dedicated solely to raising them?

8. As they arrive at the Oy Vey Corral, Teddy and Summer are introduced to Melissa and Evan Krautheimer, the teen-age children of Sidney and Heidi Krautheimer. In your opinion, what would be the best part of growing up on a ranch like theirs? What might be the greatest challenges?

9. Consider Summer's reaction to her father telling the group, "'I'm thinking about buying the Oy Vey Corral.'" Do you think she's right to be concerned? Do you believe J.J. really wants their input on the project, or might he have an ulterior motive? Explain your answers.

10. After the group's first sighting of Sasquatch the grizzly, Sidney Krautheimer tells them all, "'Sasquatch is nothing to worry about. He comes around most nights and we've never had an issue with him.'" Though grizzlies rarely attack humans unless provoked, consider your reaction to seeing a bear so close and in person. How do you believe you would respond?

11. After Teddy agrees with Summer that the Oy Vey Corral would be a fantastic location for a safari lodge, Heidi tells him, "'There's another reason we invited you here besides the lodge.'" How does Teddy react to learning that the ranch needs his sleuthing skills to help solve the mystery of disappearing bison? Why does this announcement make his parents appear tense? Though Teddy's past investigations have been incredibly successful, why are his parents continually resistant to his participation in solving them?

12. After listening to her brother complain about where they live and how remote it is, Melissa tells him, "'You have no idea how lucky you are, Evan. Can you imagine what life was like for our great-great-grandparents out here?'" Do you agree or disagree with Melissa's stance? How might life be different today versus Melissa's great-great-grandparents' time? Explain your answers.

13. Melissa offers to show Summer and Teddy the secret storage area once used to hide booze under the kitchen. How does learning that the Krautheimer home was once used as a way station for bootlegging make the visitors more interested in the home? How does this space ultimately play a larger role in one of the mysteries to be solved?

14. When Summer's mom, Kandace, arrives at the Oy Vey Corral, J.J. notices her jewelry and mutters, "'Dang it. . . . Why's she wearing that?'" Consider J.J's frustration with Kandace for wearing such an expensive necklace on this trip. Do you think he's overreacting, or does he have a right to be concerned?

15. Though Evan prefers to spend his time playing video games and seemingly shows little interest in his family's ranch, he is a gifted tracker. What might readers infer from this information?

16. What do you think would be the best part of getting to participate in an investigation such as this one? Can you think of any drawbacks to this kind of experience?

17. After Sasquatch's invasion and destruction of the Krautheimers' home, J.J. is convinced the grizzly has eaten Kandace's necklace. Consider his rationale for this argument. Do you think his logic is solid? Do you believe tracking the bear by following his scat is the best way to retrieve the lost jewels? Explain your answers.

18. When describing the value of the necklace, J.J. reluctantly tells Teddy, "'The fact is, I got a great deal on it when I first bought it for her. It was the deal of a lifetime.'" Why does J.J. choose to have Teddy investigate the missing necklace instead of going to the police? What are the benefits to this arrangement? Can you think of any risks?

19. Throughout *Bear Bottom*, readers learn a great deal about American bison, bears, elk, wolves, and other animals found in Yellowstone National Park. Were there any animal facts that excited or surprised you? What animals would you like to learn more about?

20. Why does Jericho, the Spooners' foreman, try to blame the teens for planting the bear-baiting items in the Spooners' garage shed? What might be the true culprit's motivation?

21. What makes Teddy's discovery of the hidden closet and the use of the mysterious RV on the same morning so special?

22. After Summer learns that Teddy has been secretly hired by her father to retrieve her mother's missing necklace, Teddy apologizes for not telling Summer the whole truth as he was unsure what the right thing was to do. Summer reminds him, "'We are a team, Teddy. We have to be straight with each other.'" Do you agree or disagree with Summer? How does being honest with one another ultimately benefit them both? Explain your answers.

23. At the end of *Bear Bottom*, readers discover that J.J.'s former choices and actions lay the groundwork for one of the mysteries. Does knowing the motivation behind the theft of the necklace make the crime any more acceptable? Explain your answer.

24. Once again, Teddy and Summer have solved an important case. Predict what new mystery will come their way in the next installment of the FunJungle books.

Extension Activities

1. After two years of living and working at FunJungle Adventure Park, Teddy and his parents travel to Yellowstone National Park for a much-needed vacation. Besides being the world's first national park and home to the most famous geyser in the world, Yellowstone is rife with natural wonder. Working with a small group, research Yellowstone facts. Consider learning more about the following:

- Where is the park located?

- How large is it?

- What is it best known for?

- What wildlife is it home to?

- How many visitors does it receive annually?

- What are the greatest challenges faced by the park and the park service?

• What are five unusual fun facts uncovered from your research?

Continuing your work as a team, create a Yellowstone exploration pamphlet for other young people lucky enough to visit the park. Be sure the guide offers tips on what to do and what not to do while visiting.

2. Readers learn that the Shoshone tribe, sometimes referred to as the Sheep Eaters, are native to the Yellowstone area. Using library resources, learn more about the Shoshone tribe and the Sheep Eater War in the 1800s, being sure to discover the following:

• Why were the Shoshone tribe called Sheep Eaters?

• What land did the Shoshone inhabit?

• What was the outcome of the Sheep Eater War?

• What did the US government do to tribal members?

• Has the government provided any reparations for their actions?

Then engage in a group discussion about what you've learned; to add to your knowledge, select another Indigenous group of people in the US and learn more about the history of that tribe.

3. The Wildlife and Aquatic Resources Branch of the National Park Service is at the center of the conservation and preservation work highlighted in *Bear Bottom*. Using library resources and the Internet, research to learn more about the service's essential work and the outcomes of their endeavors. Be sure to learn the following:

• What are the specific programs this branch oversees?

• What makes each of these programs unique?

• Who are other collaborators on these programs?

• What are some of the biggest challenges faced?

After gathering this information, create a visual presentation that illustrates your findings.

4. While reading *Bear Bottom*, readers learn that scat, or animal droppings, can be used to identify animals as well as learn their habits and patterns. Begin by reading "How to Identify Wildlife" from the BBC's *Discover Wildlife*:

https://www.discoverwildlife.com/how-to/identify-wildlife
/how-to-identify-animal-droppings/. After reading the
article, look for additional information shared by US parks
and zoos to learn more about ways scat is identified and
tracked. Note the facts you find most interesting; after you've
collected your "scoop on poop," be sure to share your findings with others.

5. In *Bear Bottom*, readers learn about Yellowstone's incredible geological features, including geysers like Old Faithful.
Using library and Internet resources, research the following:

• Where in Yellowstone is Old Faithful located?

• When was it discovered and by whom?

• What are the most unique features of this geyser?

• How many geysers does Yellowstone have?

• How is climate change threatening this natural splendor?

Taking what you've learned, discuss possible solutions and
ways that students can actively help with climate change
issues.

6. Readers learn that in the late 1800s there were sixty to eighty million bison in North America, but they were nearly wiped out in the space of a few decades by European settlers and the government's campaign against Native Americans. Learn more about American bison using the following resources:

https://www.nwf.org/Educational-Resources/Wildlife-Guide/Mammals/American-Bison

https://www.nationalgeographic.com/animals/mammals/facts/american-bison

After these readings, research more about today's conservation efforts for the American bison. Using a digital product of choice, take the new knowledge you've gathered and create a visual that can be showcased and shared with others.

This guide was created by Dr. Rose Brock, an associate professor at Sam Houston State University. Dr. Brock holds a Ph.D. in Library Science, specializing in children's and young adult literature.

This guide has been provided by Simon & Schuster for classroom, library, and reading group use. It may be reproduced in its entirety or excerpted for these purposes. For more Simon & Schuster guides, please visit simonandschuster.net or thebookpantry.net.

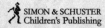

AN AN UNDERCOVER NERD BECOME A SUPERSTAR AGENT? FIND OUT IN STUART GIBBS'S *NEW YORK TIMES* BESTSELLING SPY SCHOOL SERIES!